Children and Fiction

Novels
Bed and Work
A Town on the Never
Lunch with Ashurbanipal
Games in a Dead-End Street

Critical
Word for Word
Writing with Care
Thirteen Types of Narrative
Only the Best (U.S.)

Fiction for Children
Over 10
Jim Starling
Jim Starling and the Agency
Jim Starling's Holiday
Jim Starling and the Colonel
Jim Starling and the Spotted Dog
Jim Starling Takes Over
Jim Starling Goes to Town
Top Boy at Twisters Creek (U.S.)
The Secret Winners (U.S.)
The Prisoners of Gridling Gap
Kids Commune (U.S.)
The Boy at the Window

Birdy Jones
Birdy and the Group
Birdy Swings North
Birdy in Amsterdam
Louie's Lot
Louie's S.O.S.
Mapper Mundy's Treasure Hunt
The Secret Spenders (U.S.)
The Doughnut Dropout
The Active-Enzyme Lemon-
Freshened Junior High School
Witch (U.S.)

8–11
The Questers
Calling Questers Four
The Questers and the Whispering Spy
Manhattan is Missing

Meet Lemon Kelly
Lemon Kelly Digs Deep
Lemon Kelly and the Home-Made Boy
The Nose Knows
Dolls in Danger

7–9
Here Comes Parren
Back with Parren
Lucky Les
The Dragon that Lived under Man-
hattan (U.S.)
My Kid Sister

5–7 Picture Book
10,000 Golden Cockerels
   (with Richard Rose)

Documentary Fiction for Children
The Cokerheaton Storypack
The Rushbrook Storypack

Book of the Film
Monte Carlo or Bust

Children and Fiction

A critical study in depth of the artistic
and psychological factors involved in
writing fiction for and about children

Wallace Hildick

Evans Brothers Limited London

Published by Evans Brothers Limited,
Montague House, Russell Square,
London, W.C.1.

Set in 11 on 12 point Imprint and printed in
Great Britain by Hazell Watson & Viney Ltd,
Aylesbury, Bucks.
ISBN 0 237 35186 2   PRA 3481

Contents

Chapter one   Children in fiction

Much of the fiction written for children today is about children and, looking around at many of the products and their producers, one is tempted to suggest that this is merely because much of the fiction written for children today *is* about children. Grey woolly sheep tend to follow the grey woolly tails in front of their noses.

But much of the *best* fiction for children today is about children, and the reason for this has little to do with fashion or the weary customs of wary publishers. On the contrary, it has everything to do with sound artistic choice, hinging on the question of identification common to fiction of all kinds, adult or juvenile.

The process of identification is basic to the whole writer-story-reader relationship. To realize a character – to give it bones and muscles and sweat and blood and make it live – a writer must identify with it to some extent. Even if he is not predisposed to sympathize with a character he must at least try to see through its eyes, feel the way it feels. In this way many a cardboard devil has been endowed with a touch of humanity that has made it all the more frightening if also more forgivable. At the same time, one suspects, many an axe-grinding author has been forced by the application of his artistic integrity to this matter to see the good in a living enemy or pre-judged doctrine he hoped to pillory.

The reader's function is less demanding. In the interests of identification he is not expected to bargain directly with devils. It is usually enough that he should identify with the angels – with the hero or heroine – or some neutral recorder of the proceedings. Even in the case of the modern anti-hero – the poor devil, the misunderstood devil, the defiant devil – it is the writer who has taken the first risk and drawn the fire, making identification there as easy and harmless as possible. Indeed, one sometimes feels that the soul at risk in an obscene publication case is not the fourteen-year-old girl's so dear to the heart of prosecuting counsel, but that of the poor damned author himself.

But it is the power of a work of fiction to draw the reader into this process of identification that gives that work its quality – moral as well as aesthetic. At its lowest level of operation we speak of such a process as 'taking us out of ourselves', or 'ushering us into another world', or simply 'providing an escape' from an often unpleasant reality. It can, however, do much more. By taking us into another world it can widen our experience, and by widening our experience it can help to cultivate our sympathies, giving them depth and extending their range. And we should be unwise to sneer at mere escapism, when the escape is from the confines of one's ego.

We are now talking about education, of course, and the immense importance of an adequate supply of good fiction for children. That is why we should be on our guard against any predisposition towards the too obviously educational when buying books for schools or libraries, public or private. One good story is worth hundreds of non-fictional topics books, no matter how tastefully illustrated or attractively laid-out, because for every Spanish galleon or Chippendale commode or lapwing's egg a child will be required to recognize in life there will be hundreds of Steerforths or Uriah Heeps or Huck Finns he will need to understand.

Assuming then that identification is the key to one's enjoyment of a story and to the refreshment and sustenance to be had from it, it is possible to see why so many good children's books deal with child characters. A child *can* identify with adult characters – but only if they are sympathetically drawn and simple enough. By this I am not suggesting that the only adult characters a child can get under the skin of are simple-*minded* ones. Quite complex adults – adults who can be presumed to have complex personalities by virtue of their positions in life, like kings, prime ministers, witches, wizards and wise old nurses – abound in fairy tales of high quality. But in such a context only single aspects of their personalities are presented at a time: the predominantly greedy become greed itself, the generally envious become envy, the honest honesty, the brave bravery – and so on. Moreover, they operate – these witches and princes and shrewd old apothecaries – in a world that is none the less valid because it is a dream world, for it is in effect the world of the subconscious and therefore an important part of human experience, and the trimming down of characters to single facets of personality, single humours or traits, is itself a reflection of the dream mechanism, a replica of the myth-making, symbolizing way in which the subconscious seems often to operate. But when we come to more realistic settings such simplicity – the stylized simplicity of presentation that still leaves scope for a richness of experience – becomes over-simplification. The young flying officer, the secret service agent, the football star, the nurse, the air hostess: these operate in the conscious tangible world, the 'real' world, as we say. And if we simplify them we are cheating – diluting rather than concentrating, blurring rather than focusing – unless, and only unless, we are using them in some modern fairy tale, some allegory or fantasy that is seen to be an allegory or fantasy. Certainly, because of their simplicity or over-simplification, such 'realistic' adult characters can be enjoyed by children, who will find no difficulty in identifying with them. The popularity of Biggles – that unbelievably clean-limbed British flying knight-errant figure – and the adult characters in pulp fiction and comic strips testifies to this fact. But the resultant fiction will be of inferior quality and, educatively, even possibly harmful, for it will present an unavoidably misleading picture of an absurd glandless humanity and this could lead to serious errors of judgment. Would you be happy to let your daughter marry a Biggles?

So we have a situation in which it is almost essential to have child characters if one wishes to write good fiction for children about 'real life'. In the natural way of things, children are relatively uncomplicated and in presenting them fictionally no great distortion or suppression – no artistic dishonesty – is required. They needn't of course play leading roles in the action. They can be presented, with or without irony, as observers of adults. But they need to be there in some capacity, as media through which the child reader is able comfortably and fruitfully to participate in the action and setting portrayed.

As was suggested at the beginning, the inclusion of child characters doesn't automatically make for good children's fiction. A few days spent in a classroom or children's library or the salt mines of children's book reviewing are sufficient to convince one that many of the hundreds of people writing for children about children do so without having given the matter any thought – simply because they are vaguely aware that most good children's stories are about children. Hence the horde – the hideous, cute, pert, plastic, clockwork horde – of child characters that are just as flat and lifeless as the Biggleses and comic-book night nurses and pulp Federal officers. At the same time and on the other hand, however, there are quite a number of good thoughtful writers today producing books intended for children, about children, that are really child studies much more likely to be appreciated by adults. Consider, for example, a work recently published in Britain and America, *The Oak and the Ash* by Frederick Grice. The hero is about eleven years old, the setting a Northern English mining village just after the First World War, and the background details are throughout sharply focused and, one feels, painstakingly authentic. In the following passage we accompany the boy to a soccer match. It is a real soccer match at St James's Park, Newcastle, home of a real soccer club and not one of those depressing made-up clubs like Grimchester Rangers or Coketown United, met with so frequently in cheap juvenile fiction. This is one up, one feels, to Mr Grice – especially when he introduces the fascinating element of a homing pigeon which the boy takes to the match in order to let its owner, back in the village, know the half-time score.

They dodged in and out of the crowds, overtaking man after man, and dived down short cuts as if the whole world were competing for seats; but the more they overtook the more there were still ahead of them, and the queue for the turnstile was long. This was the one thing about going to St. James's that Francis did not like. As he pushed in after his father he held the little bag with the pigeon high about his head, and did not feel easy until the great iron arm had swung away before him.

Then his father ran clattering up the stone gangway, and at last they came to the top and saw the great hollow of the stadium, vast and green before them. They shuffled along the rows of the stand until they found good seats. Then Mr. Kirtley relaxed and opened his programme; but Francis had eyes only for the vast crowd, the tiers of faces rising on the terraces until the topmost row was outlined against the sky, the policemen and ambulance men patrolling the touchlines, the sellers of chewing-gum and chocolate throwing their packages dexterously up into the crowd and catching the coins as they were pitched down to them. He sat on the bench with the pigeon in his lap, looking at the far stand with its clock, whose fingers never seemed to move. There was nothing he hated more than waiting for those pointers to go round, and nothing he enjoyed more than that marvellous moment when the crowd began to roar and the trim players, jogging up and down to flex their muscles, came running out of the tunnel, and the referee had finished testing the nets and had blown up the two captains to begin the game. From then on he could not bear to lose one kick, one movement, one moment of the game.

As soon as the first half was over he took the pigeon out, slipped a note with the score inside the ring, and threw the bird up into the air. It clapped its wings noisily, then flew out into the free air above the pitch, and began to circle the field – once, twice – and then made off deliberately and quickly until it disappeared beyond the heads of the spectators.

The game came to an end all too quickly. While the ground staff were taking up the flagposts, Francis and his father shuffled along between the seats, kicking the cigarette ends and treading on the flattened packets. Beyond the turnstiles the crowds thinned away sadly.

Now this is, on the face of it, a moderately good description of a visit to a soccer match seen through the eyes of a small boy. Apart from a few lapses – the clumsy juxtaposition of 'before him' and 'before them' and the unfortunate choice of the phrase 'blown up', with its suggestion of inflatable captains – the prose itself is moderately good too. Indeed, this could be part of a conventional novel for adults, taken from a chapter dealing with the hero's boyhood – a passage with a certain sociological interest. And, also on the face of it, this is the sort of thing a child – especially a boy of around Francis's age – might find enjoyable.

Unfortunately, however, the game does indeed come to an end all too quickly. A boy reader, stimulated by the fact that this is a real ground the hero is visiting and therefore two real teams that are to be watched and described, will be eager for details. The fact that all this took place some forty-five years ago will not be likely to put him off, for no one is keener on social history than the young sports enthusiast when it comes to examining old records. But what is he told? Nothing. Nothing about the course of the match. Nothing about the players. Nothing about the score or even the pigeon-posted half-time score. The very name of the visiting team is left unmentioned.

This is, for all its compensating virtues, bad writing for children. And, by exactly the same token, it is then seen to be less than good writing for adults, even at the child-study level. For here, we are told, is a boy who 'could not bear to lose one kick, one movement, one moment of the game' – but the telling, the authorial informing, is not enough in any branch of fiction. Everything that is at all important should be demonstrated.

Adult fiction itself is full of good studies of children. Writing of Ivy Compton-Burnett in *A Treatise on the Novel*, Mr Robert Liddell has perceptively remarked:

> Her treatment of children is particularly admirable. Children in fiction have been more sentimentalized, lied about and betrayed than any other class of being. The more intelligent the writer, the better he treats them. Henry James and Proust have written better about them than anyone. An author so unsentimental and intelligent as Miss Compton-Burnett might be expected either to leave them alone, or to deal with them perfectly, as she has done. Although her narrative takes place almost exclusively in the form of very highly developed conversation among remarkably articulate people, she has all the same managed to draw shy and even very young children brilliantly – and she knows, what most people forget, how extremely early the character is distinct.

To James, Proust and Compton-Burnett, Mr Liddell might have added many more authors, including George Eliot (one thinks especially of Tom and Maggie Tulliver), Virginia Woolf (a whole gallery, with the young Orlando, the Pargiter children and little George in *Between the Acts*), Charlotte and Emily Brontë (in the early chapters of *Jane Eyre* there are parts where the very technique reflects the workings of a child's mind), André Gide (in spite of exaggerated homosexual undertones), James Joyce, D. H. Lawrence (especially in *Sons and Lovers*), Robert Liddell himself (for a deft Compton-Burnett-like portrayal of prep-school boys in *The Deep End*) and of course, despite all his numerous lapses into sentimentality, Charles Dickens.

Examples from most of these sources, brilliant though they may be as studies of children, are likely to leave children if not cold then merely lukewarm. This is understandable. The authors in question weren't writing to entertain children and their purpose in presenting child characters was usually to further some larger design: to help explain or explore some element of an adult's character, for example, or to illustrate the consequences of certain adult actions in the central plot, or to throw an ironic light on such actions. Granted, there are occasions when the simple entertainment value of such passages can be fairly high, and children will sit up and take notice for a while, but with very few exceptions such moments are brief and rare in the work of authors writing for adults. Of such exceptions, probably the most notable and the one most worthy of close study is Charles Dickens.

If we regard the boyhood chapters of *David Copperfield* as a book in its own right, we have here a story with a tremendous appeal for children – under certain conditions. These conditions are achieved through skilful sub-editing. In this, I am not of course thinking of those grossly illustrated gift-book monstrosities that have been hacked from the parent book (and what an indication it is of Dickens's genius that it can glow through even that treatment!). I am not even thinking of any rare case where really skilful cutting and reassembling might have been done in print. I am thinking rather of the subtle, tailored, oral editing that is attempted every day by teachers and parents, story-telling librarians and baby-sitters – by anyone who is faced with the job of reading aloud from a well-loved book to a child or group of children. Because of its great importance it will be useful briefly to examine this question before going any further.

At first such off-the-cuff editing is usually hasty and clumsy – the reaction to such danger signals as the glazed eye, the straying glance, the movement of elbows above a desk lid, the hand stretched out to pull a classmate's hair. The reader is thereby warned and, if wise, takes the steps (or, more usually, the skips) necessary to reclaim attention without spoiling the story. With experience, however, one gradually becomes defter. Knowing the story and knowing the child or children, one is able to anticipate the likely booby-traps and brick walls and take quite smoothly the necessary action. And in time one comes to learn that such action need not always be evasive. A brief preliminary explanation can work wonders, and the sacrifice of an ounce of surprise can guarantee a ton of gleeful anticipation. Not all teachers and parents and other readers-aloud reach such a stage of smooth expertise, but – so long as they know and like both children and story – many do. In so doing, they win friends for books and authors who, administered straight, would have been rejected after the first sip or sniff. What, for example, would *Ivanhoe* be like for a ten-year-old without such a careful preliminary introduction? Have you read it yourself lately? Have you tried reading it straight out, unedited, to children? When adults speak or write nostalgically about such works, or enthusiastically about those modern children's authors more noted for their delineation of character or evocation of atmosphere than for their story-lines, I get an image of some anonymous schoolteacher, sitting on the edge of his desk, book in hand, eyes alert, making such judgments and impressions possible.

The second chapter of *David Copperfield* offers an excellent example of the value of the preliminary tip-off. Once a child is alerted to the fact that Murdstone is an unpleasant scamp, bent on marrying David's widowed mother (to a child an archetypal nightmare situation if ever there was one), the whole episode of the boy's trip to Lowestoft with the man can be read without editing, and the irony of Murdstone's cronies' comments on the forthcoming marriage, lost on David, will be relished by an audience who might otherwise have been as unaware as he. But where Dickens scores with children over most other writers of adult fiction is in the very texture and movement of his prose and the fresh liveliness of his mind, as nimble and challenging as any bright ten-year-old's. Apart, perhaps, from a brief explanation about the epitaph, neither foreword nor editing is required to make a passage like the following appeal to most children.

Here is our pew in the church. What a high-backed pew! With a window near it, out of which our house can be seen, and *is* seen many times during the morning service, by Peggotty, who likes to make herself as sure as she can that it's not being robbed, or is not in flames. But though Peggotty's eye wanders, she is much offended if mine does, and frowns to me, as I stand upon the seat, that I am to look at the clergyman. But I can't always look at him – I know him without that white thing on, and I am afraid of his wondering why I stare so, and perhaps stopping the service to inquire – and what am I to do? It's a dreadful thing to gape, but I must do something. I look at my mother, but *she* pretends not to see me. I look at a boy in the aisle, and *he* makes faces at me. I look at the sunlight coming in at the open door through the porch, and there I see a stray sheep – I don't mean a sinner, but mutton – half making up his mind to come into the church. I feel that if I looked at him any longer, I might be tempted to say something out loud; and what would become of me then! I look up at the monumental tablets on the wall, and try to think of Mr. Bodgers late of this parish, and what the feelings of Mrs. Bodgers must have been, when affliction sore, long time Mr. Bodgers bore, and physicians were in vain. I wonder whether they called in Mr. Chillip, and he was in vain; and if so, how he likes to be reminded of it once a week. I look from Mr. Chillip, in his Sunday neckcloth, to the pulpit; and think what a good place it would be to play in, and what a castle it would make, with another boy coming up the stairs to attack it, and having the velvet cushion with the tassels thrown down on his head. In time my eyes gradually shut up; and, from seeming to hear the clergyman singing a drowsy song in the heat, I hear nothing, until I fall off the seat with a crash, and am taken out, more dead than alive, by Peggotty.

This has all the singing bubbling quality of Dickens's prose at its good-humoured best, but it is the element of magic that gives it its special appeal to children – that concrete palpable magic created out of objects rather than the sort that is suggested by whimsy or fancily-wrought phrases. For here, in this church (and one says 'this church' rather than 'that church' advisedly), nothing much is happening but a great deal can – any second – and this is the very condition of magic. And a great deal can happen because of the nature and potency of the symbols, each of them guaranteed to strike a chord and awaken responses in a child's mind, and all strung together, in perfect order, like an incantation. Thus we have the church itself – with its awesome, rigid, confining promise of security – and the window, which offers some relief from that confinement – and the child's home, with its gentler offer of safety – and the notion of robbery and fire, threats to that safety – and the unfairness of adults, one of the prices to be paid for one's security, and something to be put up with more or less patiently – and the dread of being shown up in public – and the child's genial petulance with adults, beautifully brought out by the emphasis on 'she' – 'she pretends not to see me' – and the child's feeling of comradeship towards animals – and the passion for improvisation in play, focused on the pulpit and its potentialities as a castle, with the author acting as a brilliant older child in offering such richly circumstantial suggestions – and the final minor catastrophe, bordering on farce, of not only falling to sleep in church but falling off one's seat, and not only falling off one's seat but doing it with a *crash*. As a study of a child's mind it is brilliant. As a passage that will appeal to children it is excellent. All that is required to make it a perfect narrative for children – who like to see the splendid possibility fully worked out – is a continuation in which the pulpit really is used as a castle.

In *Tom Sawyer*, in a remarkably similar passage, Mark Twain is actually writing for children and he demonstrates his awareness of just what is required in this matter of working out – often, in adult eyes, working to death – the lively possibility. The occasion is again that of a church service seen through the eyes of a small boy – and again we have the elements of rigidity, the open window, the intruding animals, the child's fellow-feeling for them, the fear of making oneself conspicuous (augmented cleverly and accurately here with a fear of God's anger), and the improvised game. It is a pity perhaps that in a narrative for children Mark Twain should have been so self-indulgent as to give us the substance of the prayers and sermon – witty enough from an adult's point of view but likely to weigh rather heavily on a child reader – but at least he has the good sense to leaven this by his diagrammatic representation of the parson's tone of voice:

Shall I be car-ri-ed toe the skies, on flow'ry beds

of ease,

Whilst others fight to win the prize, and sail thro' blood-

y seas?

– a piece of verbal gymnastics calculated to catch a child's eye and appeal directly to his sense of fun. And after all it is the same exuberant desire to squeeze the last drop of juice from a situation that prompts him to carry the presence of the beetle and the dog to its logical conclusion, granting that farce has a logic of its own. But let us join Tom in his pew.

Now he lapsed into suffering again as the dry argument was resumed. Presently he bethought himself of a treasure he had, and got it out. It was a large black beetle with formidable jaws – a 'pinch-bug' he called it. It was in a percussion-cap box. The first thing the beetle did was to take him by the finger. A natural fillip followed, the beetle went floundering into the aisle, and lit on its back, and the hurt finger went into the boy's mouth. The beetle lay there working its helpless legs, unable to turn over. Tom eyed it, and longed for it, but it was safe out of his reach. Other people, uninterested in the sermon, found relief in the beetle, and they eyed it too.

Presently a vagrant poodle dog came idling along, sad at heart, lazy with the summer softness and the quiet, weary of captivity, sighing for change. He spied the beetle; the drooping tail lifted and wagged. He surveyed the prize; walked around it; smelt at it from a safe distance; walked around it again; grew bolder, and took a closer smell; then lifted his lip, and made a gingerly snatch at it, just missing it; made another, and another; began to enjoy the diversion; subsided to his stomach with the beetle between his paws, and continued his experiments; grew weary at last, and then indifferent and absent-minded. His head nodded, and little by little his chin descended and touched the enemy, who seized it. There was a sharp yelp, a flirt of the poodle's head, and the beetle fell a couple of yards away, and lit on its back once more. The neighbouring spectators shook with a gentle inward joy, several faces went behind fans and handkerchiefs, and Tom was entirely happy. The dog looked foolish, and probably felt so; but there was a resentment in his heart, too, and a craving for revenge. So he went to the beetle and began a wary attack on it again; jumping at it from every point of a circle, lighting with his fore-paws within an inch of the creature, making even closer snatches at it with his teeth, and jerking his head till his ears flapped again. But he grew tired once more, after a while; tried to amuse himself with a fly, but found no relief; followed an ant around, with his nose close to the floor, and quickly wearied of that; yawned, sighed, forgot the beetle entirely, and sat down on it! Then there was a wild yelp of agony, and the poodle went sailing up the aisle; the yelps continued, and so did the dog; he crossed the house in front of the altar; he flew down the other aisle; he crossed before the doors; he clamoured up the home-stretch; his anguish grew with his progress, till presently he was but a woolly comet moving in its orbit with the gleam and the speed of light. At last the frantic sufferer sheered from its course and sprang into its master's lap: he flung it out of the window, and the voice of distress quickly thinned away and died in the distance.

Like the dog the beetle and eventually the beetle the dog, Twain won't leave the situation alone. He presses, he squeezes, he persists until he has drawn the last minim of joy out of it, and throughout this performance – for persistence, though essential, is not enough – he is sufficiently in command of his craft to keep the line of the narrative taut, with the reader in suspense and anxious to know what will happen next. Or, rather, anxious to have happen next what he fervently and gleefully hopes *will* happen next. This is fiction for and about children at its best, where the author has a complete understanding of the child who is the character and the child who is the reader, and he knows precisely how the one is likely to act and the other react.

A child's love of simple chicanery, verbal trickery and the practical joke will be only too well known to all who have been asked recently what makes a Maltese cross, or what is black and white and red all over, or who have wakened some morning in April, unaware – and been made fools of. Some of the best-loved characters in children's fiction throughout the world have been perpetrators of tricks, purveyors of riddles. Thus in *David Copperfield* one of the scenes most popular with children is that in which David is gently cheated out of his ale and chops and batter pudding by the chirpy waiter.

> After watching me into the second chop, he said:
> 'There's half a pint of ale for you. Will you have it now?'
> I thanked him and said 'Yes.' Upon which he poured it out of a jug into a large tumbler, and held it up against the light, and made it look beautiful.
> 'My eye!' he said. 'It seems a good deal, don't it?'
> 'It does seem a good deal,' I answered with a smile. For, it was quite delightful to me to find him so pleasant.

Having softened up his victim, the waiter gets to work.

> 'There was a gentleman here yesterday,' he said – 'a stout gentleman, by the name of Topsawyer – perhaps you know him?'
> 'No,' I said, 'I don't think –'
> 'In breeches and gaiters, broad-brimmed hat, gray coat, speckled choaker,' said the waiter.
> 'No,' I said bashfully, 'I haven't the pleasure –'
> 'He came in here,' said the waiter, looking at the light through the tumbler, 'ordered a glass of this ale – *would* order it – I told him not – drank it, and fell dead. It was too old for him. It oughtn't to be drawn, that's the fact.'

David, shocked, orders water instead.

> 'Why, you see,' said the waiter . . . 'our people don't like things being ordered and left. It offends 'em. But *I*'ll drink it, if you like. I'm used to it, and use is everything. I don't think it'll hurt me, if I throw my head back, and take it off quick. Shall I?'

So the waiter downs David's ale. With the chops, Dickens has the waiter introducing a logical variation – as a known antidote to the bad effects of the ale – and with the batter-pudding there is the further variant, this time less devious.

'Why, a batter-pudding,' he said, taking up a table-spoon, 'is my favourite pudding! Ain't that lucky? Come on, little 'un, and let's see who'll get most.'

The waiter certainly got most. He entreated me more than once to come in and win, but what with his table-spoon to my tea-spoon, his dispatch to my dispatch, and his appetite to my appetite, I was left far behind at the first mouthful, and had no chance with him.

Psychologically, this is an extremely perceptive study of a typical confidence trickster: with the ploys becoming decreasingly plausible as the man's greed mounts. As a study of a child's behaviour it is far less accurate, however. Very few children of eight or nine would be fooled by such tactics today, and one suspects that few children of David's intelligence would have been fooled in those days either – especially over the matter of food. But children of either era and most ages would be delighted at the sport offered to them by such an encounter, even as victims (so long as it was understood that the man was kidding), and most wholeheartedly as spectators. The humour, the cunning variation – step by circumstantial step – and the appeal to their love of simple ritual, all combine to enchant them, and the fact that Dickens piles it on a little by having the waiter trick David into overtipping him, as well as grossly overcharging the boy for a sheet of letter-paper, is all to the good as far as child readers are concerned.

Here, then, Dickens has not been able to have it both ways, as in the passage quoted earlier. In *Huckleberry Finn*, however, Mark Twain does, in a similar situation, when Huck and Jim are joined on their raft by a pair of petty rogues. Their seediness and shiftiness are never in question, right from their first appearance.

One of those fellows was about seventy, or upwards, and had a bald head and very gray whiskers. He had an old battered-up slouch hat on, and a greasy blue woollen shirt, and ragged old blue jeans britches stuffed into his boot tops, and home-knit galluses – no, he only had one. He had an old long-tailed blue jeans coat with slick brass buttons, flung over his arm, and both of them had big fat ratty-looking carpet-bags.

The other fellow was about thirty and dressed about as ornery.

Almost as quickly their profession is established.

'What got you into trouble?' says the baldhead to t'other chap.
'Well, I'd been selling an article to take the tartar off the teeth – and it does take it off, and generly the enamel along with it – but I stayed about one night longer than I ought to. . . . That's the whole yarn – what's yourn?'

'Well, I'd ben a-runnin' a little temperance revival thar, 'bout a week, and was the pet of the women-folks, big and little, for I was makin' it mighty warm for the rummies, I *tell* you, and takin' as much as five or six dollars a night – ten cents a head, children and niggers free – and business a-growin' all the time; when somehow or another a little report got around, last night, that I had a way of puttin' in my time with a private jug, on the sly. . . .'

Before long, the two rogues exercise their talents on Huck and Jim, one of them claiming to be the rightful Duke of Bridgewater and the other the French Dauphin, and getting the 'victims' to wait on them and address them as 'Your Grace' or 'My Lord' and 'Your Majesty' – incongruities of a kind that children relish. But Huck isn't really fooled.

It didn't take me long to make up my mind that these liars warn't no kings nor dukes, at all, but just low-down humbugs and frauds. But I never said nothing, never let on; kept it to myself; it's the best way; then you don't have no quarrels, and don't get into no trouble. If they wanted us to call them kings and dukes, I hadn't no objections, 'long as it would keep peace in the family; and it warn't no use to tell Jim, so I didn't tell him. If I never learnt nothing else out of pap I learnt that the best way to get along with his kind of people is to let them have their own way.

Writing of this quality, making so honestly an appeal so genuinely broad, is alone worthy of such overworked blurb-phrases as 'for children of all ages, from 8 to 80'. But it is very rare.

On a smaller scale, and without touching the poetic depths of *Huckleberry Finn*, the modern American children's writer Sid Fleischman has a similarly rounded passage in *Chancy and the Grand Rascal*. Here the boy Chancy, out to seek his long-lost brother and sisters, armed with his prized axe, a few personal belongings and a little cash, meets a stranger.

The man was sitting on a butternut stump at the crossroad. He wore a leather eye patch, a tail coat and a double gold watch chain across his vest. He was fanning his plump red face with a beaver hat when Chancy came whistling along. At the man's feet stood a straw suitcase.

Fleischman, it should be noted, doesn't tip the scales heavily against the stranger as far as personal appearance is concerned. Instead, the warning signals are sounded in the man's conversation – a note of Munchausenish grandiloquence in his claims to own a nutmeg farm and to have discovered a method of developing triple-yolked eggs.

'I guarantee it. I keep a few prime chickens, you know, and raise 'em scientific. Three yolks to every shell. Folks call 'em Colonel Plugg's Ohio Wonder Eggs. The general store at Tulip Tree is always trying to buy my triple-yolkers, but they ain't for sale, usually. *Ahem.* Prefer to give them away to the poor. But if I don't exercise my leg the Doc says it'll go lame on me, so I thought I'd march down to the store and sell a few eggs.'

But the note is reasonably well muted and the timing – both the author's and the character's – is carefully handled. Not until another page and about half-an-hour's internal time have passed does the Colonel make his pitch, suddenly going lame and sitting down under a tree.

'I'm desperate sorry,' said Chancy.
'No matter. None at all. But you'd be doing me a large favor to take those eggs to the store while they're still fresh. If it wouldn't be too much trouble.'
'None at all.'
'Thank you, boy. Chancy was your name, wasn't it?'

Still both Colonel and author take it gently. The Colonel speaks of giving Chancy a dollar reward – thereby dazzling the boy – after stating the price he expects the eggs to fetch.

'But see here, Chancy, we ought to do this businesslike and scientific. Not that you don't have an honest face. I know you ain't going to skedaddle with my egg money. Bless you, the thought hasn't entered your head – I can see that.'

And after a few more blandishments he suggests that nevertheless 'a chunk of security is called for in a case like this'. Then comes the ritual series of alternatives. The boy suggests leaving his shoes. The Colonel demurs. ('I never met a boy who'd come back for his shoes.') The Colonel then feints by proposing the axe – but Chancy refuses because of its sentimental value. Then the Colonel suggests cash – with an additional safeguard for Chancy.

'You just put up five dollars. Climb this old buckeye and leave it on a high branch where I can't touch it. It'll be there when you get back . . .'

But Chancy has only three dollars – plus misgivings.

Chancy wished suddenly he were shed of Colonel Plugg and his triple-yolk eggs. And yet, what did he have to fear? With his bad leg the Colonel couldn't climb the tree if the ground were afire.

They agree on three, the gold piece is hung from a high branch, the eggs are taken to the store, to be pronounced ordinary single-yolkers and stale into the bargain, and on Chancy's return to the tree both Colonel and gold piece have gone.

Here then we have a bit of classical roguery made just plausible enough for the child character to succumb to it without looking an absolute fool. Thus some of the edge is taken off the reader's immediate enjoyment. Even so, enjoy it he will – and while the author has sacrificed something on the roundabout of risibility he has made up for it to some extent on the swings of sympathy. Having had doubts, with Chancy, and consciously given his trust to the man, the reader will all the more acutely feel the hero's indignation and – eventually – relish the moment when Chancy meets up again with the rogue.

In most of the examples quoted, the writers make use of a knowledge of children's psychology and behaviour for the purposes of motivation – to have them act and react in a convincing manner to the experiences and situations confronting them. But there is an approach whereby authors make use of such knowledge for reproducing the very mode in which children apprehend experience: the process by which new or relatively unfamiliar experience is broken down in a child's mind into constituents that can be related to earlier familiar experience.

Adult fiction about children is full of good examples of this, and one of the most striking is the way that Benjy, in William Faulkner's *The Sound and the Fury*, sees the people and things and activities around him. Now Benjy is a grown man, in his early thirties, but he is an imbecile with the mind of a very young child so it amounts to the same thing, and Faulkner's achievement in recording it is none the less remarkable. Here is how Benjy apprehends some golfers:

> Through the fence, between the curling flower spaces, I could see them hitting. They were coming toward where the flag was and I went along the fence. Luster was hunting in the grass by the flower tree. They took the flag out, and they were hitting. Then they put the flag back and they went to the table, and he hit and the other hit. Then they went on, and I went along the fence. Luster came away from the flower tree and we went along the fence and they stopped and we stopped and I looked through the fence while Luster was hunting in the grass.
>
> 'Here, caddie.' He hit. They went away across the pasture. I held to the fence and watched them going away.
>
> 'Listen at you, now,' Luster said. . . .

James Joyce, in *A Portrait of the Artist as a Young Man*, gives us a vignette of an arithmetic lesson through the eyes of a slightly feverish small boy, whose wandering attention has less and less of the consciousness of David Copperfield's in the church but is, in its way, equally valid. The boys in the class referred to are divided into York and Lancaster teams and wear small silk rosettes accordingly.

Jack Lawton looked over from his side. The little silk badge with the red rose on it looked very rich because he had a blue sailor top on. Stephen felt his own face red too, thinking of all the bets about who would get first place in elements, Jack Lawton or he. Some weeks Jack Lawton got the card for first and some weeks he got the card for first. His white silk badge fluttered and fluttered as he worked at the next sum and heard Father Arnall's voice. Then all his eagerness passed away and he felt his face quite cool. He thought his face must be white because it felt so cool. He could not get out the answer for the sum but it did not matter. White roses and red roses: those were beautiful colours to think of. And the cards for first place and second place and third place were beautiful colours too: pink and cream and lavender. Lavender and cream and pink roses were beautiful to think of. Perhaps a wild rose might be like those colours and he remembered the song about the wild rose blossoms on the little green place. But you could not have a green rose. But perhaps somewhere in the world you could.

And here is James Baldwin, in *Tell Me How Long the Train's Been Gone*, describing a scene in a condemned house in Harlem on a dark rainy Saturday night, as witnessed and apprehended by a ten-year-old boy.

I looked toward the backyard door and I seemed to see, silhouetted against the driving rain, a figure, half-bent, moaning, leaning against the wall, in indescribable torment; then there seemed to be two figures, sighing and grappling, moving so quickly that it was impossible to tell which was which – if this had been a movie, and I had been holding a gun, I would have been afraid to shoot, for fear of shooting the wrong person; two creatures, each in a dreadful, absolute, silent, single-mindedness, attempting to strangle the other! I watched, crouching low. A very powerful and curious excitement mingled itself with my terror and made the terror greater. I could not move. I did not dare to move. The figures were quieter now. It seemed to me that one of them was a woman and she seemed to be crying – pleading for her life. But her sobbing was answered only by a growling sound. The muttered, joyous curses began again, the murderous ferocity began again, more bitterly than ever, and I trembled with fear and joy. The sobbing began to rise in pitch, like a song. The movement sounded like so many dull blows. Then everything was still, all movement ceased – my ears trembled. Then the blows began again and the cursing became a growling, moaning, stretched-out sigh. Then I heard only the rain and the scurrying of the rats. It was over – one of them, or both of them, lay stretched out, dead or dying, in this filthy place. It happened in Harlem every Saturday night.

Here we have three highly individual child viewpoints. And each is employed by the author for a highly individual purpose. The narrative of Benjy – the idiot who introduces the tale that is full of sound and fury (but signifying much) – was first conceived as a means of making the story more effective, 'told by someone capable only of knowing what happened, but not why'.[1] Later the author was to see it as a prologue – 'like the gravedigger in the Elizabethan dramas. He serves his purpose and is gone. Benjy is incapable of good and evil because he had no knowledge of good and evil.' On the technical level, this purpose is brilliantly furthered by the choice of the golf scenes, where the cries of 'Caddie!' are responded to, somewhat puzzlingly at first, by Benjy's terrible anguish. This is the result of his yearning for his lost sister, Candace – nicknamed Caddy – and is indeed the reason for his haunting the course.

James Joyce has a special purpose too, in his scene with the sums and the roses – a purpose that goes far beyond the display of great mimetic skill in tracing out the very feel of a slightly swimming head through the rhythms and cadences of the prose. (Those two final sentences, faltering, each beginning weakly with a 'But' and seemingly so casual, even slapdash, are masterstrokes.) For in this passage is emphasized Stephen's essential aestheticism, the character-trait that is to become so dominant in later life.

As for Mr Baldwin's passage – this is not merely a means of ironic reflection, for which such child-views are so often used in adult fiction. It establishes, rather, a keynote of the whole book, in which love is often physically ambiguous (Leo Proudhammer turns out to be bisexual) and life, for a modern black American, is so often violent – violent in all its aspects, including those that are generally regarded as being the most tender. Assault and even murder are indeed the familiar experiences through which a Harlem child would be likely to attempt an interpretation of this new experience of sexual love. So Mr Baldwin makes a scathing social comment.

Naturally, percipient adult readers can fully appreciate such uses of children's modes of thought. But what of children? Can they be expected to relish or even follow such technical *tours de force* – even where the subject-matter is more congenial? Older children of reasonable intelligence might, certainly, especially when they are closely familiar with books and literary methods – but them I count as adult readers anyway. But younger children – the seven to tens? William Mayne's *The Yellow Aeroplane* offers a number of interesting examples in this context.

---

1. This and the subsequent quotation come from the *Paris Review* interview with Faulkner, published in *Writers at Work*, Secker & Warburg.

The book opens with the hero, a boy of about seven, being seen off by his mother at a railway station. He is going to visit his grandparents – not very far away, but far enough for a child not used to travelling alone to regard as a great distance. His mother allows him to buy the ticket himself.

Mother felt in the silky inside of her handbag and brought out a scented ten shilling note. It had taken the smell from the bag. New notes smell like roast beef.

There follows a little deadpan badinage with the booking clerk – the sort that children love and Mayne presents so well.

'You're supposed to talk through the hole up here,' said the man, pointing to another place where the glass was cut away.
'I can only reach that with my fingers,' said Rodney, touching it. The speaking hole was much too high, unless someone lifted him up.
'I can hear you just as well from down there,' said the man. 'What would you like?'
'A half single,' said Rodney.
'That should be easy enough,' said the man. 'Where do you want to go? You'll have to tell me.'

At this point the kidding has come to an end, and what we are witnessing is a small boy's genuine struggles with an unfamiliar situation.

'My grandfather's house at Kenge Common,' said Rodney.
The man pulled a ticket out from a place in the wall, put it into a machine that made a bumping noise, and then handed it to Rodney. 'That'll take you as far as Kenge Station,' he said. 'That's as far as the railway goes. You know, it doesn't go right to anybody's house.'
The ticket was green, with black writing. It had hard corners.

As he goes on to the platform, the boy enters another unfamiliar situation.

Rodney was carrying the ticket carefully, because he did not want to bend it. But the man at the little gate to the platform put out his hand, took the perfect ticket from Rodney, snipped a piece out with his things like pliers, and gave it back.
'I've just bought that,' said Rodney, looking at it. 'And you've spoiled it.'
'I have to,' said the man. 'I spoil them all.' But he very kindly bent down and looked on the ground, and picked up the piece he had cut out, and gave it back to Rodney. 'There,' he said. 'Put it together in the train. It'll give you something to do.'

Rodney's mother puts him on the train.

'There,' she said, 'there's plenty of room to sit down. Don't forget to get out of the train at Kenge. Give everybody's love to Grandfather and Granny.'

'And be a good boy,' said Rodney. 'Mother, you be a good girl.'

On the way he fiddles with the ticket.

He put the case on the seat beside him, and looked out of the window. Then he looked at the ticket, with its chopped-out piece. He put the piece in its place, and the ticket looked right again. Then the piece fell out, and he put both parts in his pocket.

He now begins to grapple with the unfamiliar aspects of time and distance.

The train stopped at a station. He went to the window again and looked out. Mother could have come very quickly to this station and got on here. But there was no one on the platform but a railway man. The train waited a moment, and then left. Rodney sat down again.

At the next station he looked out again, but there was still no Mother. But he really knew she would not be there. And at the third station he forgot to look at the platform at all.

Thus Mr Mayne does something very remarkable. He gives an accurate, almost scientifically checkable description of the boy's stage of mental development in terms of distance, time and powers of relating the two. But this subtlety would be lost on another child, of course – as indeed it would on many adults.

As the journey proceeds, the author cleverly and perceptively has the child using his recently assimilated experience to come to terms with something else that is new to him.

Kenge was among the hills. The train began to get into cuttings, where the ground had been nipped out like the nipped-out piece of ticket, in a V shape. The sides of the V went higher and higher. A bridge sped by overhead, and then another, and then a tunnel closed in over the train, and all the yellow lamps came on in the carriage, and it was noisy.

Here Mr Mayne's skill as a storyteller is in evidence, for the noise from that tunnel, which runs under a wood, is to constitute the central mystery of the book for Rodney and his playmates – who at first take it to be the roaring of some kind of monster. But the preliminary journey continues (now into its fourth page).

Grandfather was on the platform, looking into every carriage as it came by. He came to Rodney's door and opened it, and that was a good thing, because there was no door handle inside at all. Rodney was glad he had not noticed before, or he would have worried all the way to Kenge.

Here, one feels, Mr Mayne has missed a valuable storytelling trick in *not* having Rodney notice it before and thereby communicating a feeling of suspense to the reader. But back to the ticket.

He wondered whether he had to give both pieces up, or whether some more would be cut away from it, and he would be able to keep it.

This thread of minor suspense is only finally dropped, at the end of Chapter One, after Rodney and his grandfather have greeted each other and watched the train out.

The man at the barrier took both pieces of ticket, looked at them, fitted them together, and gave back the little piece. 'I don't want it all,' he said.

'He's kept the best piece,' said Rodney; and they began to walk to Grandfather's house.

A punch-line – or, rather, a playful-slap-line – worthy of Sterne.

But most of the fussing over the ticket is not a matter of deadpan kidding on Rodney's part. He genuinely wonders about the pieces – as a child would. It could be argued that in doing so, for so long, he is rather stupid for a boy of seven or so. Perhaps he is. Perhaps not. Train journeys in this motor-car age are not all that common for many young children. It could, on the other hand, be claimed with some justification that no mother who wasn't stupid would send him on the train alone – with the hazards of locked doors, unpleasant strangers, etc. But then so many parents *are* stupid in this respect.

Yet even allowing that Rodney himself is a special case, more stupid than most children of his age, that is no reason for condemning the passage. Fiction is full of special cases, is indeed largely *about* special cases, and Mr Mayne has presented this one, this highly individual young character, in an interesting and amusing way for an adult reader. What is wrong with the passage in my view is that a child reader, taking the fictional experience (the ticket, the collectors, the train, the cutting, the distances and times) on its face value, is likely to be confused by it. Rodney's perplexity in grappling with a new experience is likely to create a further perplexity – and a further breaking down, into elements consonant with the reader's own experience, of the constituents into which Rodney has already broken it down. In other words, an adult, with his vast natural fund of common experiences, can witness with understanding and appreciation Rodney's grapplings, just as he can the young Stephen Dedalus's, or Leo Proudhammer's, or Benjy Compson's, whereas a child has not yet built up a sufficiently high vantage point.

Later in the book Mr Mayne misses an even more important story-telling trick because of his preoccupation with showing things too exclusively through Rodney's eyes and in the boy's terms. Rodney makes friends with a group of children slightly older than himself who have built a tree-house in the woods. This is a marvellous den, much envied by the villainous Maureen Garley, splendidly drawn as the sort of quarrelsome child who becomes the neighbourhood *bête noire* and scape-goat. Now the children notice that some of the trees have white crosses painted on them and – understandably in Rodney's case, less so in that of his older companions – none of the children knows that they are connected with the tree-felling going on in other parts of the woods. Mr Mayne leaves it at that, without attempting to tip-off the reader in any way, so that when Maureen paints a white cross on the house tree no feeling of pleasurable horror can be experienced by readers equally unaware of the mark's significance. To my mind, not even the glorious comedy of the short painting scene can make up for that unnecessary loss of suspense.

> She knelt on the ground, and began to stir the paint with a piece of wood. It was white paint. Rodney saw the piece of wood turn from brown to white. Then she dipped the brush into the pot, and made it painty. She stood up, walked to the trunk of the tree, and began to make a mark on it.
>
> Then Rodney knew that she was making the same mark on the tree as the one they had seen in other places on the common. Maureen must have made them all, and he did not know why. Perhaps she was counting them.
>
> Rodney would have painted the whole tree white, he thought. Maureen just made her mark. Rodney forgot she was the enemy, and stepped out into the clearing to ask her what she was doing. She did not smile, she did not answer. She stepped forward with her brush, dipped it in the paint, and made it ready. Then she painted a slappy white stripe right up Rodney's front, all the way up his body and straight up his face. Then, while he stood all surprised, she brushed his hair with it, and walked off.

End of chapter.

Faced with such sound narrative technique as that, one is all the more saddened at the misdirected psychologizing analysed above.

Many other writers for children, some consciously following Mr Mayne's example, fall into this trap – urged there by the opinions of critics and editors who fail to distinguish between the demands of child characters and the needs of child readers, between what is essentially fiction about children and what is essentially fiction for children. In falling into such a trap – and it is an honourable accident, generally befalling those whose talents children can least afford to have obscured – there is a great danger that they will drive the children themselves along paths where everything is less confusing but trashy. This might be termed the McFiggin Syndrome. Hoodoo McFiggin, as lovers of Stephen Leacock's sketches will remember, was also a victim of thoughtless adult good intentions. For Christmas he wanted: skates, a puppy, an airgun, a bicycle, a sledge and a drum. He got: 'a pair of nice, strong, number-four boots, laces and all', some celluloid collars, a tooth-brush, a pair of pants, galluses and a small family Bible. He himself had saved up his pennies to buy his father a cigar and his mother a brooch. And how did Hoodoo take it?

Hoodoo had now seen all his presents, and he arose and dressed. But he still had the fun of playing with his toys. That is always the chief delight of Christmas morning.

First he played with his tooth-brush. He got a whole lot of water and brushed all his teeth with it. This was huge.

Then he played with his collars. He had no end of fun with them, taking them all out one by one and swearing at them, and then putting them back and swearing at the whole lot together.

The next toy was his pants. He had immense fun there, putting them on and taking them off again, and then trying to guess which side was which by merely looking at them.

After that he took his book and read some adventures called 'Genesis' till breakfast-time.

Then he went downstairs and kissed his father and mother. His father was smoking a cigar, and his mother had her new brooch on. Hoodoo's face was thoughtful, and a light seemed to have broken in upon his mind. Indeed, I think it altogether likely that next Christmas he will hang on to his own money and take chances on what the angels bring.

Everyone concerned with children's fiction would do well to beware of setting up the McFiggin Syndrome. Especially where the tooth-brushes turn out to be insecurely bristled and the pants a poor quality mixture of cotton and shoddy.

Already, in the various examples discussed above, we have touched on many of the elements children seem especially to look for in their fiction. Apart from the major necessity of a ready means of identification – a smooth and speedy way into the more or less unfamiliar world being presented to them – we have come across the following desiderata:

28

- A wealth of concrete accurate detail

- An element of anticipation, hopeful or fearful, that is often more attractive to children than surprise

- A constant appeal to curiosity in little matters as well as in large ones – an appeal that guarantees suspense and is created by care in revealing no more than is necessary at any given point

- Irony – but only when properly announced

- Verbal dexterity – which might vary from the higher magic of incantation to base trickery – in the prose itself

- Games and the play element – not only directly presented but also reflected in the form and texture of a story

- Plausible but easily detectable chicanery on the part of certain characters

- Great gifts of improvisation in work or adventure or play on the part of characters

- Various archetypal threats and promises in the plots, corresponding to the child's own basic fears and hopes

- The opportunity to experience known and recognized great dangers vicariously and therefore safely

- The opportunity to perpetrate known and recognized mischief or misbehaviour vicariously and therefore with impunity

- An uncluttered, preferably humorous attitude towards adults – especially where this tends to cut them down nearer to child-size

- The carrying of things to their logical conclusions and the squeezing of every drop of humour or excitement from a situation, often beyond the limits an adult is likely to tolerate

We shall be examining these elements in greater detail in subsequent chapters.

Chapter two

Likes and dislikes: Some fallacies

There is nothing like the subject of children – and especially the aspect concerned with their likes and dislikes – for attracting the instant pundit, with his dogma and his sweeping asseverations. Teachers, to their cost, know this better than anybody. It is in fact one of their chief occupational hazards: the steady driving to distraction caused by know-all parents and industrious writers of letters to local papers. Faced with such antagonists it is useless to protest that one has been a child oneself too, with perhaps a different residue of memories, or has children of one's own, or is in daily contact with a broader cross-section of children than the critic is, or even that one has, after all, undergone a more or less intensive training in child psychology. Nothing can shake the vest-pocket Spock in full cry and he will as likely as not turn your gentle protests violently against you. You had a childhood yourself? It was probably sheltered, or uncommonly rough, or in some other way quite untypical. You have children of your own, or daily contact with a classful, a whole schoolful? God help them. And for 'intensive' in relation to teacher-training, the instant pundit too often reads 'expensive' and agrees and snorts about the waste of taxpayers' money – which waste, in keeping with his general headlong tone, is almost invariably 'sheer'.

In the children's book world too it can get pretty uncomfortable at times for the producer, the conscientious professional practitioner. Here too there are areas where purely personal experience and prejudice are rationalized, elevated into dogma and thrust at him. And here too amusement ends when attempts are made to translate the more popular of such dogma into standard practice. In teaching, this can be done and is done by exerting pressure through politicians at all levels; in the book field, it is usually done directly – by whatever instant pundit happens to have the ear of a publisher. Usually he will be a staff man – a sales manager, perhaps, or a member of the promotion and publicity department, or even an editor – and any teacher who is currently having a rough time in the face of a wave of uninformed criticism may draw consolation from the fact that at least his adversaries are not as a rule close professional associates or in any position of direct control over his work.

This situation is, happily, becoming less common than it was, say, twenty years ago. But to understand why such an undesirable state of affairs could exist at all in publishing, one must realize that until quite recently 'juvenile' books – and this very designation tells us much about the way in which they were regarded – were the Cinderellas of most publishers' lists, in spite of the fact that they often provided the basic bread and butter without which a firm might be in danger of foundering. Under these circumstances, it was not uncommon for a children's department to be run by second-stringers – editors who could be spared from other departments or lady clerks more familiar with the intricacies of royalty calculations or film rights – and perhaps supervised with lax geniality by whichever junior director happened to have young children of his own. Even now, when the accountants and take-over specialists have taught general publishers to regard a substantial children's list as the gilt-edged security it is, there are places where some of the second-stringers are still in control, entrenched now and made more powerful by their employers' uneasy recognition that they hold key-posts; and where first-rate children's specialists have been appointed they still tend some-times to be regarded with feelings of mildly amused contempt by executives in other departments. The result is that if a well-informed competent children's editor doesn't also possess a strong thrustful personality he – or, still more often, she – is likely to be overshadowed and overruled by others. Thus there are sections of the field that are still comparatively wide open for the professional bright boys in publishing, usually in the sales or promotion departments, to launch their job-justi-fying diktats: to impose on their book committees, in slick pseudo-scientific terms, the same kind of spurious spur-of-the-moment rubbish as is perpetrated by any pundit-in-the-street.

As if this were not troublesome enough to the conscientious children's author, the situation is paralleled in the field of reviewing. Children's books are still regarded by many newspaper and magazine editors as unimportant trifles, to be dumped by the truckload once or twice a year on some junior member of the staff. Even where a more intelligent interest is taken, a magazine editor will still shrink from devoting more than a few pages to them three or four times a year. True, in such cases qualified reviewers will be used, but they will be expected to sift through much larger batches than the reviewers of adult books and they will more often than not be paid less for their considerable (and sometimes almost physical) pains. In this field too, then, it is not surprising that a fairly substantial number of fallacies are hastily recollected, repeated with conviction, and so perpetuated.

As the writer of a number of children's books over the past ten years or so, I have had various first-hand opportunities of observing such trends and lapses both in publishing and reviewing. One of the most glaring and persistently recurring examples is connected with my first book, *Jim Starling*. At the time it was written it was still quite rare for books about working-class children in industrial environments to be published, partly because of the prevalence of a belief that children in poor or drab surroundings disliked reading about such circumstances and craved nothing less than total escape, and partly because their parents and other relations didn't form a regular book-buying market anyway. Now I had once taught such children in such an environment over a period of several years, and I was therefore quick to appreciate the growing demand for that sort of book that was being voiced by teachers and librarians. I too had had many awkward moments in the classroom when trying to present children's books with middle-class settings and values that were often quite foreign to my pupils. I too felt that in the interests of identification and the pleasure of recognition, it would be a good thing if these children could at least occasionally read about their own kind. Consequently, I wrote such a book and, because of the unusual nature of some of the problems involved, I also wrote a number of articles about these problems. And it was then that I first realized what a lot of atrociously sloppy thinkers there are among those concerned with children's books.

Perhaps it was the mention of class that did it – causing the Blimps to reach for their mental riding-crops and the social workers their case-books. At all events, letters and counter-articles began to fly about like shrapnel – some accusing me of wanting to bolshevize children's books, some praising what they considered to be my social democratic crusade, and few, if any, recognizing that all I wished to do was help fill a certain gap. Used to administering comprehension tests to twelve-year-old backward boys I was amazed at the inability of these adult literate people – and they included critics, fellow authors and leader-writers – to read correctly what I had plainly written. Even today I am often accused – with the irritating implication that at last I have seen the error of my ways and may now be forgiven – of having wished to provide working-class children with *nothing but* stories about children like themselves, or, worse still, of having suggested that working-class children can enjoy only such stories *and none of any other kind*. (I am aware that the last six words are redundant. I am also aware that in matters of this nature one can't be too explicit.) Here then was a fallacy, born out of ignorance by prejudice, swaddled in the scraps of more general fallacies, and dumped on my own front doorstep.

on the wall would some day fall off and brain Peggotty, or that the vicar is destined to attack Mrs Copperfield behind the pulpit, a sub-editor might have given us something like this:

> We had a pew with a high back. I used to sit in it with Peggotty and my mother. Peggotty used to be cross when I looked out of the window towards our house, even though she herself was always doing it, to make sure it was safe. She expected me to look at the clergyman, which made me feel self-conscious, and often my attention used to stray – to other members of the congregation or to the memorial tablets on the wall. Often I would imagine what kind of games one could play using the pulpit, and sometimes I would grow drowsy and fall asleep and drop off my seat.

Similar facile barbarity can be inflicted on the *Tom Sawyer* church passage by anyone with a sharp pencil and an eye for bare bones and 'strict essentials', but perhaps enough has been done to show the tendency to resort to summary instead of scene – or, as some would put it, report instead of episode. To see the results of such a tendency at its worst, one need go no further than the first shelf of children's fiction one comes to – there are likely to be only too many examples. To pick one from my own shelves almost at random, let me quote from a book by Miss Elfrida Vipont, first published in 1958 as *More About Dowbiggins* and reissued, inexplicably, ten years later as *A Win for Henry Conyers*. The arrival of the Vicar is expected? At once we have slapped before us a couple of flat cold paragraphs beginning: 'The Reverend Charles Meredith had only recently arrived in Hilderstone. Previously the living had been vacant for two or three years . . . ' etc., etc. One of the children goes to put on the kettle for the visitor? Another long paragraph of explication: 'They had earned the electric kettle with the "long let" when Miss Weston and her niece Miss Geraldine had been paying guests at Dowbiggins . . .' etc., etc., etc. Earlier, in the first few pages, the fact that Father 'just paints' is mentioned by a character. There follow two long paragraphs, running to a page apiece, about Henry Conyers: 'That was true, of course. Jim's father, Henry Conyers, had been painting for years . . .' etc., etc., etc., etc. After which Jim has only to look up the sloping field towards Dowbiggins and, quick as a flash, the authoress looks in again for another paragraph, this time recapitulating the boy's school career.

This method, drearily long-winded as it seems, is actually a quicker way of getting down (if not *across*) the essential facts – and, to give Miss Vipont credit, hers are all, by and large, essential to the plot – than presenting the information in some other way, more closely integrated with the action. But in this raw state it *is*, only too obviously, information, a series of hand-outs. With a Dickens or a Twain, a book containing the same amount of information would have been longer, much longer, but far less boring for the reader, adult or child.

Now there were times, because of the sheer exigencies of space resulting from publication in monthly parts, when Dickens himself had to make fairly severe cuts, and it is as fascinating as it is instructive to read some of the passages thus snipped. Here, for instance, as it now stands, is the passage from *Barnaby Rudge* where Solomon Daisy describes to his taproom cronies his experience with the 'ghost':

A more complete picture of terror than the little man presented, it would be difficult to imagine. The perspiration stood in beads upon his face, his knees knocked together, his every limb trembled, the power of articulation was quite gone; and there he stood, panting for breath, gazing on them with such livid ashy looks, that they were infected with his fear, though ignorant of its occasion, and, reflecting his dismayed and horror-stricken visage, stared back again without venturing to question him; until old John Willet, in a fit of temporary insanity, made a dive at his cravat, and, seizing him by that portion of his dress, shook him to and fro until his very teeth appeared to rattle in his head.

'Tell us what's the matter, sir,' said John, 'or I'll kill you. Tell us what's the matter, sir, or in another second, I'll have your head under the biler. How dare you look like that? Is anybody a following of you? What do you mean? Say something, or I'll be the death of you, I will.'

Mr. Willet, in his frenzy, was so near keeping his word to the very letter (Solomon Daisy's eyes already beginning to roll in an alarming manner, and certain guttural sounds, as of a choking man, to issue from his throat), that the two bystanders, recovering in some degree, plucked him off his victim by main force, and placed the little clerk of Chigwell in a chair. Directing a fearful gaze all round the room, he implored them in a faint voice to give him some drink; and above all to lock the house-door and close and bar the shutters of the room, without a moment's loss of time. The latter request did not tend to re-assure his hearers, or to fill them with the most comfortable sensations; they complied with it, however, with the greatest expedition; and having handed him a bumper of brandy-and-water, nearly boiling hot, waited to hear what he might have to tell them.

'Oh, Johnny,' said Solomon, shaking him by the hand. 'Oh, Parkes. Oh, Tommy Cobb. Why did I leave this house tonight! On the nineteenth of March – of all nights in the year, on the nineteenth of March!'

And here is the passage that Dickens was forced to cut. It came from between the last two paragraphs.

> They waited so long, and questioned him so often, without receiving any more satisfactory answer than a wild start, that Mr. Willet had entertained serious thoughts of [throttling him *deleted*] inserting a fork in his arm or leg by way of opening a vein, and had indeed begun to polish one of those instruments with his apron, and to look intently at the little man as if considering where to have him, when Solomon Daisy, with tears in his eyes, implored them to have patience for a minute longer and to fill his glass once more, to the end that he might rally his scattered spirits and be coherent in his speech.
> 'If he don't tell us now,' said John as he stirred the liquor and held it to his lips to take, 'if he don't tell us now in a quarter of a minute what's the matter, I shall do him a mischief. Mind that.'[1]

Note that the natural inclination had been to expand – to put flesh on the bones, not take it off. Even in the deleted passage itself there had already been the magnificently rich expansion from mere throttling to the circumstantial blood-letting. And if anyone is still in doubt about which kind of writing children prefer, let him read to a group of them first the passage as it now stands and then with the cut restored. Then let him ask which version they liked better and – if they're old enough to enjoy analysis – why.

One can understand Dickens's decision, or his editor's, to make a cut in this case. There was a crisis involving space, which Dickens fully appreciated, and that was that. Certainly there was no nonsense about the cut's being artistically desirable, or about the readers of monthly instalments being unable to tolerate anything that might smack of irrelevance.

Mr Jasper Rose, in his interesting monograph on Lucy Boston,[2] is too thoughtful to repeat such a fallacy in its entirety. He can write, 'Most people, in particular young people, read a story in order to find out what happens: a dawdling tale does not appeal to them very much' – but he precedes this with the admission that:

> . . . it is possible to saunter about in the company of Laurence Sterne or Henry James without losing patience with their digressions, their dilatoriness, their lack of interest in arriving at a destination. But Sterne and James are acquired, sophisticated tastes.

This gives a clue to the whole misunderstanding, for here, surely, he has been taken in by the art that conceals art. James was – as any examina-

---

1. Quoted in *Dickens at Work* by John Butt and Kathleen Tillotson.
2. Bodley Head.

tion of his notes and prefaces will show – passionately interested in arriving at a destination. And Sterne was openly, even comically obsessed by it in *Tristram Shandy*. The reason we don't lose patience with his digressions is precisely because in each he *is* telling us what happens next, but only a fragmentary part of it. *Tristram Shandy* is in fact a great complex of minor cliff-hangers.

Quite contrary to the general dogma, children's literature is full of examples of meandering, of dwelling on incident very often at the expense of the main action, from the by-play in *Tom Sawyer*, through Arthur Ransome's preoccupation with processes, to the slapstick and knockabout and ritual exchanges in such immensely popular books as the *Billy Bunter* series or the *William* books, where, apropos of practically nothing but his own distinctive personality, a character will make a detailed display of his greed, say, or disgruntlement, or his (usually disastrous) passion for such domestic experiments as tight-rope walking across his bedroom.

The fact is that a child lives absorbed in the present, and is intensely interested in the detail of the moment. Time-patterns spreading beyond an hour or two seem to mean little to children and certainly cannot be retained in the mind with any degree of consistency. This is often evident in their own writing. Ask a child of any age up to ten to describe a friend or relation and the chances are you will be presented with something like 'My brother is twelve-years-old and he has brown hair and red socks and blue eyes' – where the temporary, if sufficiently striking, is given the same value as the permanent, and treated as such.

So, in my opinion, Mr Rose is quite right but in the wrong context. Children do most assuredly want to know what happens next, but in the context of the incident rather than the book – and if the incident is sufficiently interesting they will become totally absorbed in its working-out, without giving a thought to its place in any larger design.

But this brings us to the deeper and more difficult question of how an author ensures that a child will want to know what happens next: of what it is that makes a children's story grip the attention in spite of any straying away from the main plot line and even from what is generally thought of as 'action'.

Chapter three

Making them wait: The importance of timing

The capturing and holding of children's attention – the ability to have them 'hanging on every word' – is not simply a matter of offering them high adventure: bloody battles, fearsome monsters, fantastic happenings. If such things are badly presented attention will soon flag. Nor is it simply a question of offering them subjects less melodramatic but near to their hearts: like food, or fun and games, or security, or the love of a parent. Again, if badly presented such themes may arrest but they will not grip the attention. A more valid proposition might be this: *that an author will ensure that a child will want to know what happens next,* (a) *so long as he takes care not to tell what happens next-but-one, and* (b) *so long as he sees to it that the possibility – awful or delightful – of what-might-happen-soon is always fairly apparent.*

But this needs explaining.

Basically the method is one that is relevant to all forms of fiction – indeed to all forms of exposition where it is desired to grip the attention as firmly as possible. Wilkie Collins summed it up in the third part of his precept: 'Make 'em laugh, make 'em cry, make 'em wait.' Flaubert put it less flamboyantly with his '*Il faut interesser*'. Miss Elizabeth Bowen crystallizes it beautifully in her *Notes on Writing a Novel:* 'Stress on manner of telling: keep in mind, "I will a tale *unfold*". Interest of watching a dress that has been well-packed unpacked from a dress-box. Interest of watching silk handkerchiefs drawn from a conjuror's watch.' The crowd around a skilful market barker or a mock auctioneer succumbs to the method, as first one thing then another is brought from its carton, unwrapped and displayed. Even hard-bitten parliamentary reporters and politicians can be hooked by it, and played, as the following news item demonstrates:

41

Chancellor proves master of suspense

Calm, confident and surprising, Mr. Callaghan, Chancellor of the Exchequer, unfolded his Budget to the House of Commons tonight. Was it by chance that he had chosen to wear white heather in his buttonhole?

The main surprise which he had to give to the House was his selective employment tax. He built up anticipation for this in a manner which any theatrical producer would have applauded.

Would it be useful, asked Mr. Callaghan, to increase duty on beer, tobacco and spirits? No, he rejected these ancient expedients.

What was then left? Purchase tax and income tax, but again he proposed to set these aside.

By that time the crowded House had exhausted all its faculties for intelligent guessing. Jaws were dropping and eyes became ever more speculative.[1]

And it is of course a method that all good teachers make use of when planning a lesson or series of lessons.

In some of the examples quoted earlier in this study we see the technique at its best. Mark Twain, in the church scene with Tom Sawyer and his beetle, is not dealing with anything bloody or thunderous: just a boy with an insect in a cap-box in a familiar – some would say hum-drum – setting. But the readers already know the boy and they are told the insect nips and from these two facts the delightful-awful possibility is born immediately. *What will happen?* becomes *What form will the catastrophe take?* Given this interest – or having created it – the author takes care not to squander its potential. He knows he can 'make 'em wait' and he knows too that the longer he can continue to do so, enter-tainingly, the better. So first we have the boy himself being pinched – just to give evidence of the creature's capabilities – and then, at once, the reflex flip. Dozens of writers would then have gone straight on to the climax and had the flip carry the insect to a nearby parishioner or even into the pulpit. Twain knows better. He has the boy watching it as it lies helpless in the aisle, and so introduces another speculative element, of a less violent sort, hinging on how the owner might contrive to get it back. This is firmly kept in a secondary place, however, for the author now brings on the poodle, brings it, in fact, step by step, inch by inch, nearer the beetle until the inevitable happens – but still only on a limited scale. Again the insect nips, again it is flipped away in a reflex of pain, and again it lands in the aisle and not on priest or parishioner. And now the pace is stepped up, and the reader's pleasure in watching the unwary

---

1. Report by T. F. Lindsay in the London *Daily Telegraph* 4 May 1966.

fall into a trap is temporarily replaced by his interest in watching the outcome of open hostilities. Will the dog kill the insect? Might someone intervene – Tom himself perhaps? Patiently, careful to give nothing away, the author proceeds, step by step, to the catastrophe: with the dog being pinched in exactly the right place for maximum *comic* embarrassment and then creating the maximum amount of disturbance in the very place where this is deemed most deplorable. To all children who have ever been reprimanded for giggling or raising their voices in church the wait has been more than amply rewarded; and if any should still wistfully hanker after what might have been – hanker after the hullabaloo that might have been raised if the beetle had been flung into the folds of the preacher's gown, say – then such a reader will almost certainly be doing it as a criticism of life and not of the author, so well has Twain created the illusion.

A simpler example, but remarkable for its evidence of a born sense of timing, is provided in the second story by the six-year-old Susan – written, it should be added, without any help whatsoever save for the occasional spelling she felt unsure about. Here too there is no reliance on momentous deeds – all is peaceful domesticity. But in the second sentence the note of the awful possibility is struck by Baby Bear's *cri de coeur:* 'Oh no, not him!' Few experienced professional writers could have bettered that. With startling economy, Susan made absolutely sure that Arthur's entry would be awaited with eagerness and observed with complete attention – and although the ominous use of 'black' with reference to the taxi and Arthur's suit has much to recommend it as an example of a fine evocative touch – the sense of timing, much more important and considerably rarer, is what is really astonishing. For Susan sustains it throughout the story. As soon as Arthur arrives we are told about the 'big parcel' – always an object of fascination to children – and this fascination is voiced and therefore brought into focus by Baby Bear's immediate reaction: 'O o, there might be something in that parcel for me.' But there, for the moment, the author leaves it, turning to the equally attractive element of Arthur's unpleasantness with her reference to his mother, whom the reader has already met. This is followed by a concrete example of Arthur's unpleasantness, as he pokes Baby Bear in the ear. But before long we return to the parcel and the two elements are blended, but very carefully. We see the parcel unpacked, item by item. We wonder about the good things, speculating on whether the chocolate is for Mother Bear and the lollipop for Baby Bear, and this makes our sense of delighted outrage stronger than ever when we come to the orange peel and the banana skin. Now we begin to wonder how they will receive such presents, and again, with the skill of a born storyteller, Susan takes her time. Mother Bear looks very sad. What is she thinking? That is something else we must wait for. But the beastly Arthur is laughing. Will Baby Bear be able to show the same restraint as his mother? Yes, he does. But now Arthur is getting his sweets out of his pocket. Ah! Maybe he's not so bad after all. Maybe they're the real presents. Maybe he'll hand them around. But no . . . So then, quite surpassing herself, the author has Mother Bear reacting more positively to this behaviour – if at first only in a whisper. Even now the reader is kept agog. We are not told straight away *what* she whispered. Only *that* she whispered. Then: 'This is what she whispered. . . .' The pause, the hiatus, is fractional, but it couldn't be more effective in giving comic emphasis to the beautifully oddly phrased instruction: 'Go to your cousin and thump your cousin' – which itself embodies a further fractional delay. As I hinted earlier, many a professional writer would give ten per cent of his earnings for such a facility, and had he witnessed the scenes at the reading and many rereadings of this story in the school – the peals of laughter, the tears of pure joy – he'd probably be prepared to double it.

With the *Tom Sawyer* church scene we have the unfolding process taking place in connection with the delightful possibility (or the awful that is really the delightful to the reader). In the Baby Bear story there is a similar context. In the eggs episode from *Chancy and the Grand Rascal* there is a split: the possibility could be delightful, with Chancy earning some much-needed money, or awful, with Chancy losing what little he has. Essentially this is a gambling situation, with the author being careful to tilt the odds only slightly in the latter direction. In the following passage from *The Borrowers*, however, the possibility uppermost in the reader's mind is almost wholly awful. Arrietty is making her first excursion outside the house. Pod, her father, warns her not to stray too far, after having pointed out that there is always the danger, remote but there, that someone might make it impossible for her to climb back up the doorstep by taking away the shoescraper by which she has descended. (The Borrowers, it should be remembered, are only a few inches high and make a living as scavengers in a normal household.) Furthermore, there is always the added danger that someone might shut the front door. Pod, of course, has some borrowing work to do inside.

'. . . Well,' he said, beginning to move away, 'stay down a bit if you like. But stay close!'

Arrietty watched him move away from the step and then she looked about her. Oh, glory! Oh, joy! Oh, freedom! The sunlight, the grasses, the soft, moving air and half-way up the bank, where it curved round the corner, a flowering cherry-tree! Below it on the path lay a stain of pinkish petals and, at the tree's foot, pale as butter, a nest of primroses.

Arrietty threw a cautious glance towards the front doorstep and then, light and dancey, in her soft red shoes, she ran towards the petals.

They were curved like shells and rocked as she touched them. She gathered several up and laid them one side in the other . . . up and up . . . like a card castle. And then she spilled them. Pod came again to the top of the step and looked along the path. 'Don't you go far,' he said after a moment. Seeing his lips move, she smiled back at him: she was too far already to hear the words.

A greenish beetle, shining in the sunlight, came towards her across the stones. She laid her fingers lightly on its shell and it stood still, waiting and watchful, and when she moved her hand the beetle went swiftly on. An ant came hurrying in a busy zigzag. She danced in front of it to tease it and put out her foot. It stared at her, nonplussed, waving its antennae; then pettishly, as though put out, it swerved away. Two birds came down, quarrelling shrilly, into the grass below the tree. One flew away but Arrietty could see the other among the moving grass stems above her on the slope. Cautiously she moved towards the bank and climbed a little nervously in amongst the green blades. As she parted them gently with her bare hands, drops of water plopped on her skirt and she felt the red shoes become damp. But on she went, pulling herself up now and again by rooty stems into this jungle of moss and wood-violet and creeping leaves of clover. The sharp-seeming grass blades, waist high, were tender to the touch and sprang back lightly behind her as she passed. When at last she reached the foot of the tree, the bird took fright and flew away and she sat down suddenly on a gnarled leaf of primrose. The air was filled with scent. 'But nothing will play with you,' she thought and saw the cracks and furrows of the primrose leaves held crystal beads of dew. If she pressed the leaf these rolled like marbles. The bank was warm, almost too warm here within the shelter of the tall grass, and the sandy earth smelled dry. Standing up, she picked a primrose. The pink stalk felt tender and living in her hands and was covered with silvery hairs, and when she held the flower, like a parasol, between her eyes and the sky, she saw the sun's pale light through the veined petals. On a piece of bark she found a wood-louse and she struck it lightly with her swaying flower. It curled immediately and became a ball, bumping softly away downhill in amongst the grass roots. But she knew about wood-lice. There were plenty of them at home under the floor. Homily always scolded her if she played with them because, she said, they smelled of old knives. She lay back among the stalks of the primroses and they made a coolness between her and the sun, and then, sighing, she turned her head and looked sideways up the bank among the grass stems. Startled, she caught her breath. Something had moved above her on the bank. Something had glittered. Arrietty stared.

Stage by stage – drawn by the grass, the bank, the tree, the primroses and distracted by the various insects and birds, and always with careful reference to the increasing distance from the door and reminders of her size – Arrietty wanders away and therefore, automatically, in to greater and greater danger. And, as if this weren't gripping enough, there is the continual fascination of seeing normal things through the eyes of someone so tiny. Indeed, this sense of the awful possibility and this fascination are present throughout the whole of the book; they can hardly fail to be, given the size of the heroine and her family and their obvious vulnerability. Nevertheless, as the sample shows, Mary Norton makes the most of it by her skill at unfolding the narrative. Note, in particular, the increase in tension – already tight for the reader if not for the character – created by the last four very short sentences, producing a corresponding set of four questions, each of the first three implicitly answered by the next – but only partially. Thus: *What* had startled her? *What* had moved? *What* had glittered? *What* was she staring at? The fact that this comes at the end of a chapter makes it all the more powerful, and even at the beginning of the next – 'It was an eye' – Miss Norton is in no hurry to specify whose or what's eye, preferring instead to dwell on its size, its enormity and the voice of its owner.

Where the awful possibility is less obvious the difficulty in conveying this to children is greater. Sometimes, as in the train journey passage from William Mayne's *The Yellow Aeroplane*, and in the situation arising from the marking of the trees in the same book, an author will, intentionally or otherwise, make no attempt to do so – thereby sacrificing some of the narrative's power to grip. When this is not a simple failure to use the opportunity and is intentional, it is often because of a quite worthy but, I think, misguided aestheticism, which cautions an author against obtruding himself too much – against making the warning noises in his own voice. This has more to commend it in the case of adult fiction where one can count on the reader to respond from a greater fund of experience than a child's and therefore to subtler promptings – though even here some of the finest works, certainly of pre-nineteenth-century fiction and now of the newest wave of novelists, make use of the minatory voice of the omniscient author. Personally, I am all in favour of a wider use of this in children's fiction, where, after all, it is more urgently required and can pay greater dividends. It needn't be altogether as clumsy as might be feared, for there are various tones that even a minatory aside can have. Rabelais, for instance, makes great comic as well as attention-focusing play with it in the middle of some of his soberly detailed actions. ('Now note that Panurge had tied on to the end of his long codpiece a fine silken tuft, red, white, green, and blue, and inside he had hidden a beautiful orange.') In a modern children's story, *The Flight of the Doves*, Walter Macken handled the problem rather less blatantly if not as crisply in a passage in which a runaway brother and sister are cornered at the top of a deserted castle by a stranger who has been pursuing them. They don't know, nor does the reader at this point, that the man has orders to kill them. They only know that he is unpleasant and up to no good.

It was a terrible situation to be in. They couldn't run any more. They couldn't go over and climb down the steep sides of the castle. They couldn't run down the steps into the arms of the man, if it was he. Why did he come into the castle? It was the last place he should have come. The rain had stopped. There was still some pools of water on the flags. It would be easy to slip on them and fall down to the cold dung-covered floor at the bottom.

Then the opening was filled with this man.

He had to bend his head to come through.

He looked at the two children crouched against the wall. He held out his hand.

'Don't be frightened,' he said. 'I'm your friend.'

He advances slowly; they back away. He continues trying to reassure them; they remain suspicious.

He moved another step towards them.

They moved away from him. Finn reached his hand out to the broken wall and found a stone that fitted his fist.

'Don't be like that, kid,' Nicko said. 'It will be all right, I tell you. Come with me. We'll have a good time. You'll see a new land and you'll have fun.'

They backed away from him.

He didn't want to look at it, but he knew the flags were broken behind them, that they had only another few paces to go and they would fall. He hoped he didn't have to put his hands on them. If they fell on their own, that would be an accident, wouldn't it?

Finn knew this too. He raised the stone.

'Keep away from us,' he said. Derval was gripping him around the hips, her head hidden in his back.

To an adult nurtured on post-Jamesian fiction, the intrusion of the man's thoughts in a scene that had so far been viewed exclusively through Finn's eyes might seem jarring. But the increase in tension when it is known for sure what the man intends to do is terrific – and while Macken might have hesitated to use such a device in one of his adult novels I think he was quite right to do so here and so show an artistic sensibility transcending that displayed by rule-of-thumb purists.

Another interesting example occurs in one of my own early books for children, *The Boy at the Window*. In this I set out to write a story that would be gripping despite the fact that it was all to be seen through the eyes of a bedridden boy, confined to the same room throughout the action. My model here seemed impeccable for an undertaking of this sort: Alfred Hitchcock's film, *Rear Window*, in which the hero, immobilized by a broken leg, observes a number of seemingly insignificant but rather strange incidents in an apartment opposite, which eventually add up to a murder.

Now embarking on this exercise I had, in my inexperience as an author, overlooked a number of things. The film was for adults; my book was for children. The film was directed by Hitchcock, which was all an adult needed to know by way of a warning that the incidents observed were not to be dismissed as trivial or innocent. The film was in fact a who's-going-to-do-what rather than a who-done-it. Somewhat fool-like, then, I rushed in with my who's-going-to-do-what, with the boy observing all sorts of comings and goings to and from a block of shops opposite his window, and I had written the whole thing and submitted it to a publisher and had it rejected and roared with anger at the vagueness of the reasons given (for it was neatly enough written, carefully thought out and brought to an exciting climax) before I realized what was wrong. Children, picking it up and starting cold, as it were, couldn't be expected to know that the series of tiny incidents observed by the boy in the first four or five chapters were not as trivial as they seemed, and they would therefore soon become bored. What was wanted, obviously, was that the reader should be properly alerted to the fact that something dreadful was to happen as a result of those incidents, and, thus alerted, induced to draw conclusions of his own from the incidents. Since this went on for chapters, a mere warning note sounded however openly in the body of the first few pages of text seemed insufficient, therefore I decided to use italicized introductory passages of about half a page each above the first twelve chapter headings, the first beginning with: '*You may say: "There was this boy at the window, with nothing to do but look out all day. Why didn't he realize what was going on in the sweet shop over the street? Why did it take him so long to discover who was the ringleader of the crooks?"* . . .' – and the last, half way through the book, beginning with: '*David now had all the basic information about the plotted crime, the criminals, the victim and even the time when the crooks were likely to strike. But it was still mixed up. It still needed sorting out. Could you have sorted it out?*' In this way I was able to obtain a far stronger grip on the child reader's attention and still leave my aesthetic cake – my single point of view – intact within the text, which needed little further alteration.

It will have become quite apparent by now that although the same principles are applicable to adult fiction and other forms of exposition there are important differences of degree. One, which we have touched on in the last few examples, is that adults, with their greater experience, are generally able to apprehend the what-might-happen – the awful or delightful possibility – far more readily than children, without much or indeed any prompting from the author. Hence the fact that many of us can be gripped by a story or play of which the more child-minded of adult critics might complain that 'nothing much happens' – precisely because we can discern in the nature of the situation or characters certain signs that tell us that much *can* happen, at any time. Harold Pinter – to name just one of a growing number – is a master of this kind of writing. The other important difference in degree is that to a child, with a far smaller fund of experience, many more things possess exciting – frightening or pleasing – possibilities, simply because they are new to him. A promised half-day trip to the sea will seem to have immensely greater value in the eyes of a child than a reduction in, or even the complete abolition of, income tax; a lost doll can create in a little girl far greater distress than the fall of a government; and, in short, the quite literal slip between the cup and the lip is often sufficiently gripping a subject for children's fiction – generating much drama especially if a new carpet or new dress is in jeopardy.

Arthur Ransome is obviously keenly aware of this last aspect. Note how often he intermingles with relatively high adventure sprightly passages of the low, using the second to regulate the pace of the first. In the opening paragraphs of *Secret Water*, for example, the Swallows' high hopes of exploring a group of islands with their father are dashed when the Commander is ordered back to London by the Admiralty. By the end of that first chapter, however, they are somewhat cheered to learn that their parents have a secret plan.

'Something to do with us,' said Titty. 'Didn't you hear what he was saying?'
'What did he say?'
'He said, "Better keep mum about it till the morning".'

End – very effectively – of chapter. The next opens at breakfast.

'All hands!' said Daddy, as they sat down to breakfast.
'Wait till they've had their porridge,' said Mother.
Daddy laughed.
'Oh do tell us now,' said Titty.
'You heard what your mother said.'
'Oh Mother!'
'You get your porridge down,' said Mother. 'But don't go and eat it too quickly.'

'Or too slowly,' said Roger, swallowing fast. 'Slop it in, Bridget. Bridget doesn't know how to eat porridge. When you've got a mouthful in, don't just wave the spoon about. Get it filled while you're swallowing.'

'Don't you hurry, Bridgie,' said Daddy. 'News'll keep.'

'Anybody want any more porridge?' said Mother presently.

'Nobody does,' said Titty.

'What about Roger?'

For a minute or two everybody had been watching Bridget, whose eyes wandered from face to face as she worked steadily on, spoonful by spoonful. Roger looked at the porridge still left in her plate. He could have a little more and yet be done as soon as she was.

'Yes, please,' said Roger, and passed his plate.

Bridget eyed him balefully and put on speed. It was a very close thing. Roger was still swallowing his last mouthful while Susan was wiping a stray bit off Bridget's chin.

Daddy looked at Mummy. She nodded.

There was a breathless pause.

'Now look here,' said Daddy . . .

And so the momentous secret is finally divulged.

The risk that Mr Ransome has taken here is really quite considerable – that of making the delay as bothersome to the readers as it is to the characters – for it is a firm rule in any branch of fiction that the boring must never bore, always entertain. Here the author resolves the problem by interrupting, or braking, the larger drama with one of the miniature dramas of childhood, involving the technique of eating porridge, Roger's agonizing decision, and the brief race – the real prize for which is the justification of Roger's decision, the evident accuracy of his calculations. It is done so skilfully that one is able to bear the main delay without being moved to skip – an ever-present temptation where child readers are concerned, the succumbing to which can be ruinous to true appreciation.

Ransome's books are full of such passages, not all of them concerned with techniques as relatively unimportant as that of porridge-eating. Navigation, map-making, surveying, fishing, fire-making, cooking: readers can learn a lot about these and similar subjects from this author's pages of fiction – and learn about them almost unconsciously (a) because they are presented as situations arising naturally out of the basic story, and (b) because the author handles them with great technical skill, taking care to unfold them in an atmosphere of possibility, good or bad. This is didacticism at its best.

The problem of didacticism has puzzled many children's authors and commentators on children's fiction, and it has not been made any easier by the assumption that the didactic is necessarily bad in the artistic sense. This assumption probably arises from the fact that so much of the didactic in fiction – any kind of fiction – is bad: so many pills, so many clumsy attempts to sugar them. One thinks of all those abominable fictionalized nature walks, with the know-all uncle and the know-nothing twins, of pat answers to a stream of timely questions, and of such modern instances as government department advice to farmers being pasted between the lines of *The Archers*, the British radio soap opera about countryfolks. No wonder even so percipient an observer as Geoffrey Trease[1] can speak about the didactic story as 'filling the modern adult with horror'. Yet what he is really talking about is the bad didactic story. The good is rarely even thought of as being didactic. So Mr Trease can, a few paragraphs later, in conjuring up and answering a hypothetical critic, write:

> You could never accuse Arthur Ransome . . . of being didactic. . . . True, so long as one does not try to give *much* information, one escapes the charge.

But surely it is, as I have already suggested, much more a matter of quality than quantity. Mr Ransome does in fact convey quite a considerable amount of information in his stories. So did the author of *Swiss Family Robinson*, also cited by Mr Trease in this connection. So do the authors of the pony-books and career novels he mentions in passing. Not all of these are as skilful as Mr Ransome in unfolding a narrative, admittedly, but the examples do have one thing in common: the instructive matter to be conveyed is almost always concerned with a process. Building a boat or a house or a fire, saddling a horse, seeking a job as a juvenile actor – these in themselves possess all the ingredients of stories. Each consists of a series of actions requiring thought, care and foresight. Each presents penalties for going wrong, bonuses for perfection. Each is a prey to attendant circumstances. Given such ingredients, a competent storyteller can hardly fail to hold his readers' attention.

It is not difficult to see why young children, with comparatively little experience of their own to draw upon for information, should be less shy of this sort of didacticism than adults or older boys and girls. What is more difficult to understand is why so many writers, with such examples before them, should strain so hard to sugar their pills by introducing into career novels, say, all manner of claptrap from contrived skulduggery to novelettish Romance – when in reality the well-placed, well-timed, well-told process is capable of generating far more interest, even of stealing the scene from apparently more momentous happenings.

---

1. In *Tales Out Of School*.

Indeed, this is what tends to happen in that most adult novel, James Baldwin's *Tell Me How Long the Train's Been Gone*, where the hero's struggles to become an actor, to learn and perfect his craft, often overshadow what the author intends to be the more important theme of race relationship. Here, for example, is how Leo Proudhammer begins to play a prepared scene from *Waiting for Lefty*, before an audience of fellow drama students and a renowned and highly critical teacher:

My first line was, *Hello, Florrie.* I couldn't use my book. I put it back down on the sofa. I hoped I knew the scene well enough just to be able to go with it. The assistant picked up my book, and opened it. He stood there, waiting. I looked at him. Then I realized that he was going to read the short scene which precedes my entrance, between Florrie and her brother, Irv, who doesn't want Florrie to marry me.

I smiled, and said, 'Sorry', and left the alcove.

'Nerves, nerves,' said the assistant, and there was a little burst of laughter.

They started.

'I got a right to have something out of life,' Barbara said, and she moved, sullenly, restlessly, about the alcove. 'I don't smoke, I don't drink. So if Sid wants to take me to a dance, I'll go. Maybe if you was in love, you wouldn't talk so hard.'

'I'm saying it,' read the assistant, flatly, 'for your good.'

I knew that Jerry had cued Barbara for this scene many times, and yet it was odd to see her play it in a vacuum. I had no idea whether she was any good or not, and the way the assistant was reading the lines made it impossible – for me – to believe in the scene at all. Barbara looked far too young, it seemed to me, to be saying any of the things she was saying; if *I* had been her brother, I would have turned her over my knee. Still, she was sullen, she was upset, she was terribly nervous; only, I couldn't tell whether it was *she* who was nervous, or Florrie. She certainly sounded very close to hysteria by the time she shouted, 'Sure, I want romance, love, babies. I want everything in life I can get!' And she didn't seem so young then. She seemed to know what was in store for her.

Here came my cue: '. . . Take the egg off the stove I boiled for Mom.' Then she looked up, and insisted on a rather long silence – long enough to make one wonder. The assistant nervously looked at his – or, rather, *my* book. Barbara turned away. 'Leave us alone, Irv.'

I stepped into the alcove. The assistant and I stared at each other a moment, and then he disappeared – with my book. Then Barbara turned back, and looked at me.

'Hello, Florrie,' I said.

'Hello, honey. You're looking tired.'

When she said that, I thought of our walk through town.
'Naw,' I said. 'I just need a shave.'
And so we hit it. . . .

And so too Mr Baldwin presents his process, the building of a scene by a couple of acting students, and makes it a thousand times more enthralling than any conventional piece of 'excitement' – than a backstage fire, say, or the dressing-room hysterics of a leading lady, or the phantom sniper, lurking above the curtains. And primarily he does this (a) because he realizes that to most people the technique of acting is interesting in itself, and (b) because the situation is so well integrated with the characters involved. To Leo and Barbara, success or failure at this point means practically everything they have to live for, and so we have the perfect balance between the awful and delightful possibilities. Thus what might amount to no more than a piece of information or local colour – a sample slice of stage life – becomes a compelling scene in its own right. We hardly know we are being told something of the difficulties experienced by any actor – difficulties involving one's assessment of the playwright's intention, of the quality of the material and of one's colleagues, and questions of timing. Instead, we are holding our breath, hoping that neither of the protagonists will falter, slip and so make a mess of the scene. Baldwin makes sure of this by revealing nothing beyond each cautious step, by taking us along the high wire, as it were, with Leo and Barbara, into the ever-increasing danger that could bring total failure or brilliant success. Towards the end of the scene the suspense is terrific.

Then she threw her head against my chest, buried her head in my chest, and held me. This was not the way we had played the scene before. I held her, and I said, 'You worried about your mother?'
'No,' she said. But she had not moved; and I was taking my cue from her.
I said, gently, 'What's on your mind?'
'The French and Indian war,' she said, and I now understood, holding her by the shoulder, that I could move her slightly away from me, and look into her face. 'What's on your mind?'
'I got us on my mind, Sid.' She looked at me. 'Night and day, Sid!'
Well, now I was in the scene and so I couldn't know – it didn't matter – whether we were any good or not.

Acting is constantly presenting complex technical situations of this kind. So do most professions. This explains the popularity of career novels for older children. Even where the material is clumsily handled it is difficult for an author to go too far astray, given a learner character who badly wants to succeed. It is when a job involves too simple and too few processes that it fails to lend itself to extensive treatment in fiction. That – as much as the question of the class of the potential reader – is why there are so few, if any, career novels dealing with, say, factory work of the usual repetitive kind. It is a devastating indictment of the working life to which most school-leavers are condemned that such a book would soon exhaust the intrinsic interest of the job and would have to do one of three things: (a) break out in a rash of adventure or melodrama of which the factory was only a fortuitous or, at best, a likely setting; (b) become didactic in the bad sense, stodgy with facts about the industry generally – handed out information about raw materials, by-products, factory legislation, 'prospects' and matters of that sort; (c) become what would perhaps be most satisfactory on several counts – artistic, social and moral – an *anti*-career novel.[1] Yet even in the case of a job involving just one basic process, a good writer can make a most entertaining and absorbing short story or episode. The work of a shoe-shine boy, for instance, could hardly provide material in itself for a full-length book. It is not, as a craft, capable of development even though it might well be capable of acting as a starting-point or nucleus for a series of extra-curricular incidents. Yet here is Piri Thomas making what there is to make of it in his fictionalized autobiography, *Down These Mean Streets:*

In the morning I stood on Lexington Avenue in Spanish Harlem, one finger poked through my pants pocket, scratching myself, while I droned, 'Shine, mister – good shine, only fifteen cents. Shine, mister. . . .' It was hard to shine shoes and harder to keep my corner from getting copped by an early-rising shine boy. I had to be prepared to mess a guy up; that corner spot wasn't mine alone. I had to earn it every time I shined shoes there.

When I got a customer, we both played our roles. The customer,

---

1. Which essentially is what most good – i.e., truly reflecting – adult novels of factory life are: the accounts of collective struggles for better pay and conditions, or of fiddles and evasions on the factory floor, or of individual from-lathe-to-boardroom ambition involving patience and cunning. The play of individual skills and judgement accounts for very little of the action in such books, precisely because it accounts for so restricted a proportion of actual factory work, and to present a child with a picture of factory life in which patience and future rewards are at a premium is to ask of him what so many employers do ask of him – to put any thought of immediate enjoyment of working life in abeyance, to endure that life in the hope of riches to come. Well, employers can get away with this, for the young factory worker hasn't much choice in the matter. But he does have some choice in what he reads, and any author peddling that sort of dishonesty is more than likely to have his offering rejected with the contempt it deserves.

tall and aloof, smiled, 'Gimme a shine, kid,' and I replied, '*Sí, señor*, sir, I'll give you one that you'll have to put sunglasses on to eat the bright down.'

My knees grinding against the gritty sidewalk, I adopted a serious, businesslike air. Carefully, but confidently, I snaked out my rags, polish, and brushes. I gave my cool breeze customer the treatment. I rolled his pants cuff up – 'That'll keep shoe polish off' – straightened his socks, patted his shoe, assured him he was in good hands, and loosened and retied his shoes. Then I wiped my nose with a delicate finger, picked up my shoe brush, and scrunched away the first hard crust of dirt. I opened my bottle of black shoe cleaner – dab, rub in, wipe off, pat the shoe down. Then I opened my can of polish – dab on with three fingers, pat-a-pid, pat-a-pid. He's not looking – spit on the shoe, more polish, let it dry, tap the bottom of his sole, smile up at Mr. Big Tip (you hope), 'Next, sir'.

I repeated the process on the other shoe, then picked up my brush and rubbed the bristles very hard against the palm of my hand, scientific-like, to warm the brush hairs up so they would melt the black shoe wax and give a cool unlumpy shine. I peeked out of the corner of my eye to see if Mr. Big Tip was watching my modern shoe-shine methods. The bum *was* looking. I hadn't touched his shoe, forcing him to look.

The shoe began to gleam dully – more spit, more polish, more brush, little more spit, little more polish, and a lotta rag. I repeated on the other shoe. As Mr. Big Tip started digging in his pocket, I prepared for the climax of my performance. Just as he finished saying, 'Damn nice shine, kid', I said, 'Oh, I ain't finished, sir. I got a special service,' and I plunged my wax-covered fingers into a dark corner of my shoe box and brought out a bottle of 'Special shoe lanolin cream for better preservation of leather.'

I applied a dab, a tiny dab, pausing long enough to say very confidently, 'You can't put on too much or it'll spoil the shine. It gotta be just right.' Then I grabbed the shoe rag firmly, like a maestro with a baton, and hummed a rhythm with it, slapping out a happy beat on the shoes. A final swish here and there, and *mira!* – finished. Sweating from the effort of my creation, I slowly rose from my knees, bent from the strain, my hand casually extended, palm flat up, and murmured, 'Fifteen cents, sir,' with a look that said, 'But it's worth much more, don't you think?' Mr. Big Tip dropped a quarter and a nickel into the offering plate, and I said, 'Thanks a mil, sir,' thinking, *Take it cool*, as I cast a watchful eye at his retreating back.

But wasn't it great to work for a living? I calculated how long it would take to make my first million shining shoes. Too long. I would be something like 987 years old. Maybe I could steal it faster.

Instinctively understanding the limitations of the job as material for his larger narrative as well as he understood its economic limitations, Mr Thomas universalizes the situation, positing a typical customer, before particularizing. But when he does particularize – when, as he might say, he 'gets down to the nitty-gritty' – the writer makes us hang on every movement of the operation even as the boy hoped to make the customer do. And he does this as all good writers will: by taking us step by step through the process in such a way that we become as desperately anxious about that tip as the young Piri was, as if for us too nothing matters in the world at this particular moment as much as that one 15-25-30 cents question. Certainly there is not quite the same suspense here as that in the Baldwin passage. No real disaster is imminent. But to have played for such a heightened sense of disaster would have been to play the passage false, given the smaller scale of its material. Instead, Thomas keeps our feelings focused on the small delightful possibility, and the passage correspondingly short. Within that framework he relies, very successfully, on such elements as changes of tense, sharply detailed expertise and a sense of humour – keeping us alert for the next little trick of the shoeshine trade, the next wisecrack. All these things, plus the additional element of likeable roguery, would make this passage from an essentially adult book immensely appealing to most children, especially as the rogue in question is a child and the victim an adult. As it is, it is sufficiently engrossing to detain the adult reader even in the middle of the more pressing, often quite terrible events of the main narrative.

In a sense, that shoeshine passage is analogous to the writer-narrative-reader situation under discussion. The reader/customer comes expecting a service; the writer/shoeblack makes a promise; certain careful preparations are made in both cases, preliminaries that boost the confidence as well as clear the decks; then, sentence by sentence, dab by dab, the work proceeds; straying attention is watched for and brought back by a tap or a striking statement, even by a silence or odd reservation; and, as the climax is approached, the writer/shoeblack always has something in reserve: the extra twist or the spot of lanolin. Note the timing, too, employed by both writer and shoeblack: the dab, the 'tiny dab' and then the pause, followed by the more vigorous swing of words and shoe-rag into the climax itself.

We have to go back to Mark Twain and *Tom Sawyer* for a more striking and instructive analogy of the writer-narrative-reader situation than that: to the famous fence-whitewashing episode, in fact. And since in addition it involves more directly teachers and pupils, besides summarizing much of what has been dealt with in this chapter, it will be worth our while to consider it in some detail at this point.

Tom, it may be remembered, is being punished by his aunt, who has given him the Saturday task of whitewashing a fence. It is a beautiful morning, but:

> He surveyed the fence and the gladness went out of nature, and a deep melancholy settled down upon his spirit. Thirty yards of board-fence nine feet high! It seemed to him that life was hollow, and existence but a burden. Sighing he dipped his brush and passed it along the topmost plank; repeated the operation; did it again; compared the insignificant whitewashed streak with the far-reaching continent of unwhitewashed fence, and sat down on a tree-box discouraged.

Jim, the hired help, comes along, on his way to fetch water. Tom suggests that they exchange tasks for a while, backing this up with the offer of a white marble – but Aunt Polly intervenes and sends Jim about his business 'with his pail and a tingling rear'. Tom then whitewashes 'with vigour' for a while, but soon flags.

> He began to think of the fun he had planned for this day, and his sorrows multiplied. Soon the free boys would come tripping along on all sorts of delicious expeditions, and they would make a world of fun of him for having to work – the very thought of it burnt him like fire. He got out his worldly wealth and examined it – bits of toys, marbles and trash; enough to buy an exchange of work, maybe, but not enough to buy so much as half an hour of pure freedom. So he returned his straitened means to his pocket, and gave up the idea of trying to buy the boys. At this dark and hopeless moment an inspiration burst upon him! Nothing less than a great, magnificent inspiration.

The author doesn't explain what this is. He simply goes on to describe Tom's 'tranquilly' resuming the whitewashing. Then Ben Rogers comes along, carefree, imitating a steamboat and eating an apple. Tom takes no notice, goes on whitewashing. Then Ben says:

> 'Hi-yi. You're up a stump, ain't you?'
> No answer. Tom surveyed his last touch with the eye of an artist; then he gave his brush another gentle sweep, and surveyed the result, as before. Ben ranged up alongside of him. Tom's mouth watered for the apple, but he stuck to his work. Ben said:
> 'Hallo, old chap; you got to work, hey?'
> 'Why, it's you, Ben! I warn't noticing.'
> 'Say, I'm going in a-swimming, I am. Don't you wish you could? But of course you'd druther work, wouldn't you? 'Course you would!'
> Tom contemplated the boy a bit, and said:
> 'What do you call work?'
> 'Why, ain't that work?'

Tom resumed his whitewashing, and answered carelessly:

'Well, maybe it is, and maybe it ain't. All I know is, it suits Tom Sawyer.'

'Oh, come now, you don't mean to let on that you like it?'

The brush continued to move.

'Like it? Well, I don't see why I oughtn't to like it. Does a boy get a chance to whitewash a fence every day?'

That put the thing in a new light. Ben stopped nibbling his apple. Tom swept his brush daintily back and forth – stepped back to note the effect – added a touch here and there – criticized the effect again – Ben watching every move, and getting more and more interested, more and more absorbed. Presently he said:

'Say, Tom, let me whitewash a little.'

Tom considered – was about to consent; but he altered his mind: 'No, no; I reckon it wouldn't hardly do, Ben. You see, Aunt Polly's awful particular about this fence – right here on the street, you know – but if it was the back fence I wouldn't mind, and she wouldn't. Yes, she's awful particular about this fence; it's got to be done very careful; I reckon there ain't one boy in a thousand, maybe two thousand, that can do it the way it's got to be done.'

'No – is that so? Oh, come now; lemme just try, only just a little . . .'

After a further show of reluctance, Tom finally agrees, in exchange for the half-eaten apple.

And while the late steamer *Big Missouri* worked and sweated in the sun, the retired artist sat on a barrel in the shade close by, dangled his legs, munched his apple, and planned the slaughter of more innocents. There was no lack of material; boys happened along every little while; they came to jeer, but remained to whitewash. By the time Ben was fagged out, Tom had traded the next chance to Billy Fisher for a kite, in good repair; and when he played out, Johnny Miller bought in for a dead rat and a string to swing it with; and so on, and so on, hour after hour. And when the middle of the afternoon came, from being a poor poverty-stricken boy in the morning, Tom was literally rolling in wealth. He had, besides the things I have mentioned, twelve marbles, part of a Jew's harp, a piece of blue bottle-glass to look through, a spool-cannon, a key that wouldn't unlock anything, a fragment of chalk, a glass stopper of a decanter, a tin soldier, a couple of tadpoles, six fire-crackers, a kitten with only one eye, a brass door-knob, a dog-collar – but no dog – the handle of a knife, four pieces of orange-peel, and a dilapidated old window-sash. He had had a nice, good, idle time all the while – plenty of company – and the fence had three coats of whitewash on it! If he hadn't run out of whitewash, he would have bankrupted every boy in the village.

It is not difficult to see why this particular passage should have been a favourite with one of the senior education lecturers at the college where I was trained for teaching. Year after year, very early in the course, he used to read it, with a great deal of relish and many an appreciative pause, to the assembled freshmen. For this is essentially what education at the classroom level is all about. We have on the one hand the apparrently dull project, the whitewashing of a fence; and on the other the unenthusiastic pupil, Tom Sawyer. There is the element of punishment, of a punishment task, which does nothing to render the project any less repellent. There is, in those grim statistics, thirty yards by nine feet, the element – always to be avoided in teaching, even with more promising assignments — of overfacing the young student. There is the futility of threats, of trying to get the work done with the aid of a stick, in this case resulting in nothing more than a brief spurt of activity, dropped as soon as Aunt Polly is out of sight. There is too the futility of bribes, of the too obvious, too withered a carrot, deemed not enough in this case by the pupil's own reckoning as he toys with the idea of using the method on his peers. And then there is the showmanship – the conmanship, if you like – with which the project is finally presented to the others, as something difficult, exclusive, precious, challenging.

Now in quoting this passage – and doing it, as I have already suggested, with a zest and a feeling for timing that reinforced the passage's intrinsic ability to keep an audience transfixed – the lecturer was warmly commending to us the methods of the character, Tom. And this was all very well, in its more negative aspects of warning us against a too placid reliance on certain expectations and approaches in the classroom. When it came to the positive, however, it merely threw out a guideline, telling us to make the task seem tempting, challenging and so on without explaining how to go about it. For that, we should have been recommended to go one further step and study the methods of the author of the passage.

Mark Twain, too, was presenting, on the face of it, a potentially dull subject. As the whitewashing of the fence was to the boy, so might the boys' whitewashing of the fence have been to the reader. But almost at once the author introduces the notion of a delightful possibility: in this case a brief escape from the task even if only by an exchange of work, and we are drawn into the negotiations with Jim. These break down, but within a few sentences a second delightful possibility is raised: the prospect of buying a longer respite. Certainly the original means are quickly rejected, the bribes being considered too meagre, but the possibility remains – brought nearer and made even brighter by the inspiration: 'Nothing less than a great, magnificent inspiration'.

So far, Twain has kept our interest alive by presenting certain possibilities and certain plans for transforming them into reality. The fence itself is pushed into the background as we follow with him, step by step the workings of these minor machinations. By this point, however, our attention requires another stimulant – a stronger one still – if it isn't to flag. We shan't, for instance, be too happy about another half-cock plan at the level of the earlier ones. Something promising spectacular success (or spectacular disaster) is required. And this, the spectacular success, the author promises: 'Nothing less than . . .' etc.

But he doesn't specify. We are not told why this inspiration was so great, so magnificent. We are made to wait. With our curiosity aroused and the author's promissory note in our pocket, we watch what follows with sharpened interest, reassured by Tom's obvious confidence. So Ben comes along. We study him with all the amused carefulness with which one does study a marked man, the destined victim of a trick. Twain gives us plenty of time to do this – three paragraphs of what might have been rather tedious by-play in any other circumstances. But we watch Ben's capers as an imaginary steamboat and smile at his vulnerable innocence – relishing in advance the trick by which somehow he is to be made to prefer the prosaic physical toil of whitewashing a fence to these idle daydreams. Twain then allows him to notice Tom and us to return to a closer figuring of just how the switch is to be achieved. And now, little by little, as Ben is conned so we are enlightened, and even when we do see fully Tom's line, Twain still has him play the victim along, until we begin to fear that Tom will overdo it and Ben escape, or maybe that Tom will actually fall for the patter himself. In either case it is an intriguing situation and our interest is maintained.

Thus, one way or another, the author has us eager to know, at any given moment, what happens next – with possibility succeeding possibility. And thus, one feels, a teacher would do well to present his material, never leaping too far ahead yet always keeping the most attractive aspects of the next few steps in view, drawing attention to them with a swirl of mist here and a glitter there. Nor should another characteristic of the passage be overlooked in this connection: Twain's never failing to particularize wherever possible. Note especially the way he marks the passage of the late morning and the afternoon and at the same time obviates the necessity either to go through every encounter in similar fashion or baldly to summarize. The fascinating catalogue of highly diverse objects extracted from the victims does it all, and does it so entertainingly. Children seem to have an insatiable appetite for such precise concrete details – whether served up in stories or lessons – and it is this appetite with which we shall be dealing in the next chapter.[1]

---

1. For further examples of the use of various aspects of narrative techniques employed outside prose fiction, see Appendix C.

Chapter four   Wealth of detail

Some of the funniest fiction in the junior library I used as a child was to be found in the reference section, in a series of volumes ostensibly devoted to non-fictional subjects. And it was presented not in words but line drawings. The name of the series escapes me – it was something like the *Discovery Books* or *Wonder Books* or *Marvel Books*, embodied in such titles as *The Discovery/Wonder/Marvels of Modern Engineering* and so on – and if my life depended on it I couldn't recollect a single page, passage, photograph or diagram from the body of any one of those no doubt quite instructive tomes. But I can remember vividly their end-papers: endpapers that crawled and seethed and exploded with the activities of a tribe of goblinlike creatures, the clowns who came before as well as after each parade of Wonders or Marvels. The crawling and seething took place in the endpapers at the front; the explosion at the back. Thus, if the book's main topic should be aircraft, the goblins – singly, in pairs, in family groups or comradely bands – would crowd into the front endpapers with Brueghelian busyness: some on the brink of experimenting with soapbox airplanes, or umbrella parachutes, or home-made hot-air balloons, others simply noting the aeronautical activities with a placid gravity, maybe with cameras or ready notebooks or half-extended helping hands. Then – slap! bang! – one turned to the end-papers at the back to find the same general scene depicted a few seconds later, cataclysmically transformed. It may have been the bursting of a balloon or the shedding of a propellor – sometimes it would have required a public inquiry to find out for certain what originally caused these disasters – but whatever had struck the single initial spark everything now fell beautifully, comically, satisfactorily into a logical chainlike pattern of cause and effect. The occupants of the balloon would fall on the parties of observers below, causing cameras to be flung into the air, to strike prematurely off-balance the umbrella parachutist who'd been dithering on his branch . . . and so on. Here then, with an almost literal vengeance, was the awful/delightful possibility used to its best advantage, and many was the time when a child was evicted from the library for illiberal laughter or a fit of uncontrollable giggling.[1]

Now as far as those goblin endpapers were concerned, one had of course to be in the know to get the maximum pleasure from them. One had to be aware in fact that the possibilities were destined to be fulfilled at the turn of a wrist. But before that condition existed, each newcoming observer had to be attracted and held, made to study the scene and become familiar with its various aspects, to take pleasure in it for its own sake, and this initial attraction could never have been ensured without the very multiplicity and sharp definition of the detail presented.

Children love such detail. The youngest look for it in their picture books and it is, surely, the teeming detail of comic-strips – clear if crudely drawn – that is one of that medium's most attractive elements. Older children insist on it in their toys – from model cars to imitation weapons – and they love to pore over the smallest distinguishing marks in books about birds or flowers or flags or locomotives. And at all ages it is their hunger for detail that prompts their streams of questions. 'Hunger' in fact is probably a more accurate word than 'love' in this context, so strongly instinctive is the urge of a growing child to get his bearings in the world. At times its manifestation seems to the more completely orientated adult to be irrational. After a while one will suddenly become irritated by a child's persistent questioning, forgetting that the details sought are far from trivial to him. And I shall always remember being pulled up with a jerk, when I asked a nine-year-old girl

---

1. Oddly enough, the comic possibilities of this before-and-after technique have been neglected by children's writers, who might hope to put its starkness to the best use. Indeed, as far as I know, it is only in the work of that highly cerebral adult novelist, Thomas Love Peacock that we have anything approaching it. This occurs in *Headlong Hall*, where the landscape artist, Mr Milestone, discusses his plans for Lord Littlebrain's park in the following terms and patterns:

> Here is another part of the grounds in its natural state. Here is a large rock, with the mountain-ash rooted in its fissures, overgrown, as you see, with ivy and moss; and from this part of it bursts a little fountain, that runs bubbling down its rugged sides. . . . Hideous. Base, common, and popular. Such a thing as you may see anywhere, in wild and mountainous districts. Now, observe the metamorphosis. Here is the same rock, cut into the shape of a giant. In one hand he holds a horn, through which that little fountain is thrown to a prodigious elevation. In the other is a ponderous stone, so exactly balanced as to be apparently ready to fall on the head of any person who may happen to be beneath: and there is Lord Littlebrain walking under it.

which of the two opening pages of *The Boy at the Window*[1] she liked better: the revised version, with its preamble tipping off the reader that a criminal plot was brewing in the shops across the way, or the first version, which led straight in with a description of the boy in bed.

'This one,' she said emphatically, pointing to the revised version.

Gratified, I asked why.

'Because of the custard,' she said.

I was nonplussed at first, until I had a look at the typescript and remembered that after adding the preamble I'd done a little tinkering with the original opening paragraph, which described the sunlight falling on the bed, the quilt, a comic-book and the dozing boy himself. Between quilt and comic-book, the sooner to establish the fact that he was an invalid, I'd inserted: 'It fell on the stain on the sheet, where he'd spilt some of the custard he'd had for dinner'. Now I'm quite sure the girl had no conscious appreciation of the purpose for which the detail had been inserted. It was simply because of its vividness and the very fact that it was there at all that she applauded it.

Detail is of great importance to fiction writers. They too have a pressing need to establish their bearings – not so much in the real world as in whatever worlds they are constructing. And in the first instance they need to establish these bearings for their own satisfaction, even before they begin to consider their readers' requirements. This is what Robert Louis Stevenson had to say about it:

It is, perhaps, not often that a map figures so largely in a tale, yet it is always important. The author must know his countryside, whether real or imaginary, like his hand; the distances, the points of the compass, the place of the sun's rising, the behaviour of the moon, should all be beyond cavil. And how troublesome the moon is! I have come to grief over the moon in *Prince Otto*, and so soon as that was pointed out to me, adopted a precaution which I recommend to other men – I never write now without an almanack. With an almanack, and the map of the country, and the plan of every house, either actually plotted on paper or already and immediately apprehended in the mind, a man may hope to avoid some of the grossest possible blunders. With the map before him, he will scarce allow the sun to set in the east, as it does in *The Antiquary*. With the almanack at hand, he will scarce allow two horsemen, journeying on the most urgent affair, to employ six days, from three of the Monday morning till late in the Saturday night, upon a journey of, say, ninety or a hundred miles, and before the week is out, and still on the same nags, to cover fifty in one day, as

1. See p. 48.

may be read at length in the inimitable novel of *Rob Roy*. And it is certainly well, though far from necessary, to avoid such 'croppers'. But it is my contention – my superstition, if you like – that who is faithful to his map, and consults it, and draws from it his inspiration, daily and hourly, gains positive support, and not mere negative immunity from accident. The tale has a root there; it grows in that soil; it has a spine of its own behind the words. Better if the country be real, and he has walked every foot of it and knows every milestone. But even with imaginary places, he will do well in the beginning to provide a map; as he studies it, relations will appear that he had not thought upon; he will discover obvious, though unsuspected, shortcuts and footprints for his messengers; and even when a map is not all the plot, as it was in *Treasure Island*, it will be found to be a mine of suggestion.[1]

Sometimes the need for such preliminary charting will go beyond mere topography. In *Nostromo*, for instance, Joseph Conrad – as Walter Allen has pointed out[2] – 'invents a whole country, the South American republic of Costaguana, with its especial geography, history, and economy, its political struggles and its revolutions.' But the most important aspect of the activity – whether it take the form of a sketch-map of a hamlet or the blueprint of an empire – is the positive one mentioned by Stevenson. There is created in this way something containing elements for the characters to react against, and be acted upon by, that have not been *directly* preordained by the author. By these means, too, there is brought into play a positive aspect of chance. If, for example, one pins the action of a story down to a certain place and time, it can be immensely useful to look up the relevant meteorological records for that period and agree to be bound by them – thus introducing a natural, plausible upsetter of apple-carts or lifter of spirits that may cause a little extra trouble but will help to break down any contrived stiffness, or any too facile mingling of grey clouds with tears, sunshine with smiles. Similarly, an eye on the news reports of the period can produce some healthy unplanned catalytic repercussions in a too-tight plot.

It is not of course necessary to present to the reader all or even the bulk of such known background details. Indeed, as Tolstoy has pointed out, a superabundance of details can obscure for the reader the feeling the author might have for the objects dealt with, and so impair the communication of that feeling. Usually, in adult fiction, the tip of the iceberg is all that a writer needs to reveal in this connection. So Tchehov, in a

---

1. 'My First Book', reprinted in *The Art of Writing*, and quoted by Miriam Allott in *Novelists on the Novel*.
2. In *The English Novel*.

few short strokes, can convey the beauty and boredom and mystery of the steppes by focusing on the flight of a hawk:

> The music in the grass was hushed, the petrels had flown away, the partridges were out of sight, rooks hovered idly over the withered grass; they were all alike and made the steppe even more monotonous.
>
> A hawk flew just above the ground, with an even sweep of its wings, suddenly halted in the air as though pondering on the dreariness of life, then fluttered its wings and flew like an arrow over the steppe, and there was no telling why it flew off and what it wanted. In the distance a windmill waved its sails. . . .[1]

But when an author is writing for children his interest in having the details right will coincide more frequently with his readers' interest in having the right details, and he will be able to afford, and in fact will be wise, to show more of the basic structures and patterns and mechanisms. That is why a child can enjoy, in a book with a definite geographical setting, details which an adult might consider boringly didactic – but only boring because they are superfluous to *his* needs.

Another aspect of the overt use of detail by writers of fiction – for adults or children – is its function in helping to establish authenticity. This is not merely a question of displaying knowledge of a setting – for a setting may correspond to no known place on earth – but to make the story 'ring true'. In some respects this function is closely related to the circumstantiality of the accomplished liar, the con-man's stock-in-trade, a piece of necessary semantic legerdemain. The speech of Dickens's Mr Jingle is peppered with such detail – ('Sudden disappearance – talk of the whole city – search made everywhere – without success – public fountain in the great square suddenly ceased playing – weeks elapsed – still a stoppage – workmen employed to clean it – water drawn off – father-in-law discovered sticking head first in the main pipe, with a full confession in his right boot . . .') – and of course the waiter who hoodwinked David Copperfield out of his chops and ale was fully proficient in this black art. But it is a white form that authors themselves use, in that it is practised with the reader's consent, as an aid to that willing suspension of disbelief which forms the basis of the bargain.

So there is a place even in adult fiction for details that are not immediately relevant to plot (as the playwright's much-quoted gun on the wall, which must go off by the end of the third act), nor immediately relevant to character (as (Uriah Heep's writhings), nor even immediately relevant to underlying themes or moods, forming 'objective correlatives' with them (as many of Hardy's landscapes) – but simply to help construct a convincing reality or, rather, to give the illusion of reality. Some of the

---

1. From 'The Steppe', translated by Constance Garnett.

more exuberant older masters were fond of using details in this way: writers like Sterne, Rabelais, Dickens and Balzac. It was as if the abundant richness and clarity of the worlds they were building went to their heads, causing them to allow so much to spill over, regardless of any formal relevance – much as the unknown masons and carvers who helped to build the great Gothic cathedrals seemed unable to forbear from enriching the structures with the totally irrelevant but highly individual physiognomical details of their friends and enemies and acquaintances and pet animals. Nowadays in adult fiction such outpourings tend to be released in a dourer spirit, often grimly purposeful.

Thus, while we could have in Sterne such passages as this:

The moment my father got up into his chamber, he threw himself prostrate across his bed in the wildest disorder imaginable, but at the same time in the most lamentable attitude of a man borne down with sorrows, that ever the eye of pity dropped a tear for. – The palm of his right hand, as he fell upon the bed, receiving his forehead, and covering the greatest part of both his eyes, gently sunk down with his head (his elbow giving way backwards) till his nose touched the quilt; – his left arm hung insensible over the side of the bed, his knuckles reclining upon the handle of the chamber pot, which peeped out beyond the valance, – his right leg (his left being drawn up towards his body) hung half over the side of the bed, the edge of it pressing upon his shin-bone. – He felt it not. A fixed, inflexible sorrow took possession of every line of his face. – He sighed once, – heaved his breast often, – but uttered not a word.

An old set-stitched chair, valanced and fringed around with party-coloured worsted bobs, stood at the bed's head, opposite to the side where my father's head reclined. – My uncle Toby sat him down in it

– we now get M. Alain Robbe-Grillet presenting descriptions of this sort:

The pier, which seemed longer than it actually was as an effect of perspective, extended from both sides of this base line in a cluster of parallels describing, with a precision accentuated even more sharply by the morning light, a series of elongated planes alternately horizontal and vertical: the crest of the massive parapet that protected the tidal basin from the open sea, the inner wall of the parapet, the jetty along the top of the pier, and the vertical embankment that plunged straight into the water of the harbor. The two vertical surfaces were in shadow, the other two brilliantly lit by the sun – the whole breadth of the parapet and all of the jetty save for one dark narrow strip: the shadow cast by the parapet. . . .

66

– with, somewhere in between, such passages as this one from Joyce's *Ulysses:*

A sofa upholstered in prune plush had been translocated from opposite the door to the ingleside near the compactly furled Union Jack (an alteration which he had frequently intended to execute): the blue and white checker inlaid majolicatopped table had been placed opposite the door in the place vacated by the prune plush sofa: the walnut sideboard (a projecting angle of which had momentarily arrested his ingress) had been moved from its position beside the door to a more advantageous but more perilous position in front of the door: two chairs had been moved from right and left of the ingleside to the position originally occupied by the blue and white checker inlaid majolicatopped table. . . .

One: a squat stuffed easychair with stout arms extended and back slanted to the rere, which, repelled in recoil, had then upturned an irregular fringe of a rectangular rug and now displayed on its amply upholstered seat a centralized diffusing and diminishing discolouration. The other: a slender splayfoot chair of glossy cane curves, placed directly opposite the former, its frame from top to seat and from seat to base being varnished dark brown, its seat being a bright circle of white plaited rush

–where the displacement of the furniture does indeed have some relevance to the internal world of the novel, indicating to the observer, and symbolizing, the act of adultery that had taken place in the room earlier in the day.

And again where children are concerned, because of their craving for small hard facts, there is at once greater justification and greater scope for such an exuberance, an overabundance of detail, a presentation of detail for its own sake. Many of the best children's writers seem to have sensed this, even where the habit of economic relevance has been dominant. So we get a creative superfluity in the form of afterthoughts and droplets of information in Kastner, flying from the basic surge of narrative like spray. Emil takes out his sandwiches on the train, 'though it wasn't very long since he had had his dinner. He was half-way through the third, *and there was sausage in it*, when the train drew into a big station.' The italics are mine, the unnecessary but vivifying detail Kastner's – as later in the book, after the chase in the taxi: 'The rest of the boys clambered out, and Emil paid the fare, *which was a shilling*' – and after another, this time triumphant, taxi-ride, when Emil tells the driver to buy a cigar with the change and the man replies: 'Thank you, my boy . . . *but I don't smoke, I chew.*' That was outside his Grandma's house at *15* Schumann Street, and again the italics are mine – for throughout the book, with little regard for relevance, Kastner gives numbers of houses, hotels, telephones, streetcar route numbers. With similar throw-away speed, he shows Emil's cousin answering the door in an apron and holding out an elbow for him to shake because her hands are wet with washing the dishes, or has the girl announcing earlier in the story precise details of her Grandma's threatened punishment: '. . . she'll make you eat fish every day you're here . . .' Here indeed the flow is momentarily diverted, as one of Emil's companions is made to ask: 'What's the matter with fish?' – as intrigued by the detail as any young reader might be.

In E. Nesbit we have more frequently the same sort of thing: a good swift narrative flow that is diverted, sent twisting a little off course rather than being checked, by ostensibly irrelevant but vivid items of information. When the original momentous suggestion is made that the Bastable children go seeking treasure 'to restore the fallen fortunes of your House', we are told not only that Dora was mending a large hole in one of Noel's stickings, but that he'd torn it playing shipwrecked mariners, and that the game had taken place on top of a chicken house, and that it was the day H. O. had fallen off and cut his chin, and that he had the scar still. We are then told that Dora was the only one who mended things – but that Alice tried to make things and once 'she knitted a red scarf for Noel because his chest is delicate, but it was much wider at one end than the other, and he wouldn't wear it. So we used it as a pennon, and it did very well, because most of our things are black or grey since Mother died; and scarlet was a nice change. Father does not like you to ask for new things . . .' – and so, after this meandering, this *brisk* meandering, back to the fallen fortunes and the plans for restoring them.

With some writers there is little attempt made to integrate details of this sort – but they are given with such verve and clarity that here again the narrative flow does not seem to be held up nor even in these cases diverted, but is simply bridged attractively at particular spots. So when Dr Dolittle learns that one of the swallows wishes to speak to him at the beginning of *Doctor Dolittle's Post Office*, we are told not only the name of the bird and the fact that he was the swallow leader, but that he

> was the champion flycatcher and aerial acrobat of Europe, Africa, Asia, and America. For years every summer he had won all the flying races, having broken his own record only last year by crossing the Atlantic in eleven and a half hours – at a speed of over two hundred miles an hour.

Many writers would have been content to mention the bird's championship without the figures involved.

Charlotte M. Yonge, a much better children's writer than many people realize, was even more deliberate in establishing details not strictly necessary to a story but so wonderfully capable of giving it life and making it interesting or amusing for a child. The following is a passage from her story *Left Out* – a surprisingly fast-moving account of a school trip to the sea and a girl who stowed away on it, hoping to be overlooked by the organizers. There is nothing about this character or her predicament in the paragraph; nevertheless, it is hardly likely to be skipped by a young reader.

> But on shore there was quite as much fun, for there was a little strip of beach edging the castle walls, first of stones and then of sand. To those who knew what the shore of the open sea could be, it seemed a poor affair, but to these inland children it was perfectly delightful. They all tasted the water: to be sure it was salt, and what faces they made at it! The boys took off their boots and stockings, turned up their trousers, and paddled in the shallow water, and Miss Hilda did the same, calling to Emma Nowell to come with her. Then all the girls joined, except Frances Gale, who could not feel as if it was proper thus to run about with bare feet, and preferred trying how far she could creep round under the walls, and being told by Miss Edith the names of the odd plants that grew on the rocks, and the seaweeds that were left upon the stones.[1]

We may smile a little at the implication that Miss Hilda turned up *her* trousers (though much better writers have made similar syntactical slips – Tchehov himself perpetrating 'a wide boundless plain encircled by a chain of low hills' a paragraph or two before the hawk passage quoted on page 65) – but we must still admire the dynamic way she presents her details, the human interest she manages to invest them with, and the freshness of the resultant picture.

Equally coolly – refusing to be browbeaten by any demand for strict relevance, Joan Aiken decorates her stories with an excrescence of lively detail. Sometimes she seems to bend over this work with great care, comma by comma, as in her description of the room Sylvia shared with her Aunt Jane in *The Wolves of Willoughby Chase*.

> It was in Park Lane, this being the only street in which Aunt Jane could consider living. Unfortunately, as she was very poor, she could afford to rent only a tiny attic in such a genteel district. The room was divided into two by a very beautiful, but old, curtain of white Chinese brocade. She and Sylvia each had half the room at night, Aunt Jane sleeping on the divan and Sylvia on the ottoman. During the daytime the curtain was drawn back and hung elegantly looped against the wall. They cooked their meals over the gas jet, and had baths in a large enamelled Chinese bowl, covered with dragons, an heirloom of

---

1. From *Village Children*.

Aunt Jane's. At other times it stood on a little occasional table by the door and was used for visiting cards.

Sometimes she seems to sprinkle the details in passing. So the stranger in the train offers Sylvia chocolates from a box 'about a foot square by six inches deep, swathed around with violet ribbons', which she refuses, even though her tea had 'not been substantial – two pieces of thin bread-and-butter, a cinnamon wafer, and a sliver of caraway cake'. So she is further tempted by the stranger's 'pasteboard carton filled with every imaginable variety of little cakes – there were jam tarts, maids of honour, lemon cheese cakes, Chelsea buns, and numerous little iced confections in brilliant and enticing colours.' Later, when the wicked governess indulges herself in the absence of her employers, we learn that she orders 'a light luncheon at one o'clock: chicken, oyster patties, trifle, and a half-bottle of champagne' and has been dressing in Lady Green's 'draped gown of old gold velvet with ruby buttons' – to say nothing of the 'rose-coloured crape with aiguilettes of diamonds on the shoulders. It did not fit her very exactly.' Besides her details of food, dear to all children, Miss Aiken never lets her girl readers down by neglecting this other aspect – dress. Sylvia is given on her second morning at Willoughby Chase 'a soft, thick woollen dress in a beautiful deep shade of blue that exactly matched her eyes' and her Cousin Bonnie wears 'a dark-red cashmere with a white lace collar' – and so, sparklingly, colourfully, but not always entirely relevantly, on.

Some writers for children show signs in their work of a slight uneasiness over this question of detail – as if one side of them, the adult-orientated side, demanding relevance, occasionally pulls up the more liberally disposed children's side. Walter de la Mare practically debates the matter openly, at the beginning of his story *Dick and the Beanstalk* when mentioning the tales Dick had been brought up on.

These tales not only stayed in Dick's head, but *lived* there. He not only remembered them, but thought about them. . . . He not only knew almost by heart what they told, but would please himself by fancying what else had happened to the people in them after the tales were over or before they had begun. He could not only find his way about in a story-book, chapter by chapter, page by page, but if it told only about the inside of a house he would begin to wonder what its garden was like – and in imagination would find his way out into it and then perhaps try to explore even further. It was in this way, for example, that Dick had come to his own conclusions on which finger Aladdin wore his ring, and the colour of his uncle the Magician's eyes; on what too at last had happened to the old Fairy Woman in *The Sleeping Beauty*. . . . *He* knew why she didn't afterwards come to the Wedding!

And as for Blue-Beard's stone-turreted and many-windowed castle, with its chestnut gallery to the east, and its muddy moat with its carp, under the cypresses, Dick knew a good deal more about *that* than ever Fatima did! So again, if he found out that Old Mother Hubbard had a *cat*, he could tell you the cat's name. And he could describe the crown that Molly Whuppie was crowned with when she became Queen, even to its last emerald. He was what is called a *lively* reader.

Thus de la Mare seems to be putting forward for examination the view that some commentators on the subject have: that there is no need for an abundance of detail in children's stories – as witness many of the great fairy tales, with their stark but compelling outlines, inviting the reader to fill them in themselves, as Dick was said to do here. But de la Mare himself points out that this was a particularly lively reader, and it is significant that he assumes no such spin-it-yourself liveliness on the reader's part in the tale he goes on to relate, itself a further Dicklike exploration of an older tale, in which, after setting out 'due north-west into the morning', the hero finds out what happened to Jack's old bean-stalk and the Giant's descendants. (As might be expected from such a sample passage, this story itself is not particularly good as a children's story, being of much greater interest, because of the parabolic nature indicated, to grown-ups concerned with children's stories.)

This uneasiness over the supply of detail seems also to have disturbed Professor Tolkien – mercifully only for a moment – in the following passage from *The Hobbit*, where Bilbo is told his visitor's name:

'Gandalf, Gandalf! Good gracious me! Not the wandering wizard that gave Old Took a pair of magic diamond studs that fastened themselves and never came undone till ordered? Not the fellow who used to tell such wonderful tales at parties, about dragons and goblins and giants and the rescue of princesses and the unexpected luck of widows' sons? Not the man that used to make such particularly excellent fireworks! I remember those! Old Took used to have them on Midsummer's Eve. Splendid! They used to go up like great lilies and snapdragons and laburnums of fire and hang in the twilight all evening!' You will notice already that Mr. Baggins was not quite so prosy as he liked to believe, also that he was very fond of flowers.

'And also,' the author seems falteringly to suggest, 'that all this wealth of detail is not a sign of verbal profligacy on my part and that it has relevance, in this case to character.'

James Thurber obviously had no such qualms in his stories for children. Details tumble after details in a glittering profusion. It was as if he were glorying in the opportunities offered not to be consistently relevant, not to be cool and sparing, not, in short, to be too much in the

New Yorker style – which he once defined as 'playing it down.'[1] Here, for example, is the opening paragraph of *The 13 Clocks*:

Once upon a time, in a gloomy castle on a lonely hill, where there were thirteen clocks that wouldn't go, there lived a cold, aggressive Duke, and his niece, the Princess Saralinda. She was warm in every wind and weather, but he was always cold. His hands were as cold as his smile and almost as cold as his heart. He wore gloves when he was asleep, and he wore gloves when he was awake, which made it difficult for him to pick up pins or coins or the kernels of nuts, or to tear the wings from nightingales. He was six feet four, and forty-six, and even colder than he thought he was. One eye wore a velvet patch; the other glittered through a monocle, which made half his body seem closer to you than the other half. He had lost one eye when he was twelve, for he was fond of peering into nests and lairs in search of birds and animals to maul. One afternoon, a mother shrike had mauled him first. His nights were spent in evil dreams, and his days were given to wicked schemes.

To an adult, this might seem like exuberance carried to a fault – the fault of lapsing into swinging verse rhythms and even rhyme. But few children are going to cavil at this, even if they notice it, dazzled and enthralled by the detail as they are likely to be. On the other hand, the effect could well be extremely boring even for them without such close particularization – if, for instance, the passage above were left with its vague general 'wickeds' and 'evils' and 'gloomys' and 'lonelys' but deprived of its *thirteen* (try *many*), its *pins, coins, kernels*, its *nightingales* (try *birds*), its *six feet four* (tall? very tall?), its *forty-six* (*middle-aged?*), its *velvet, twelve* (try *a boy*) and *shrike* (try *bird* again). Such details as that help to peg down the fantasy, give credibility to the incredible, and to sense the underlying reality of the tale, we don't need to know that Thurber himself had lost an eye in his boyhood. (Itself – really the result of a bow and arrow accident – transmuted into a fantasy-incident by E. B. White, one of his *New Yorker* colleagues, who wrote that Thurber as a young man had once helped out as a ship's cook, tried to make pancakes out of stump powder, blown up the galley and lost his eye as a consequence – an anecdote that rumour sufficiently invested with truth, helped no doubt by the circumstantiality of the specified pancakes and stump powder, as to induce Dale Kramer into solemnly refuting it in *Ross and the New Yorker*.)

---

1. 'With humor you have to look out for traps. You're likely to be very gleeful with what you've first put down, and you think it's fine, very funny. One reason you go over and over it is to make the piece sound less as if you were having a lot of fun with it yourself. You try to play it down. In fact, if there's such a thing as a *New Yorker* style, that would be it – playing it down.' *Writers at Work*.

But there is an important aspect of the use of detail in children's fiction that should never be overlooked – an aspect that gives rise to a kind of double-standard where fantasy is concerned. The larger details of context in time and space can be most outrageously distorted (with the reader's agreement) but the internal details, the functional ones, those that have any relation to universal reality – such as types of trees or animals or people or cars or processes or forms of behaviour or institutions – must be accurate. Hence Joan Aiken, with a keen understanding of her intended readership, took the precaution of displaying prominently, at the very beginning of some editions of *The Wolves of Willoughby Chase*, this:

NOTE

The action of this book takes place in a period of English history that never happened – shortly after the accession to the throne of Good King James III in 1832. At this time, the Channel Tunnel from Dover to Calais having been recently completed, a great many wolves, driven by severe winters, had migrated through the tunnel from Europe and Russia to the British Isles.

Just as the amassing of facts is of tremendous importance to children, so any failure to present them truly is, when discovered, regarded as a tremendous betrayal. That is why an author who has taken pains to check and cross-check gets so annoyed with the illustrator who can't even make sure that the details of his pictures correspond with the details given in the text. That is also why such an author gets so furious with the occasional publisher who – still clinging to some outdated view that anything will do for the kids – regards such illustrators' lapses as being of no importance. Happily, far more publishers are beginning to appreciate the fact that to a child text and illustrations are aspects of the same thing, products of a collective imagination, and they take care to let the author (who, after all, is likely to retain a more vivid picture of what has been written than anyone else) vet the illustrations and so obviate discrepancies that could be disastrous to any suspension of disbelief.

This in fact is where even the best of illustrators most frequently go wrong. They have their own standards to look to – questions of composition, light and shade, and so on – and so long as they check the obvious details – of architecture, dress, car design, etc. – they tend to become quite cavalier with regard to the author-originated details. So, if a group of three children make a better picture in a certain setting than a group of two, an artist might put the third child in for the sake of the composition, even if the text states clearly that that particular child is not present at that point in the story. So, if a splash of black is required, an artist might have a character wearing a dark raincoat that he happens to have had stolen in the previous chapter. So, if an artist likes to draw children's limbs, he might put a thirteen-year-old boy in short trousers, even when the text implies and all heaven cries out that a lad of this age and type would sooner die than wear them. So – even when getting everything, intrinsic and extrinsic, right – an artist might design a *book-jacket* showing a missing dog in the arms of a former owner, a person whose identity the author has been careful not to disclose before the last chapter. All these and more have happened to me, and I squirm to think of the damage they might have done had I not had publishers enlightened enough to let me see the drawings before the blocks were made.

Perhaps the greatest danger nowadays vis-à-vis illustrations – given the fact that most publishers are fully alive to the need for such checking – lies in books that are translated from another language or, in the case of Anglo-American interchanges, produced by a different publisher in each country. In such cases they are often reillustrated. Why, I am not sure, beyond the fact that currently fashionable styles of illustration seem rarely to coincide in the various countries. What I am sure of is that a great deal of damage could be – and indeed must be – done, because in such cases it is rare for the author to be given the chance to vet the new illustrations. As a result, discrepancies which could have been avoided tend to get through and, what is in some respects worse, facts like those concerned with forms of behaviour or dress or geographical features are often distorted. One of the most striking cases of this general distortion was presented to me through my own book, *Jim Starling*. The setting is the industrial West Riding of Yorkshire, and the British illustrator, Roger Payne, made an excellent job of getting the background – with its mill chimneys, crowded terrace houses, warehouses, old chapels and Victorian school buildings – right. The Swedish edition, reillustrated, transforms all this into a bosky, leafy, utterly rural haven; very pleasant but totally impossible; while the Polish, just a little nearer the mark, makes Smogbury into a neat clean market town, with some half-timbered houses, of the kind much more likely to be found in the agricultural Midlands or southern counties of England. Again, where Jim Starling, a devoted cricketer, is shown bowling off-spinners, the Swedish illustrator has him half-whirled round and bent-elbowed in a stance much more likely to be seen at the Connie Mack stadium than at Lords, while the Pole – again nearer the mark – has him half-kneeling after a crown-green type of delivery that looks as if it merits the caption of 'Good wood, lad!' The meticulous Dutch, thank heavens, retained the original British illustrations, though even they managed to pick up an original British mistake – spotted and corrected in the home edition – of showing a crouching character wearing the headgear that is supposed to have been in police hands – alleged proof that he'd committed the crime that he's being hunted for.

There are of course obvious physical difficulties involved in vetting at a distance. These are by no means insurmountable, however, as I discovered when I had to see through the press several of my British-published children's books from a Central Ohian base, and various American-published children's books from England.[1] But in any case there is much to be said for retaining original illustrations of foreign publications. A scrupulous attention to detail is infinitely more important than current trends.

---

[1]. Regarding Anglo–American publication, changes of illustrations are usually completely overshadowed, in an author's eyes, by proposals or requests to make changes in the text itself. For a detailed discussion of this much-debated, pundit-peppered question – which does not quite fall within the framework of the present chapter – see Appendix A. And for an amusing but, I trust, horrific ultimate example of the extent to which illustrations can diverge from the text, see Appendix B.

Chapter five

Variations in technique and content

We have noted already a number of differences in treatment that hinge on the question of whether one is writing fiction for children or adults. There are however certain important variations inside the children's field – general variations that have little to do with the styles and approaches of individual authors. These are primarily determined by (*a*) the age or (*b*) the ability of the intended readership, and secondarily by (*c*) the medium through which the fiction is presented (comic-book, movie, television or radio play, and so on) or (*d*) in the case of content, the general outlook of the periods in which the works were written. It is true that the two secondary instances are important in the adult field also, but not to the same extent as in the juvenile, where the impact of fiction presented through media other than prose can have a very significant effect on the still unformed reading habits and attitudes of a child, and where content has always to be thoroughly checked for suitability and – what is not always the same thing – acceptability.

A. Variations according to age

To a great extent this aspect is bound up with ability, particularly in the earliest stages of a child's schooling. Here the books that are to be read *by* children must be carefully designed and manufactured as precision instruments – skill-acquiring instruments – with strictly limited and graded vocabularies, sentence structures and lengths. That these instruments are usually constructed in fictional form – very simple, bare, gutless narratives – is at once a tribute to fiction's powers to attract and engage and a very dangerous hazard: a threat to a child's future capacity to enjoy prose fiction and thereby derive from it the immense educative benefits it has to offer. Indeed, without certain balancing factors, an initial diet of such drab, lifeless, skill-acquiring narratives can completely cancel out the real value of the skill acquired.

For example:

Mother, see baby.
See baby play ball.
Baby can catch the ball.
See baby catch it.

(Beacon Readers, Book 1)

See the little kitty!
It is up in the tree.
It ran and ran.
It ran up the tree.
Can you catch it?
It may fall.
O Sam, you are good!
You have the little kitty.

(Beacon Readers, Book 1)

This is fiction, of course. It has characters – of a sort. It has narrative movement – of a sort. Granted, the authors are doing their best in the second example to give that narrative some pace. 'It may fall' comes at the end of a page, and between that minor cliff-hanger and the words 'O Sam, you are good!' the narrative line is carried by a picture showing Sam climbing the tree and lifting down the kitten. There is even the introduction of the comparatively sophisticated flash-back device in the two lines after 'It is up in the tree.'

But with character -- the staple of all good fiction – hardly anything is done at all. Sam might as well be John, the two girls are only differentiated in size, Mother is a cardboard nonentity, nobody is greedy or bad-tempered or fat or thin or strong or weak or clever or dull. A mild kindliness is about the only discernible characteristic, shared by all – a feature that would make a fascinating adult satire or piece of science fiction, to be sure, but is insipid to the point of meaninglessness here.

Yet one cannot – as some try to do – blame the authors for this. Those words must be strictly rationed and controlled. So must the very consonants, vowels, diphthongs. These, in more than one sense, are the true characters, and the true tension that grips the reader is the extremely personal one: 'Shall I be able to read this next word, or page?' rather than 'Will he kill the dragon?' (A tension experienced more often than is admitted, one suspects, at the other end of the scale by highly sophisticated readers of avant-garde fiction.)

It is easy to applaud the freshness of the primer that strives to break through the veil of insipidity – of Leila Berg's *Fish and Chips for Supper*, say:

One day,
as Dad got out of bed,
a drip fell down from the ceiling,
and wet his head.
'Ow' he said. And he hid under the sheets.
Dad, Dad, go to work.
Then you can bring home your pay.
And we can have fish and chips
for supper.

After the traditional Janets and Johns and Sams and Ruths and Kittys and Rovers, Miss Berg's Dad looms up, delightfully, as a veritable Oblomov. But this – in such a context – is not the criterion. Do her primers introduce the words, consonants, diphthongs etc., as skilfully as the others? Has any of the science been sacrificed to art? Should the scientific aspect be impaired at all, in the interest of art?

I think not – passionately as I am concerned about the dangers of dulling or even killing a child's capacity for appreciation of good fiction. If competently engineered, such skill-acquiring instruments are indispensable – drab, unspeakably drab but indispensable – just as beginners' exercises in music are drab but indispensable. But – and this is the point not always recognized – in music the learner is usually fed and sustained on a rich diet of good music, far beyond his powers of performance but within his capacity for appreciation. And that is why fiction written to be read *to* young children is every bit as important as that which is written to be read *by* them. So every child who is presently struggling with such passages as this:

Look at the boats.
Big boats and little boats.
John has a red boat.
I like big boats, John.
Look at the big red boat.
I want to go in the big boat.

(*Janet and John*, Book 1)

– should be systematically regaled and refreshed by such passages as this:

But the Mole was very full of lunch, and self-satisfaction, and pride, and already quite at home in a boat (so he thought) and was getting a bit restless besides: and presently he said, 'Ratty! Please, *I* want to row, now!'

The Rat shook his head with a smile. 'Not yet, my young friend,' he said – 'wait till you've had a few lessons. It's not so easy as it looks.'

78

The Mole was quiet for a minute or two. But he began to feel more and more jealous of Rat, sculling so strongly and easily along, and his pride began to whisper that he could do it every bit as well. He jumped up and seized the sculls, so suddenly, that the Rat, who was gazing out over the water and saying more poetry-things to himself, was taken by surprise and fell backwards off his seat with his legs in the air for the second time, while the triumphant Mole took his place and grabbed the sculls with entire confidence.

'Stop it, you *silly* ass!' cried the Rat, from the bottom of the boat. 'You can't do it! You'll have us over!'

(*The Wind in the Willows*, Kenneth Grahame)

And this:

'Right!' shouted Mr Brown, as he braced himself once more. 'Here we go. Cast off, Paddington. Hold on, everyone!'

'Do what, Mr Brown?' cried Paddington, above the splashing of the water. Having a picnic on the river was much more complicated than he had expected. There were so many ropes to pull he was getting a bit confused. First of all Mr Brown had told him to untie the rope. Now he had shouted to everyone to hold on.

Paddington closed his eyes and held on to the rope with both paws as tightly as he could.

He wasn't quite sure what happened next. One moment he was standing on the boat – the next moment it wasn't there any more.

'Henry!' shouted Mrs Brown, as there was a loud splash. 'For goodness' sake! Paddington's fallen in the water!'

'Bear overboard!' cried Jonathan, as the boat shot away from the bank.

'Hold on, Paddington!' called Judy. 'We're coming.'

'But I *did* hold on,' cried Paddington, as he came up spluttering for air. 'That's how I fell in.'

(*Paddington Helps Out*, Michael Bond)

And this:

Then the Cyclops, in his wrath, broke off the top of a great hill, a mighty rock, and hurled it where he had heard the voice. Right in front of the ship's bow it fell, and a great wave rose as it sank, and washed the ship back to the shore. But Ulysses seized a long pole with both hands and pushed the ship from the land, and bade his comrades ply their oars, nodding with his head, for he was too wise to speak, lest the Cyclops should know where they were. Then they rowed with all their might and main.

(Church's *Stories from Homer*, quoted in *Myths Every Child Should Know*, ed. Hamilton Wright Mabie)

79

Thus, as the skill is being mastered – as it must – an experience of the delights of character, fast flickering action, comedy, word-play, high adventure and myth, to which that skill is the key, is being offered – as *it* must.

Many teachers and parents are aware of this need, of course. They do their best to supplement the primer diet. But even these enlightened ones tend to regard this reading-to as an intelligent indulgence rather than as the vital basic necessity it is. Thus, while no education authority would regard money spent on primers as wasted or of doubtful value, very few would accord equal importance to money spent on building up a large stock of books to be read *to* the same children. Similarly, while most teachers would automatically allocate time for regular primer-using periods, few would give an equal, let alone a greater, amount of time for reading stories to their classes.

This is because of a serious underestimation of the importance of fiction in education generally – of the paramount importance in the whole educative and civilizing process of the powers of imaginative and speculative projection: powers that are as applicable to the best work in science and mathematics as they are to politics, history and other more obviously 'literary' subjects. That such powers can only be cultivated by a sustained contact with good fiction from the earliest possible moment onwards is something I shall be developing in a later chapter. At this stage, however, it is worth pointing out the irony of the unconscious recognition of the power of fiction by the severer, rule-of-thumb educators who might be inclined to regard systematic storytelling as a 'frill'. For primer material could quite easily be presented in non-fictional form. Fleetingly, here and there, it is, as in some books for backward readers, where the subjects tend to be practical hints on making simple models or mending punctures. But generally there is a tendency to stick to fiction – a feeble personalizing of the material – as being potentially more attractive, engaging if not gripping.

This irony is worth dwelling on, because the instinctive adherence to fiction without giving it its full due respect is probably at the root of a problem that vexes so many teachers and librarians at the later stages of a child's reading career. Aware of the shortcomings of the fiction presented in the earliest reading books, authors, publishers and educationists tend to hasten on to the so-called 'supplementary' stages of the various courses – anxious to prove that reading can be fun. So they produce narrative booklets that are livelier, more attractive but still of necessity severely restricted (for these too are meant to be read *by* the children), which in turn, quite naturally, build up into the full but miserably thin spate of Blytonian-type books that tend to become addictive long after the reading skills have been consolidated. (Just as a diet of light television entertainment can become addictive among quite highly intelligent adults.) It would seem to be a problem that could very effectively be avoided if a rich enough and consistent enough complementary stream of material were presented in story-reading sessions from the beginning.

What then should one look for in fiction designed to be read *to* young children?

In content, as we have seen, there should be a richness of character and a diversity of plot, setting and incident to make up for the necessary thinness of these elements as presented in primers. Quite rightly, these skill-acquiring instruments generally restrict themselves to familiar subjects – homes, families, friends, toys, pets – but fail to explore them in any depth at all, or develop them in any direction. Books to be read to children at this stage are therefore not the least valuable when, starting with the same familiar subjects, they do in fact explore them and explore them vigorously, viewing them from different, often strange or amusing angles, and developing their comic (particularly) or tragic possibilities. Indeed, one of the most helpful lines of action a parent or teacher can take is to extract from the reading course a child happens to be taking a list of topics dealt with (e.g., in the *Beacon Readers*, Book 1, such a list would include Mothers, Kittens, Dogs, Balls, Babies, Lost Pets, Bells, Toys, Apples, Trees, Picnics, Cars, Dolls, Ragmen) and to select suitably rich and stimulating stories, or passages from stories, on similar topics, to be read aloud in conjunction with the basic course. Thus, as in the examples quoted on page 77, a child working his way through the boat passages in *Janet and John*, Book 1, might be presented with Kenneth Grahame's, Michael Bond's and Homer's treatments of the same theme – to mention only three possibilities.

As for technique in books designed or chosen to be read aloud, one must take into account the amateur status of most readers-aloud-to-children – the fact that, teacher, parent, or friend, such a reader will not generally have the skill of a trained actor. Therefore a style that sings *itself* is desirable – a style that as far as possible imposes its own rhythms and emphases and pauses and inflections on the reader. Further, it should ideally be a style that fits the story*telling* situation, that suggests a definite voice, that is, in some measure at least, colloquial. A care over dialogue is also to be looked for in such books.·Moods and characteristics should be projected in speech through rhythms and sentence structure rather than through indicated outlandish accents or modes of delivery that might require the interpretative skills of trained actors. Indeed, very often in the storytelling situation, reported speech is at once more natural and easier on the ear than the snatches of straight dialogue one comes to look for and to regard as attractive in one's private fiction reading.

Where the narrative methods are concerned, again the story*telling* situation makes certain treatments desirable if not preferable. When one's reading aloud has to be done, and is probably better done, and is certainly most comfortably done, in twenty-minute snatches, the briskly episodic, even serial-like rise and fall of incident is generally better than the long slow build-up. And in such a context nothing could be more suitable or more useful than a certain open-endedness – a hint of life going on before and after and all around the presented situation – demanding and stimulating speculation.

Most of the foregoing requirements or desiderata are met with in good folk tales, and this is not surprising when it is remembered that such narratives are deeply rooted in the oral tradition. But it would be a mistake to fall back on such material exclusively for these purposes. Folk tales give a rich and fascinating cast to the familiar staples of home, parents, sisters and brothers, pets, toys, food and drink, and so forth. They often delve quite deeply into personality types and forms of behaviour. They generally swing along with a vigour that even the dullest delivery fails to obscure, and this often after a genteel hack translator has already done his or her worst. But they do lack one important element: modernity. There are no cars in them, no telephones, no aircraft, no refrigerators, no television sets. . . . And since these features form so large a part of a growing child's experience – long before he has been confronted by the opinions of Merrie Englanders, pseudo-Lawrentians and others, seeking to warn him, for reasons rarely explained, how spurious and worthless such things are – since a car is as real and interesting to a child as a cat, or a can of beans as an old rooster, it is important that objects of this sort should figure imaginatively and interestingly in a reasonably large number of the stories we read to him.

Here, unfortunately, the field of choice is not as wide, and it is littered with specimens of the gimcrack lightweight kind we are hoping the child will learn to avoid, or at least not over-indulge in, when he comes to read fluently for himself. But the supply is growing and, with care, one should be able to make a satisfactorily ample selection from works like *The Wind in the Willows*, some of E. Nesbit's stories, the Doctor Dolittle series, perhaps the Uncle books of J. P. Martin (for the more gifted amateur actor-readers), the Paddington adventures, the Borrowers books, and others of that general quality.

Finally, before leaving the subject of fiction for children who are just learning to read, one must mention a category they are likely to have encountered – and should have encountered – at an earlier stage: the books designed to be read (and looked at) *with* children, as distinct from those to be read *to* them or *by* them. These, of course, are what are generally described as picture books. Skilfully done, as so many of them are, they form an excellent introduction to the *feel* of books, to their power to delight. Naturally, the active elements here are the illustrations, with the text playing a minor prompting and nudging role. Visual description, for instance, tends to be superfluous and the good writer will leave this to the illustrator – as he will leave, in fact, any function that can be more immediately and vividly fulfilled pictorially. But his will still be the basic inventive, organizing and controlling responsibility, and he will still remain alert for opportunities to add to the roundness or density of the story by inserting a sonorous word here or describing a smell or a sound there, or, by skilful repetition, striking an echo that can give new perspective to, or cast a different, remembered light upon, the juxtaposed picture. Pictorial artists, aware of the limitations of their medium, are often quite grateful for the help that can be given by a few words in the right place, and that perhaps is why so many of them do so well at writing their own texts. But they will still need to have a good writer's storytelling skill and gift for timing to produce a completely satisfactory piece of fiction in this genre, and also, one senses, a schizophrenic ability to approach the subject as two distinct personalities that are to be reunited only through the finished work.

Given the large numbers of excellent productions in this category – vivid, imaginative, resonant pre-reading experiences of storybooks – it is all the more a pity that such direct experience should tend to thin out so suddenly and drastically with the introduction of school primers and the failure to supply sufficient compensatory material in the form of stories to be read aloud. At the same time, however, the example of this early wealth does point to one way of alleviating the otherwise inevitable fictional insipidity of the primers themselves. That is through pictorial richness. Far more attention could be paid to detail in the illustrations contained in most of these reading-course booklets. Characters could be more sharply individualized. Backgrounds could be given greater authenticity, depth, potentiality. Incidents could be given stronger dramatic propensities. Let us, by all means, continue to have the learner 'Look at the little dog' or 'See the kittens'. But let him look at the little dog as it does more than run or jump in a greeny-yellowy no-man's-garden. Let him watch it, apprehensively, as it dashes out into a busy street, or, gleefully, as it snatches a newly washed napkin from the crotchety neighbour's clothes basket and trails it through the mud. Let him see Kitty scratch John's arm (and maybe take that placid booby look off his face). To their great credit, the publishers of the *Beacon Readers* seem to be aiming at something of the sort. As we have noted, they do at least contrive to have the pictures carry, often quite dramatically, some of the story-line, and they do show a realization of the suggestive value of pictorial detail. Even so, there is room for a much sharper delineation of character in the illustrations and for more by-play, understandably unmentioned in the limited text, but sure to be noticed and speculated upon by the young reader. Would it be too distracting? No more, surely, than the activities going on in the classroom around him, or in the street outside, the traditional resorts of the fairly bright but unutterably bored young mind.

Assuming a child has passed through the initial reading course and acquired basic skill, what sort of fiction should be provided for him to practise this skill on? First let us remember the eagerness that accompanies a recently acquired skill – an eagerness experienced by anyone, at any age, to put that skill to use, to enjoy it and revel in it, whether it concerns driving a car or swimming or speaking a foreign language or reading. Where reading is concerned, this access of eagerness, this first flush of voracious enthusiasm, at once gives teachers and parents an advantage and an obligation. Sadly, it is an advantage that isn't generally exploited, an obligation that is left unfulfilled, because of the dearth of good fiction designed to be read by these new readers, these 7–8 year-olds.

Obviously, anything written for them will have to be relatively simple. The stories can be rather longer, with richer and less rigidly controlled vocabularies than those in the later primer stages, but it is desirable that they should be short enough to be read in two or three sittings. And while the length of words needn't be restricted to two syllables, the sentences should certainly be kept quite short. In content, it is generally desirable that they keep to the homely familiar settings of the primers – for the enthusiasm generated by the use of a new skill tends to be enhanced and the skill more keenly enjoyed when applied to the familiar – but these backgrounds can now be more vigorously and thoroughly explored, just as the child's real home background is beginning to be more fully explored and its boundaries extended. What is over the hill, then or round the corner, or shut away in the attic, or lurking in the wood-pile – these tend to make the most tempting objectives in fictional as well as in real life at this stage, rather than what is over the sea or at the other side of the moon.

To a good writer – especially one with growing powers of his own – all this can still seem depressingly restricting. Fantasies, tales to be read aloud to young children, yes. Such a writer may feel quite happy to produce something in such categories – where he can still give his imagination and skill a reasonably loose rein. Even texts for picture-books will appeal to him more, for these are so short as to occupy little of his time. But stories to be read *by* children of six, seven or eight – no.

Yet these are the writers most needed at this age – writers of a quality to match the hopeful enthusiasm, and capable of ensuring that it is not betrayed and left to dwindle gradually into an indifference about reading. And it is doubly a pity, since if they were to examine the question more closely they would see that much could be done within the limits suggested, that working skilfully within those limits might produce some fascinating and considerable artistic results. After all, as I shall indicate later in this section, when discussing books for older backward or reluctant readers, certain major writers have produced some of their best effects in the adult field by confining themselves to similar syntactical and vocabulary restrictions.

Furthermore, there are at this stage of a child's growth certain intellectual developments that offer such a writer additional challenges and possibilities. There is the beginning of an interest in word-play – in the punning and game elements of language that authors as distinguished and cerebral as James Joyce, Lewis Carroll, Samuel Beckett and William Burroughs have found it rewarding to explore. There is also the awakening of the passion for detail mentioned earlier – manifesting itself physically in crazes for collecting.

At present, far too many stories for children at this stage neglect such possibilities. Thinness all too often accompanies brevity, and superficiality simplicity. Even the more intelligent attempts to supply books for these children tend to do no more than meet their bare needs without fully responding to their enthusiasms and going on to do them proud. So the bulk of reading material at this stage continues to be of the insipid kind, large in quantity but in quality merely an extension, a continuation of the stuff provided in primers.

Earlier I referred to this as Blytonian, and in fact much of what was written by Enid Blyton for children in this group – particularly her stories of solitary children who come into contact with elves and pixies and fairies with tired feeble anaemic names like Mr Feefo and Pop-up and Dumble-dee – is exactly what I mean by 'thin'. But Enid Blyton was by no means as bad a writer as such stories and her innumerable detractors would lead us to believe, and when she came to write for children in the next stage – roughly the eight to elevens – she could be quite startlingly good in certain departments. Let us take, for example, one of her Famous Five stories: *Five Run Away Together*.

At the most obvious levels it is fully in line with a number of the strongest requirements of readers of this age-group. It is a long story – a children's novel – running to some 190 pages, thus satisfying the demand for more prolonged immersion or escape, the antithesis to which produces the grumble, increasingly heard from children at this stage, that 'I don't like short stories because they end just when you're getting into them'. Then it carries exploration of the familiar to the running away, fending for oneself stage, as the title proclaims. And, at a period – the pre-pubertial – when the clean-limbed sexless outlook reaches its snowiest peak, the readers are presented with paragons of such an outlook in the four leading characters – with the girl Georgina dressing like a boy and being called George, and frequent references to the smelliness and pimpliness of their adversaries.

A critical reading of the book discloses other features that are equally attractive to the intended readership and some that are not to be underestimated by the most discriminating adult. For example, the author never loses sight of the fact that she is unfolding a tale: hardly a page passes without the dramatic insertion of a piece of necessary information or the sounding of a bugle-note of alarm. The basic situation is exquisitely prickly: Georgina's mother's illness and her being rushed with her husband to the hospital miles away, shortly after the girl's three cousins arrive for the holidays, leaving them for over a week in the company of the unpleasant Mrs Stick and her equally unpleasant husband, son and dog. The timing here is, as in most parts of the book, excellent, the reader being given just enough time before the bombshell of the parents' departure to begin intensely to dislike the Sticks, and the child characters equal time to show their dislike and so lay themselves more fully open to retributive unpleasantness. As a band, the characterization of the Four (the Five includes George's dog) is quite brilliant. Here we have fully portrayed the nasty, snobby, cruel selfishness that most children are capable of when they collect in packs of this sort – a dark side to children that very, very few children's authors ever touch on, and then usually only in their hero's and heroine's adversaries. Here for instance is George putting the verbal knife into Edgar Stick, as the Five set out on a picnic:

> On the way they met Edgar, looking as stupid and sly as usual. 'Why don't you let me come along with you?' he said. 'Let's go to that island. I know a lot about it, I do.'
>
> 'No, you don't,' said George, in a flash. 'You don't know anything about it. And I'd never take *you*. It's *my* island, see? Well, *ours*. It belongs to all four of us and Timmy, too. We should never allow you to go.'
>
> ''Tisn't your island,' said Edgar. 'That's a lie, that is!'
>
> 'You don't know what you're talking about,' said George, scornfully. 'Come on, you others! We can't waste time talking to Edgar.'

There, in its nakedness, is all the moral brutality of a certain almost universally experienced phase of childhood. And it is all the more convincing because the writer – probably unconsciously – shows approval of the brutality. Note the authentic ring of merciless, petulant, childish viciousness in the authorial '. . . Edgar, looking as stupid and sly as usual'. So characters, readers and author become one in their pack-hunting, and if it is somewhat nauseating it must also be allowed that it is absolutely true, far truer to human nature than the work that would present Edgar as the normal child hero and the spiteful ones as his abnormal antagonists, or the Four as normal 'nice' children, with Edgar as the spiteful outsider.

The same note also occurs in the exchanges that Julian, the older boy, has with the Sticks from time to time, with the additional spice of class warfare. Here he is, caught in the act of pulling Edgar's nose – punitively, of course:

Mrs. Stick came hurrying into the kitchen. She gave a scream when she saw what Julian was doing. She flew at him. Julian withdrew his arm, and stood outside the window.

'How dare you!' yelled Mrs. Stick. 'First that girl slaps Edgar, and then you pull his nose! What's the matter with you all?'

'Nothing,' said Julian, pleasantly; 'but there's an awful lot wrong with Edgar, Mrs. Stick. We feel we just *must* put it right. It should be your job, of course, but you don't seem to have done it.'

'You're right down insolent,' said Mrs. Stick, outraged and furious.

'Yes, I dare say I am,' said Julian. 'It's just the effect Edgar has on me. Stinker has the same effect.'

'Stinker!' cried Mrs. Stick, getting angrier still. 'That's not my dog's name, and well you know it.'

'Well, it really ought to be,' said Julian, strolling off. 'Give him a bath, and maybe we'll call him Tinker instead.'

And here he is, putting the whole family in its place:

'Good riddance to bad rubbish,' murmured Edgar to himself. He was lying sprawled on the sofa, reading some kind of highly-coloured comic paper.

'If you've anything to say to me, Edgar, come outside and say it,' said Julian, dangerously.

'You leave Edgar alone,' said Mrs. Stick, at once.

'There's nothing I should like better,' said Julian, scornfully. 'Who wants to be with him? Cowardly little spotty-face!

'Now, now, look 'ere!' began Mr. Stick, from his corner.

'I don't want to look at you,' said Julian at once.

'Now, look 'ere,' said Mr. Stick, angrily, standing up.

'I've told you I don't want to,' said Julian. 'You're not a pleasant sight.'

'*Insolence!*' said Mrs. Stick. . . .

And so, one is tempted to add, say all of us. For Julian *is* an insolent brat, and none the less so for the author's approval. But insolent brats abound, alas, and she must be congratulated for providing such an accurate chillingly convincing picture – as accurate and chilling and convincing as Mr Robert Liddell's in his acid, perceptive, Compton-Burnett-like novel of prep-school life, *The Deep End*. Here are a few of his insolent brats discussing a boy they have sent to Coventry and who is present during the exchange:

> 'Fancy reducing the fees for such a stupid boy!' said Ralph. 'If he scrapes into a public school, it's the most he'll do.'
> 'No good school would take him now,' said Michael. 'They've all got pretty well booked up. No need to take a boy of bad character.'
> 'He won't get into the Army now,' said Ronald.
> 'Not as an officer, of course,' said Michael. 'But I've no doubt he could get in without a commission – they'll take any trash.'
> 'He could hardly do that,' said Tony. 'After all, he's a gentleman.'
> 'I suppose his father's a gentleman,' admitted Ralph. 'But his mother's a very common little person; my mater said so.'

Perhaps one reason for the inordinate venom with which Enid Blyton's name is mentioned by many librarians and teachers is the discomforting accuracy with which she reflects some of the nastier traits of children of the middle-classes to which they themselves belong.

Enid Blyton can also be quite perceptive about some of her characters' less unpleasant foibles. George's father, the Uncle Quentin of the story, has an uncertain temper.

> The three children did not very much like George's father, because he could get into very fierce tempers, and although he welcomed the three cousins to his house, he did not really care for children. So they always felt a little awkward with him, and were glad when he was not there.

This is refreshingly unusual enough, in a field where the heroes' and heroines' fathers are usually stereotyped as bluff hearties or mild eccentrics. But Miss Blyton goes on to explore Uncle Quentin's character a little further, a little deeper, with commendable precision, uncovering the vein of remorse that so often lurks under the surface of such personalities.

> 'What are you going to do today?' asked Uncle Quentin, towards the end of breakfast. He was feeling a little better by that time, and didn't like to see such subdued faces round him.

A vein that is, as I say, often there – but rarely noticed by most children's authors – just as the following shrewd observation can't often have been made in this field:

> '. . . Let's do it each night if we stay a week on the island. George, did you ask your mother?'
> 'Oh yes,' said George. 'She said she thought we might, but she would see.'

'I don't like it when grown-ups say they'll see,' said Anne. 'It so often means they won't let you do something after all, but they don't like to tell you at the time.'

– a comment worthy of Miss Compton-Burnett herself.

Pockets of shrewdness, then, an awareness of the elementary needs of children of this age in the way of length and subject-matter, and a remarkable, probably quite unconscious knack of identifying with them in some of their more primitive if least pleasant urges – these are the qualities we are bound to respect in such books. But their deficiencies are equally considerable. They lack density. There is no fixing in time or space, no richness of circumstantiality. The sea could be any sea, or no sea at all. The Five could be anywhere, or nowhere. Even worse, apart from the *collective* personality, the pack personality already described, and Julian's insolence, the children are characterless, the only real differentiation made between them being in size or age or sex (and hardly that in George/Georgina's case). Worst of all, because of the moral unevenness, the startling candour in some respects and the gross distortion in others, there is this tendency to give approval to thoroughly bad natural instincts – to corrupt, in fact, and this I shall be taking up later in the chapter on the responsibility of children's authors.

Fortunately, this 8–11 group is on the whole much better served than the younger children, and it is not difficult to see why. Technical restrictions are far less severe. A normal child's vocabulary is rapidly widening at this stage. His mechanical reading ability is increasing equally rapidly, reaching almost adult proportions towards the end of the period. And, as far as his comprehension of what he reads is concerned, the widening of his experience ensures a corresponding speeding up in the process of understanding and assimilating new words. Then again, in content the author's choices are widening with this widening of experience – geographically, historically and scientifically. Granted, in the arrogance born of so vast and heady an influx of material information, children tend at this period to be at their most severe over lapses in presenting facts; but with this same broadening of experience there is a deepening process that makes certain refinements of tone possible. As a child progresses through this stage, moral blacks needn't be *quite* such solid blacks or whites so utterly spotless, while – apparently paradoxically – clearer distinctions between the sexes of characters can be drawn. What is perhaps even more important, irony and a gentler humour than the broad slapstick of the kindergarten can now be appreciated. And of course even fantastic distortions of the hallowed Facts are permitted, if sufficient provenance is made for such liberties and an honest pact entered into at the outset.

All this is why many of the outstanding children's classics were written with children of this age-group in mind; or – where the authors had no such precise designs – received their first enthusiastic response from such children. *The Story of the Treasure Seekers, Alice's Adventures in Wonderland, Swallows and Amazons, Emil and the Detectives. The Borrowers, The Wind in the Willows* – one could fill several pages with the titles of such books. (But see Appendices D and E.)

After this period, in the stage roughly spanning the years from 11 to 13 or 14 – to puberty in fact, and the time when a normal child's mechanical reading ability becomes fully adult – a more generally critical spirit begins to develop. Fact lapses are still pounced upon, but now a child will be readier to reject or scoff at books for their attitudes towards facts, for the pictures they present and the tones adopted by their authors. This is the beginning of the cynical period that continues well into adolescence – and while such cynicism might be justly condemned as 'cheap' (i.e., not sufficiently tested by experience) when adhered to at those later stages, it has a natural and honourable and most useful function here. After all, there are so many phoney, gimcrack, cant-ridden opinions thrust upon young children in the earlier stages, through books and conversation and radio and television programmes – patent mush that is tolerated by parents and teachers only because it is vaguely 'uplifting' in tone, that such a reflex – vicious, callous and brutal as it may seem – can only be beneficial. Granted, the swing tends to go too far the other way – the mealy-mouthed philosophies of one group of arrested developers to be replaced in esteem by the glib-tongued sophistries of another – but the idea of an adult world fully committed to the ideals of jingoist scoutmasters or the Stick-persecuting Miss Blyton is even more depressing to contemplate than that world as it is presently constituted.

Which brings us to that currently fashionable non-category – of fiction for 'young adults'.

It seems to me that there are two undercurrents here, converging to support the vogue: a well-meaning attempt on the part of some of the would-do-gooders to extend their province – or, rather, to recapture the following lost in the first years of the cynical reaction – and a commercial move to invent and promote a new 'demand' in order to exploit it. Obviously, there will not be the biggest money in such a demand – the money to be made in the teen-age market in clothing or records, say. But there isn't the biggest money in books anyway, and moves to exploit something commercially aren't by any means always initiated by the keenest financial brains. All that is necessary is a feasible opportunity to push up small profits or extend small empires and small men and women will be tempted to work just as hard and ruthlessly to seize it as any bleak-eyed international property tycoon. But let us examine some of the basic elements of the situation and ask a few necessary questions.

To begin with: what is meant by a 'young adult'? Are we to use as our base-line the traditional 'coming of age', and say that the category is entered at 21? Or shall we begin at the U.S. drafting and the British drinking and voting line and say 18? Or the driving and cigarette-purchasing point: the 16s and upwards? Or shall it be a biological criterion, starting at the onset of puberty – say around 13, to split the legalistic difference between boys and girls? Perhaps, since we're considering reading maturity, the last is as good as any.

Having established that, however, where are we to assume that 'young adulthood' *ends*? With marriage? With parenthood? After some suitably traumatic experience, as in the cliches of sports commentators who are fond of describing a young player after a particularly good performance in adversity as 'growing up' at the wicket, or in the seventh inning or at the eighteenth hole? What, to take the matter further in logic, are the biological or emotional points at which the *next* stage begins and ends – the stage we should presumably have to classify as 'middle' or 'mature' or 'late-young' or 'early-elderly' adulthood. And what shall be *its* characteristics?

When one tries to answer these questions accurately and conscientiously one soon becomes aware of the impossibility of giving such a concept any clearly-defined basis. Let us assume, however, that there is one for the 13–18 group that most of the producers of books for 'young adults' have in mind. Are they justified in pointing to a demand for or need of special fictional material? What sort of fiction have young persons of this group tended to read? Very roughly it can be said that they have chosen and, wisely, do continue to choose adult material according to their intellectual capabilities and capacities. The very bright ones will, at 13 or 14, already have started on or be starting on all sorts of authors: Dickens, Bellow, Saroyan, Greene, Salinger, Hemingway, and in some cases writers like Kafka, Joyce, Dostoevsky. Certainly they will not be able to understand all of what they read – who does? – but they will be enjoying the works of such writers at the levels they can understand, and any first-class novel or story is, by definition, rich in levels. On the other hand, 'young adults' of average intelligence will tend to stick to the mid-brow fields, reading mainly straight detective stories, the better-class thrillers, best-sellerish novels of the adventurous variety, and maybe Wodehouse and similar humourists, while those of below-average intelligence will, where they read prose fiction at all; veer towards pulp fiction: 'adult' comic-books, paperback thrillers of the Micky Spillane type, cheap romance novelettes.

As I have indicated, this is a very rough sorting. That is all such grading can ever be. And of course there are movements within the total grouping, mainly downwards. The more intelligent members will be seen to be quite voraciously catholic, turning from Faulkner to Creasey or James Hadley Chase as easily as one moves out of the National Gallery into a Soho coffee bar, or the Museum of Modern Art into the Café Metropole – which is as it should be. But upwards? Is there ever much of a movement in that direction? Occasionally some top-level author will exert a kind of personal hypnotic pull on a lower-level reader. I once saw it happen with a young woman who, attracted by a crinoline skirt on a dust jacket, asked if she could borrow the book. It promised to be about a period that had always fascinated her, she said. Since her usual reading was *Woman's Own* and the volume the collected works of Thomas Love Peacock, I tactfully diverted her attention to Balzac's *Cousin Bette*, on the same shelf, which seemed to me to stand a much better chance of fulfilling that other volume's promise. And indeed it did fulfil that promise, to the extent that the woman became hooked on Balzac. But Balzac it *was*, and, as far as I know, she never did stray from that author's Human Comedy series during her trips into the upper regions of fiction. True, Balzac – of all the great authors – was prolific enough to continue to meet the needs of such an addict for years, but I have the feeling that where such upward excursions are made into any one author's realm, that is more likely to be the pattern, this type of reader being this type of reader often because of a lack of confidence or exploratory zeal – a factor the formula-binding concocters of popular magazines rely upon. As for readers of the pulp category, even such rigidly vertical sorties are so rare as to be practically non-existent.

This, to give their more sincere advocates their due, is really what is bothering the 'young adult' brigade, I think. What they would like to do is steer the lower intelligence group away from pulp and offer them something they are fond of describing as 'more wholesome', on the assumption that all cheap easy-to-read adult fiction is unwholesome. Very well; granting them this (very shaky, very sweeping) assumption, we must now ask what form this something should take.

So far, judging from the productions I have seen, the answer seems to be emasculated, cleaned-up little tales with modern settings, featuring coffee-bars, motor cycles, drugs, and the occasional bastard, that offer a kind of church-hall amateur-dramatic parody of the squalor that exists in such settings and is only too well known to exist there by most of the intended readership. Humour is in markedly short supply, because humour in such a real-life setting is so often – heaven spare us – ribald. The language lacks vigour because – alas – the vigour of the language to which people in such circumstances are accustomed is so often derived from what some might describe as its saltiness or raciness and others frown upon as unwholesome. Why the producers of these books should allow themselves to get into such a false position – where the blatant dishonesty of their subsequent whitewashing brings down on their heads the well-deserved contempt of the people they're trying to reach – can be attributed, I think, to their basic muddle-headedness, to a bourgeois reluctance to let the devil have all the best tunes. So, in the teaching situation, we have well-meaning but equally disastrous attempts to kindle an interest in poetry by presenting all the bloodiest ballads, and in the scriptures by dwelling on the holocausts and murders, the swords and clubs and slings. One can't help thinking how willing the devil must be to part with such tunes, how brightly his eyes must sparkle to see the well-meaning get on with his work so assiduously.

What is really required is, simply and logically, *good* easy-to-read adult fiction. Contrary to popular opinion, a good sensitive writer of adult fiction needn't be *difficult* to be good. That is another fallacy of our quick-to-label age. Admittedly, good sensitive fiction writers will never write down to an audience, but many will be capable of – and indeed be in the habit of – expressing their fables simply. And since there are far more writers in this category than is often realized – even by quite literate people – I believe that the solution lies in seeking out the existing work of such authors and attractively presenting it to adolescents in our third group rather than by creating a hideously faked non-literature.

One such attempt – to sort out suitable adult material for adolescents in the two lower general intellectual categories – has been made by educators in the University of Bristol's area, in collaboration with the publishers, Hodder and Stoughton. This has resulted in a periodically revised list of books – most of them novels – that have been published in the usual way for adults by that firm, and have been studied and graded by a panel of teachers and lecturers. Each is briefly described and most are given special ratings. An M, for example, warns that 'the book demands more than average maturity of experience and reading skill', while a B mark 'indicates that the book may be helpful for readers with less than average reading ability'. So Arnold Bennett's *The Old Wives' Tale* is given an M – with the following annotations:

> Here is a celebrated novelist who should be rediscovered by the readers we have in mind. In this novel he speaks straight to the condition of girls leaving school, however different the circumstances. The length of the book is taxing for the inexperienced so that the teacher's help in presenting it as a whole would give the necessary impetus. Strongly recommended as the kind of book which would satisfy the reader who is gaining experience and which would create an urge to tackle more of this quality.

Jane Gaskell's *Attic Summer* – an interesting example of the type of adult book the 'young adult' fictioneers most usually produce in watered-

93

down versions – also gets an M, with the following clumsily-put but intelligent and perceptive comments:

> The crux of the problem of teenage reading is in this book: how innocence becomes experience. The author has a vivid imagination and an ear for the use the young make of language. The heroine of the story spends the summer between school and secretarial college in an attic in the Fulham Road. She works in a supermarket, then in a cinema. She is preoccupied about boys. Bed-sitter life is accurately and humorously analysed. The dialogue is excellent. But although readers in their teens will identify themselves at once with the heroine or with the rapscallion 'Teds', and share their exasperation with their parents' generation, they may not have the necessary maturity of reading skilfully to appreciate the integrity at the core of this picture of Chelsea life. It would be a pity if they confused the details of the plot with the importance of the theme and thus they will need help from teachers and librarians.

Accordingly it is also marked with an L, to indicate 'that the librarian or teacher is advised to read the book before putting it on the shelves'.

Two examples of B-categorized books are Mary Patchett's *In a Wilderness* and Francis Durbridge's prose version of his television serial *The World of Tim Frazer*. The Patchett is annotated thus:

> A dingo pup is saved by a small boy against all the rules of farming. The dog becomes a sheep-killer and the boy suffers from an intense conflict of loyalties. A compelling tale for those who like animal stories; easily read by the less experienced.

The Durbridge:

> A relatively brief, quite fast-moving adventure story with values neither markedly bad nor good. Useful for those who need the enticement of novels which are easy to read and make few demands.

The value of such a list is that it is compiled and kept up to date by practising teachers, in daily touch with large numbers of the type of readers we are concerned with – who themselves are invited to offer their opinions on the books listed. Its limitations are its extreme brevity – just under 100 titles in the edition in front of me – and the fact that it is drawn from the output of one firm only. The fact that Hodder and Stoughton's fiction is predominantly mid-brow is in some respects an obvious help, in others a drawback. Were such a list to be derived from the output of many publishers – the net to be cast much wider, as it were – some very pleasantly surprising discoveries might have been made.

But as a model, *Timely Reading* is excellent. It shows what can be done and how to set about it, and there is no reason why other educational institutions, or librarians, or groups of teachers, or individuals shouldn't follow suit – combing the lists of *all* publishers for possible titles.[1] Most of all, individuals – for there can be nothing more valuable than investigations undertaken, and compilations made, in the light of immediate personal acquaintance with the problems and tastes of the actual group to be served. In this, the individual will have as yet little expert guidance, other than rare publications like *Timely Reading* itself, or the regular adult novel reviews written with adolescent requirements in mind which Margery Fisher regularly publishes in her magazine *Growing Point*. But in this matter the individual's personal knowledge of the prospective readers makes him his own best expert, so long as he is prepared to undertake the rewarding and surely not unpleasurable task of widening his own reading interests.

But to get back to the author – the primal producer – one thing is certain. Some effort of the sort outlined above will have to be made, for we will never get really good writers to work on false or treacherously unsound premises. Such a writer may be willing to write for children up to 13 or 14. He'll sometimes be prepared to control his style and vocabulary to meet the needs of the inexperienced or the backward or reluctant readers. These are true categories and measurable needs, and truth and limitations are aspects of the angel to be wrestled with in all art. But when the talk turns to categories of adulthood based purely on age, the good writer will smell a rat: an artificial cotton-wool rat. To him, at whatever level of difficulty he operates, an adult is an adult: young or old or middle-aged. In fact the absurdity of the whole movement begins to make itself most clearly seen at this stage. If we are to have books for 'young adults' why not have books for 'middle-aged adults'? Because young adults have special biological and emotional problems? But so do middle-aged adults. Because young adults are just cutting their intellectual teeth and need a kind of literary rusk? Then how about a special literary gruel for aged adults who are losing theirs? *Dodderbooks*, say.

B. Special variations according to ability

As we have already noted, certain variations of technique and content in children's fiction are determined by the age of the reader and particularly – in the earliest years – by his mechanical reading ability. But this question of ability – as every teacher knows – is not in all cases geared

---

1. Something on these lines has in fact been undertaken in Britain by the County Libraries Group of the Library Association in their list *Attitudes and Adventure* – though in announcing this the expert compilers of *Timely Reading* point out that it assumes a 'higher degree of reading skill' than they themselves thought wise.

directly and proportionately to age. Large numbers of children fall behind the normal for various causes and to varying extents. These are generally referred to as the 'backward readers'. But backwardness is a relative term, most precisely used in connection with the individual's potential. Thus a 10-year-old child of below-average intelligence – with a mental age of 8, say – might be loosely described as backward when a more precise designation would be 'dull' or any of the kinder synonyms which educational psychologists advance from time to time. Strictly speaking, if such a child had a reading age to match his mental age he could not be described as backward in that subject. He would be fulfilling his potential. Only if his reading age were below 8 could he be classified as a 'backward reader'.

Granted, much of this is based on a fiction itself – on the convenient psychological fiction, or what Mr Frank Kermode might call the 'complementary fiction'[1] – that one is born with a certain fixed level of intelligence and that the best one can hope to do is to live up to that level, making use of every particle. Already in recent years this concept has come under heavy fire, being challenged on scientific as well as on certain obvious political grounds – and, in my view, quite rightly. But as a working hypothesis, offering teachers a practical method of measurement and indicating the first solid achievable remedial steps – which must be taken no matter how optimistic or pessimistic a view might be held about ultimate potentialities – it is most convenient, extremely useful and, if the problem is to be tackled with any system at all, hardly dispensable. In just such a way is it necessary for us still to work at certain levels on the assumption – the scientific fiction – that electricity generally behaves as liquids do, flowing in currents, disseminating in waves, and so on. We may be aware that in fact it does no such thing, but a whole apparatus of sub-concepts – of conductivity, potential difference and condensation, to name only a few – have been derived from this key figure and have been found to work as elements of the language by which we have been able to contemplate the subject and to speculate on it and – what is most important – using the bases such language provides, to explore the subject further.

But to return to backwardness in reading and the problems it presents to the fiction writer, let us first examine a case of extreme backwardness – of a boy of 12, say, with a mental age of 9 and a reading age of 6.5. Obviously, something has gone badly wrong with his early schooling; equally obviously, any remedial teaching material offered to him will have to be as simple and carefully controlled as the basic primers, even if the content is to be made to appeal to a boy of his real age. And, as in

---

1. For a fascinating study of the fictions that are found so useful in subjects other than literature, see his *Sense of an Ending*.

the case of the youngest children, no author can be expected to produce good stories under those conditions. Again the child's experience of good fiction will have to be supplied orally, in conjunction with his efforts to master the mechanics.

But there will come a time, under careful remedial treatment, when such a boy's reading ability will be equal to that of a child of 7 or 8. Then he will still be backward by some two or three years, but his greatest need will be – as it is with average readers of that age – for plenty of material on which to exercise his newly acquired skill. In fact, since this skill has been locked away inside him for so much longer than in a normal child, more or less to his embarrassment, such a boy's hunger for material is likely to be keener still.

As a teacher of backward readers, I used to find that nothing could be more discouraging, after testing for and gladly noting improvements in reading ability, than to realize how even scantier was the supply of such consolidatory material for children of this age than it was for normal 7- and 8-year-olds. As an author now my sympathy for pupils (and their teachers) in this predicament is all the stronger for knowing that the deficiency is not only still acute but is as capable of remedy as the individual pupil's original incapacity – and by good sensitive writers. Some years ago, the National Book League of Britain held a working party on the subject and dwelt on this aspect of the deficiency. 'It is very rare', their report lamented, 'to find close cooperation [i.e., between the good writer and the educational technician] in a creative venture.' It then went on to say that 'even if such a writer could be found, unless the subject of backward reading were so important to him, he would be unlikely to want to give up his other creative writing.'

No mention seems to have been made of money, but there is more than a hint here, I fancy, of the secondary difficulty of getting a professional, and therefore royalty-conscious, author to produce books for a public that is, on the face of it, so restricted in numbers. Is this, then, the impasse it seems? Are such pupils condemned to having to rely at best on fiction hack-produced especially for them, or at worst on fiction hack-produced for their younger brothers and sisters. How can good sensitive writers be tempted – creatively and financially – to help meet the deficiency?

To take the creative problem first, let us see whether in fact one does have to lower one's standards when cutting one's cloth in this particular way; whether simplicity of vocabulary and sentence structure, and the repetition of words, phrases and complete sentences – essential ingredients of books at this level – do necessarily result in work that is humdrum, flat, vitiated, 'uncreative'. Perhaps it is only in the context of writing for children – where the good is still too often equated with the ornate, the purple or the whimsical – that such questions can have arisen. For elsewhere, of course, the answers are implicit in the work of some of the best creative writers of our time.

Let us take, for example, a couple of typical passages from Harold Pinter's play, *The Caretaker*. In the first, Davies is complaining about the treatment he received from a fellow worker at a café from which he's just been fired:

'Comes up to me, parks a bucket of rubbish at me, tells me to take it out the back. It's not my job to take out the bucket! They got a boy there for taking out the bucket. I wasn't engaged to take out buckets. My job's cleaning the floor, clearing up the tables, doing a bit of washing-up, nothing to do with taking out buckets!'

The second is even simpler, with Davies explaining to the sceptical and aggressive Mick what he happens to be doing in Mick's brother's room.

'I was brought here!'

'Pardon?'

'I was brought here! I was brought here!'

'Brought here? Who brought you here?'

'Man who lives here . . . he. . . .'

'Fibber.'

'I was brought here, last night . . . met him in a caff . . . I was working . . . I got the bullet . . . I was working there . . . bloke saved me from a punch up, brought me here, brought me right here.'

'I'm afraid you're a born fibber, en't you? You're speaking to the owner. This is my room. You're standing in my house.'

'It's his . . . he seen me all right . . . he. . . .'

'That's my bed.'

'What about that, then?'

'That's my mother's bed.'

'Well she wasn't in it last night!'

'Now don't get perky, son, don't get perky. Keep your hands off my old mum.'

In vocabulary and style this is nearly at the level of simplicity we have been discussing – as indeed is the everyday speech of most of us, backward or not. Therefore no author need grumble about uncreative restrictions as far as dialogue is concerned, and if he should choose to write playlets for backward readers this aspect of the problem is, one would think, solved at once. But what of the narrative elements of fiction, should he decide to stick to stories? He may want to write of an encounter. For example:

The fire was bright now, just at the edge of the trees. There was a man sitting by it. Nick waited behind the tree and watched. The man looked to be alone. He was sitting there with his head in his hands looking at the fire. Nick stepped out and walked into the firelight.

Or, for adult backward readers, about a not uncommon predicament:

> Mr. and Mrs. Elliot tried very hard to have a baby. They tried as often as Mrs. Elliot could stand it. They tried in Boston after they were married and they tried coming over on the boat. They did not try very often on the boat because Mrs. Elliot was quite sick. She was sick and when she was sick she was sick as Southern women are sick.

Self-imposed simplicity of style and vocabulary did nothing to vitiate Hemingway's work.

And now, when we come to examine the second aspect of the problem – the question of reaching a wide enough readership to make the project commercially practicable – it is to find that it has been very largely solved with the solving of the first. For if we can manage to write good imaginative books for, say, 11-, 12- and 13-year-olds with reading ages of, say, 7 or 8, suitable not only in subject-matter for children in the older age group but also – as is possible – in style and tone and general ambience, then there is nothing to prevent those books from being sold on the wider market. In fact such a project, properly handled, could have a very gratifying two-way effect, because the very fact that books of this sort had a wide general readership would give them a considerable extra natural advantage educationally: the therapeutic value to a backward reader on finding that a book he can read and enjoy is also being enjoyed by his less handicapped fellows.

This, it seems to me, is the only way of satisfactorily tackling the problem. It is creative, positive, capable of offering something much more than effective instruments. It is fully in concordance with the broader aims of education, which are so often understandably but lamentably ignored in the struggle to provide the basic skills. In short, an approach that respects high creative quality will *result* in works of high creative quality, while an approach without such respect – and I include here all attempts to cut and chop down to size existing works of high quality – will, however effective in producing skill-developing instruments, only tend to devalue that skill, making the finally competent but uninspired reader wonder, with justification, what all the fuss was about anyway.

C. Variations according to media

Back in 1954 I wrote an article describing my mistrust – as a teacher of backward boys – of even the best-intentioned comic-books. My main contention was that they made reading seem unnecessary.

> There are words, of course, in captions and speech balloons, but it isn't really necessary to read them; the pictures are usually self-explanatory. And even where they're not – where, as in Mr James

Hemming's series of strip-cartoon schoolbooks, there has been a deliberate attempt to make the continuity and sense dependent on caption and speech – I've seen my boys skim contentedly from page to page, no doubt making up for themselves what isn't explicit in the pictures.[1]

Expanding on this, I described a pupil's probable reactions, based on my own observations.

His eyes flit from picture 1, past that blank, tombstone-looking thing with a bit of writing in it, to picture 2. He frowns. He looks again at picture 1. He works out a connection, *any* connection – he's easily satisfied – and on to number 3.

Nowadays my attitude is somewhat different. Having a much increased respect for the value of fiction as an educative, civilizing force far beyond its value as mere entertainment, high or low – as in fact a terribly badly needed stimulator and feeder of the imagination – I am bound to admit that the imaginative exercise thus adopted by the boy probably did him far more good than any conscientious tracing out of the original quite trivial little story would have done. At the same time, however, it must be stressed that this was an unusual occurrence, something that could only have happened with a backward reader. For with children of normal reading ability, that use of the imagination – of the *visual* imagination especially – is just what the strip-cartoon tends to restrict, cramp, nullify. That is why, looking back on the comic-book heroes of our own childhood, we see the more or less crude, always rigid, constant, confining outlines presented to us by the artist. Li'l Abner wears for ever the same oily shock of hair, with the same droplets of perspiration flying off at the same angles. Little Orphan Annie has eternally the same blank discs for eyes, the same round-shouldered stance, the same bubble curls. And so on.

With such characters – or perhaps we should say *with characters so presented* – there are, there can be, no visual pockets of speculation, no enticingly blurred edges, no independent growth and flowering and fruiting, as with comparable heroes and heroines of prose fiction. Everything about them is bare, two-dimensional. Yet even where there are blanks that no strip-cartoonist can fill and fix in this way without recourse to words – descriptive blanks concerning the feel of things, smells, sounds, flavours – we are not often moved to fill them in ourselves. Why?

Probably because of the element of pace, common to fiction in all media but differently affected by them. 'Reading' a comic-book, a normal child is able to pass swiftly from frame to frame, balloon to balloon.

---

1. 'Comics, Carrots and Backward Readers.' *Use of English*, Vol. 5, No. 4.

Even where the artist attempts richness or subtlety of detail – and how rare that is! – the 'reader' is not compelled to linger over such things. Skipping is made extremely easy because the medium is temporal only by virtue of the consecutive actions in the consecutive frames. Within each frame, if we exclude any printing in speech balloons or elsewhere, *spatiality* predominates. That is to say we are at liberty to focus our attention on any part of the picture we wish to – and this is usually the next step in the action. With prose fiction, however, one is much more at the mercy of the creator in so far as *sequence* is concerned, because the medium, as we use it, is predominantly temporal: built up of consecutive words in consecutive sentences on consecutive pages. Skipping may be done, of course, but only with comparative difficulty, and it is a difficulty that increases with the skill of the writer, who usually takes care to integrate the various elements of narrative, to mingle with the action-words words of qualification, reminders, comparisons, catalysts, accelerators, brakes – all the elements that give a narrative its breadth and depth, its overtones and undertones, and at the same time control its pace. Timing, as we have earlier considered at some length, is the essence of good fiction. In prose it can be controlled with micrometer precision; in television or film it can still be quite closely – though by no means *as* closely – controlled by good direction and cutting; but in a series of static pictures this control is reduced to a clumsy crudity, a dragging of the foot on the ground. Illustrators can't say to their 'readers': 'Now observe this frame very closely,' or 'Come on, hurry up – just a glance at these four then on to the next'.

So the subjects of strip-cartoons themselves tend to be as crude as the means to depict and control them: crude action, crude slapstick comedy, or – leaning heavily on the prose opportunities offered by the speech balloons – short snatches of brisk repartee. Anything remotely reflective is shunned, there being a limit to the number of think bubbles a strip can support – though satire, of all the intellectual modes, can often be well done where the butt is visual, as *Mad Magazine* has shown in its lampoons of television shows and movies.

So far we have viewed the medium from the standpoint of the 'reader'. Turning to the creator and his special problems, one is able to see how the circumstances of production help to reinforce the pervading crudity of comic strips. Above everything else there is the question of time – the 'real' time binding the artist rather than the internal one of his narrative – and the fact that it generally takes so much longer to draw a picture than to write a couple of sentences or so. This means, in modern market conditions, that the artist simply cannot afford to dwell on subtleties or intricacies – the expression on the face of a character, say, or the true feel of a roomful of fighting men, ranging from glee to terror – so that even if a story is well constructed and clearly visualized in a script-writer's head, it is usually marred by the rushed illustrations. And even where this doesn't spoil the story completely, it tends to produce flatness, dullness, the ubiquity of the stereotype. Examine a few comic-strip stories and notice how the heroes tend to look alike, and the villains too. Poor prose writers often do this themselves, certainly – using stock phrases like 'a shifty-looking individual' and 'his handsome square-jawed features' – but at least the reader is able to exercise his own imagination here, picturing his own idea of a handsome or shifty-looking man, and often building it up out of actual living people known to him. On the other hand, as I mentioned earlier, the comic-strip dummy leaves little room for the individual imagination. It is there: thickly and crudely drawn, fixed for ever.

One way of closely examining these differences between the media is to look out for a strip version of a prose work one has read and enjoyed and compare the two treatments as given to a single passage from the original. Another and perhaps more revealing way is to take a prose passage and, as conscientiously as possible, draft out instructions for a picture sequence covering the same ground, assuming the services of a first-class illustrator who is not particularly pressed for time. Most of the passages quoted in this book have been selected for their qualities as pieces of prose – that is, passages in which the author has made the most of the medium's potentialities and limitations. Even the best of strip-cartoon artists would be hard put to it to do full justice to the quality of either the Dickens or Twain church scenes, for example. But let us select a passage that is, as they say, 'full of action', from a book that doesn't pretend to indulge in great subtleties: the passage from *Treasure Island* in which Jim Hawkins is pursued by Israel Hands. On the left-hand side of the page is Stevenson's prose account, with the sentences barbarically but I hope usefully numbered for easier reference; on the right, suggestions for a pictorial sequence. Jim, it will be remembered, is alone on the *Hispaniola* with Hands, who has so far – because it has required the two of them to get the ship out of difficulties – allowed himself to be Jim's 'prisoner'.

(1) The excitement of these last manoeuvres had somewhat interfered with the watch I had kept hitherto, sharply enough, upon the coxswain.	(1) A point that cannot be expressed pictorially, though its absence may cause some 'readers' to regard Jim as stupidly negligent.
(2) Even then I was still so much interested, waiting for the ship to touch, that I had quite forgot the peril that hung over my head, and stood craning over the star-	(2) This can be shown pictorially – this standing and craning, etc. – but without, alas, the note of peril and therefore suspense. To picture that would be to picture

board bulwarks and watching the ripples spreading wide before the bows.

(3) I might have fallen without a struggle for my life, had not a sudden disquietude seized upon me, and made me turn my head.

(4) Perhaps I had heard a creak, or seen his shadow moving with the tail of my eye; perhaps it was an instinct like a cat's; but, sure enough, when I looked around, there was Hands, already halfway towards me, with the dirk in his right hand.

(5) We must both have cried out aloud when our eyes met; but while mine was the shrill cry of terror, his was a roar of fury like a charging bull's. (6) At the same instant he threw himself forward, and I leapt sideways towards the bows.

(7) As I did so, I left hold of the tiller, which sprang sharp to leeward; and I think this saved my life, for it struck Hands across the chest, and stopped him, for the moment, dead.

(8) Before he could recover, I was safe out of the corner where he had me trapped, with all the deck to dodge about.

(9) Just forward of the mainmast I stopped, drew a pistol from my pocket, took a cool aim, though he had already turned and was once more coming directly after me, and drew

Hands creeping up and therefore bring on (4) too quickly.

(3) The turning of the head can be done pictorially, with an expression of disquietude on the face – but without the extra tension created by the almost simultaneous what-might-have-happened note, so difficult to express in a drawing.

(4) Hands, with the dirk, can be illustrated quite adequately, but the lifelike blurring concerning the warning – so useful for making the tale ring true – will have to be omitted, or a creak settled for (the word CREAK! slanting from Hands's foot) or just the shadow.

(5) and (6) Picture can show them with their mouths open – though even here the convincing uncertainty of 'we must' is lost. So too is the precise quality of each cry. Most strip illustrators would try to solve this with an EEK! from Jim's mouth and a YEEARRRGH! from Hands's.

(7) Fairly straightforward to illustrate, but again without the possibility of including the qualifying note ('I think this saved my life') with its urgent reminder of the seriousness of the danger.

(8) Fairly easy to illustrate, but difficult to underline the heartening point about the room to dodge in.

(9) Straightforward illustration.

the trigger. (10) the hammer fell, but there followed neither flash nor sound; the priming was useless with sea water. (11) I cursed myself for my neglect. (12) Why had not I, long before, reprimed and reloaded my only weapons? (13) Then I should not have been, as now, a mere fleeing sheep before this butcher.

(14) Wounded as he was, it was wonderful how fast he could move, his grizzled hair tumbling over his face, and his face itself as red as a red ensign with his haste and fury. (15) I had no time to try my other pistol, nor, indeed, much inclination, for I was sure it would be useless. (16) One thing I saw plainly: I must not simply retreat before him, or he would speedily hold me boxed into the bows, as a moment since he had so nearly boxed me in the stern.

(17) Once so caught, and nine or ten inches of the blood-stained dirk would be my last experience on this side of eternity.

(10)–(13) A close-up of the pistol can be illustrated, with trigger squeezed. The lack of report poses a problem – the sort usually solved by recourse to a word, flying from source, probably CLICK! But the subsequent details cannot be shown accurately – the cause of the failure, the regret, the irony and the grim undertones about sheep and butcher. Above all, the timing is now all awry – the few seconds' suspense experienced during the reading of these sentences is lost.

(14) Fairly straightforwardly portrayable – though the wonderful fastness will not be easy to suggest – the wonderfulness in spite of wounds, that is.

(15) Impossible to convey in a drawing. Explanation – and a little more suspense – gone.

(16) Very difficult – almost impossible – to convey review of situation without words. More suspense lost.

(17) Also impossible to portray. More suspense lost – and Stevenson, be it noted, had very skilfully graded these reminders of danger, these intimations of mortality, from the mere mention of 'peril' in (2), through the 'struggle for life' in (3) and the charging bull figure in (5) and the more immediate 'sheep and butcher' figure in (13), to the precise murderous, naked literalness of the 'nine or ten inches of blood-stained dirk' here.

The reason I have dwelt on the comic-strip medium at some length is that it is the nearest and most serious rival to straight prose fiction for children – one that could, and in many cases does, offer a child's sole private experience of fiction. Many parents and teachers condemn comic-book fiction as inferior to prose fiction in an indiscriminate manner, forgetting the sheer awfulness, the worthlessness of much prose fiction. The point is – as examinations of the technical possibilities and limitations of the medium show – good prose fiction can do far more than even the best comic-strip fiction, and the reasons for this should be discussed with children. They are pretty shrewd at assessing such things for themselves, once the facts are clearly presented – just as they are apt to react instinctively against what they usually think of as the *unfairness* of indiscriminate condemnations.

But other media impose limitations of their own on any fiction they are required to convey and – while none of them constitutes quite such a strong threat to children's prose fiction as the comic-strip – it is worth looking at them briefly.

Television fiction, when presented largely live or on video tape, as for financial reasons it most often is, is hampered by lack of variety in settings, and lack of fluidity from setting to setting, because of the restricted space of studios and the need to keep down the number of sets used. Then there is a certain artificiality, a staginess, imposed on those scenes of brisk action which for safety reasons can't be taken at the necessary pace by the actors involved. Fights, horse-play, dangerous leaps – staples of much children's fiction – tend to come across choppily, jerkily, unconvincingly unless costly film is used, when the jerkiness can be removed and the whole thing be made to look as swift and perilous as it should.

Again, as with comics, reflective passages, especially those dealing with the thoughts of solitaries, can't be made to flow as naturally, intermingled with the action, as they are in prose. Though better than the strips' think-bubbles, the use of a spoken commentary is not satisfactory, being unnatural and obtrusive, and anyway even that is really a recourse to prose itself rather than an element deriving from the medium. There is also the danger of stereotyping with such a visual medium – the danger that the characters become fixed for ever in the stamp of certain actors and actresses – losing the organic qualities, the capacities for growth and change that in prose fiction our imaginations, combining with the imaginations of the original creators, give rise to. Many a splendid prose character has been ruined for ever in the minds of many readers after translation to the screen. In certain visually impressionable minds Jim Hawkins himself, for example, still continues to wear – quite distractingly – the sulky pout of Jackie Cooper, even after some thirty years.

Finally – in so far as television is concerned – there is the casting problem presented by child characters. In most countries the law about the use of child actors can be very restricting, and this, quite apart from the fact that good child actors are comparatively rare, causes producers to be wary of, if not indeed fight shy of, stories involving children. And those, as was discussed at length earlier in this study, form a very important proportion of prose fiction for children. (See also Appendix F.)

Film as a medium (and here we must include movies shown on television) is much more flexible. The range of settings and the fluidity in switching from one to another are much greater than in live television, and it is, for the same reasons, much easier to fake dangerous actions and so heighten the verisimilitude of a story containing such actions. Again, reflective passages cannot be presented as smoothly and effectively as in prose; and again there is a much greater risk of stereotyping character.

Radio is a much better medium than all except prose for reflection – particularly in the form of the long soliloquy – though here again it doesn't have the facility of prose for smoothly, often unnoticeably mixing action with reflection within a single short sentence. It is also a much better medium than all except prose for mobility and range in presenting settings – as good as film in being able to switch from a room in Harlem to a helicopter over Vietnam in a second, and better than film when it comes to deal with fantastic settings, such as another planet or a fairy grotto. Here radio enjoys the advantages of prose with the additional help of sound effects or music, whereas a film or television producer has to rely on papier mâché or strip-cartoon techniques that are often ludicrous and rarely convincing. Similarly, because radio fiction is so close to prose fiction – is indeed spoken prose fiction, when left undramatized – it is good for stimulating and exercising the imaginations of the audience. Where it lags badly behind all the other media, though, is in the presentation of swift silent action. Here the commonest device is to put the onus of the description of such action on to the dialogue – to have it reflected in the comments of the characters. This is not too bad when the action is of the sort that is likely to be commented upon by the participants (the 'to you, Alf – easy does it round this corner' of furniture removers, for example) or by witnesses. But when the action involves a single person, or two people in a life and death struggle requiring every cubic centimetre of breath they can snatch, such dialogue begins to sound very stilted and unconvincing. Henry James – writing of stage drama, where the same problem crops up in a milder but broader condition – referred to the use of dialogue for similar unnatural purposes as 'harking back to make up'. Mr Robert Liddell quotes an excellent example, including a wry comment on the practice, from Sheridan's *The Critic:*

SIR WALTER: You know, my friend, scarce two revolving suns
   And three revolving moons have closed their course,
   Since haughty Philip, in despite of peace,
   With hostile hand hath struck at England's trade.
SIR CHRISTOPHER: I know it well.
SIR WALTER: Philip, you know, is proud Iberia's king!
SIR CHRISTOPHER: He is.
SIR WALTER: His subjects in base bigotry
   And Catholic oppression held, – while we
   You know, the Protestant persuasion hold.
SIR CHRISTOPHER: We do.
DANGLE: Mr. Puff, as he *knows* all this, why does Sir Walter go on
   telling him?
PUFF: But the audience are not supposed to know anything of the
   matter, are they?
SNEER: True, but I think you manage ill: for there certainly appears no
   reason why Sir Walter should be so communicative.
PUFF: 'Fore Gad, now, that is one of the most ungrateful observations
   I ever heard – for the less inducement he has to tell this the more,
   I think, you ought to be obliged to him; for I am sure you'd know
   nothing of the matter without it.[1]

It is a passage, one feels, that ought to be pinned to every radio drama-
tist's wall, as a reminder and a warning, as well as to the wall of every
writer of prose fiction who fancies his chances of emulating the all-
dialogue or nearly all-dialogue novels of Henry Green and Ivy Compton-
Burnett.

All in all, prose fiction is a far superior instrument to the others,
in delicacy, range and penetration. Yet even in this single field there are
certain special conditions, creating special techniques and preferences
for certain subjects, arising from the nature of the medium as it is used
in magazines and periodicals. Mainly I am thinking of the serial story.
This has to be presented in a number of roughly equal instalments, each
ending with a more or less strong cliffhanging predicament. The technique has thus to be tailored to the readers' situation: the taking of the
story in half-hour snatches at weekly or monthly intervals. Now the
technique used in writing a full-length book is based on different
assumptions concerning the reader: roughly, that it will be read in three
or four sittings (few authors dare count on *one*) each lasting an hour or
more. And with such assumptions in mind the skilful writer varies his
pace, stringing out his sub-climaxes irregularly (for nothing can be more
deadening than a regular clockwork alarm bell) and building up
gradually to the big one.

---

1. Quoted in *Some Principles of Fiction* by Robert Liddell.

That is why serialization of existing books is rarely successful. To get the required symmetry of suspense, the original almost invariably has to be pummelled out of shape – squeezed here, padded there – and usually by other, less sensitive hands than the author's, with the result that that most delicate and precise element, the timing, is ruined. On the other hand, a story written as a serial cannot usually nowadays be presented successfully as a full-length story without drastic alterations to get rid of that dreadful death-watch regularity. Because of this, in the two major serializations I have personally been involved in,[1] I chose to write each story as a serial first and completely rewrote it for volume publication.

Where children's serials and magazine stories are concerned, there are usually no special pressures exerted on choice of setting or situation – apart from the fact that editors generally prefer, for obvious and quite sensible reasons, a tale that covers a time-span of at least a few weeks (and will not therefore be too much at odds with the necessarily pro-tracted reading time). In the adult sphere, however, there is a very real sense in which the medium of the popular magazine or newspaper tends to influence the content of the stories. For the producers of such organs, unlike the editors and proprietors of book publishing concerns, tend to look on the contents not so much as the expression of a single person or the varied expressions of a group of single persons, but more as the single expression – concerted, blended – of the journal itself, as largely pre-determined by a policy involving the proprietors and advertising managers as much as the editors. Thus P. G. Wodehouse was right to advise a friend:

> It seems to me that if you are to go on writing for popular magazines you will deliberately have to make your stuff cheaper. At present you are working from character to plot, and what they want, I'm con-vinced, is the story that contains only obvious characters who exist simply for the sake of the plot. Take a story like that one I thought was your very best, *In the Stokehold*. It was all subtlety. What they would have liked would have been the same idea with all the motives obvious.[2]

D. Variations according to the outlook and conditions of the period in which a story is written

Mr Wodehouse wrote the advice quoted above in 1924, but what he said about popular magazine fiction is as valid for the adult field now as it was

---

1. *Jim Starling and the Colonel* (serial in *Eagle*, volume by Heinemann, London, and Doubleday, New York) and *Jim Starling and the Spotted Dog* (serial in *Eagle*, volume by Blond, London).

2. *Performing Flea.*

then. Not so valid now, however, are the observations he made in a subsequent paragraph about children's magazine fiction.

> Here is an exact parallel. Remember *The Luck Stone*, which with your assistance I wrote for *Chums*. School story full of kidnappings, attempted murders, etc. They were delighted with it. Then I tried them with a real school story and they threw a fit. 'What, no blood?' they cried, and shot the thing back at me.

Today, while such a tale might receive the same treatment at a few children's magazines, its bloodlessness would certainly be no drawback with the majority, while its reality could be a positive asset. This is probably because of the increasing interest shown in children's fiction that has accompanied the growing interest in education and children's psychological needs – especially since World War Two. Similarly, but not so encouragingly, when writing above about serials I had to qualify my comment by saying that *nowadays* a story written as a serial can't usually be presented successfully in volume form without drastic alterations. That is because nowadays the space given to serial instalments is generally very limited, especially in children's magazines, where it is often in the region of 1,200–1,500 words (i.e., about four or five pages of a typical children's novel). In the last century, however, the situation was vastly different. Many if not most major adult novels and a number of surviving children's stories (including *Treasure Island*) first appeared as serials in magazines or as instalments in self-contained booklets, and they required little alteration[1] because the instalments were usually so long that they corresponded much more closely to the reader's sittings a novelist tends to count on, consciously or otherwise, when controlling his timing.

Regarding changing fashions in content, the British school story presents a striking example. As Orwell noted in his famous essay on 'Boys' Weeklies':

> the school story is a thing peculiar to England. So far as I know, there are extremely few schools stories in foreign languages. The reason, obviously, is that in England education is mainly a matter of status. The most definite dividing line between the petite-bourgeoisie and the working class is that the former pay for their education, and within the bourgeoisie there is another unbridgeable gulf between the 'public' school and the 'private' school.[2]

---

1. Though Thomas Hardy, writing *Tess of the D'Urbervilles* for a popular newspaper, did come up against certain moral difficulties concerning the content – to the extent that some passages were provided with more daring alternatives in different coloured ink and labelled 'For volume publication'.

2. *Critical Essays*.

That was in 1939. After the war, however, and the democratization of the educational system in England, there was a rapid dropping off in popularity of the boarding-school story about which Orwell was writing. No longer did the subject have quite the glamour of the unattainable for the working-class readers who, in their hundreds of thousands, had previously been eager buyers and borrowers of magazines like *Gem* and *Magnet* – for while they may still have had little chance of actually *living* in such schools, the grammar school, now open to many more of them, did offer a recognizable substitute, with such trimmings as gowned masters, and house systems, and well-equipped laboratories and gymnasia.

Yet this exclusiveness had not been the only reason for the genre's popularity. Another lay in its very fertility as a subject – in the splendid opportunities it offered to the writer of children's fiction. In the boarding school he had a small closed community with sharply set bounds and firmly fixed rules – the sort of compact world that any reasonably compe-tent author would find fairly easy to manipulate. Within such a framework he could experiment as much or as little as he pleased, content to know on the one hand that when dealing with such a strongly defined *milieu* there could be little danger of the plot line's straying far and, on the other, that even the flattest flimsiest set of characters would soon take on a plausible appearance of life when caught up in the currents of boarding school routine. In fact, plots shoot up so readily in this setting that if ever a fiction-fabricating machine is invented there might well be a substantial batch of traditional British school stories among its first products. For example, on such a machine there might be a BOUNDS, BOARDING SCHOOL slot, through which a given character card could be fed into a network of mixers and separators organized on the following lines: *Boarding schools have bounds: bounds may be broken deliberately or unwittingly. If deliberately it may be that the breaker has to do so for the ultimate good of the school, or a section of it, or himself; or for the ultimate harm of the school, or a section of it, or an individual. If the bounds are broken unwittingly it may be a simple mischance, or it may be that the breaker is the victim of a plot or joke (depending on the story's tendency to melodrama or farce). The discovery of the bounds-breaker by someone in authority, or the miscreant's attempts to avoid discovery, or the misunder-standing of his motives for breaking the bounds, or his discovery by someone not in authority. . . .* These variations on the theme of boarding school bounds could go on for pages, as could similar sets based on topics like Lights Out, Dormitories, School Servants (Sinister or Comic), and so on.

Furthermore, when the writer comes to consider the boarders them-selves, it is to find another richly productive vein of mystery and romance. By the very nature of the situation they are unlikely to know much about one another's parents and homes. Who is the ragged stranger who lurks among the elms? Why does Rodney go pale at the sight of him? And what of the foreign princes' and secret-weapon scientists' sons who attract the attention of picturesque members of the Russian secret police or the Mafia or the Followers of Kali? Are the antecedents of even the teachers all they seem to be? In the monastic remoteness of some moorland Greyfriars isn't it only too possible for a runaway convict to pose as the new sports master, whom he now holds captive in a cave in a deserted quarry?

In the past, the British grammar school and pre-1944 elementary school could never match the boarding school either for the simple glamour of the unknown that Orwell wrote about, or for sheer technical fecundity as a subject. After all, the only really firm limits in such places were temporal ones – 9 to 4 on weekdays – and within those limits school tended to be simply a series of lessons: so much listening, so much pen- or pencil-pushing. In other words – from the writer's point of view – so much intractable material. Certainly, one could base scenes of disobedience or stupidity on these lesson periods, but at best this would be mere light relief, and at worst padding of the dreariest kind. One could perhaps explore the possibilities of the temporal limits by drafting them along the lines of the bounds-breaking possibilities, but the gamut wouldn't extend very far, and is really only good for a series of tales about truancy.

So there was no easy way with day schools. They were places of work rather than ways of life, and writers had to labour too hard to get the subject to yield plots.

Today, however, the day school is coming into its own as a setting for children's stories. It will probably never enjoy the immense popularity of the boarding school because it lacks the glamour of exclusiveness. But every year, as modern educational methods spread and increasing emphasis is laid on the practical and actual, work in the day school is losing that monotonous chalk-and-talk, listen-and-scratch predictability, and this makes it a much more tempting prospect for the fiction writer.

My own *Jim Starling* stories are a case in point. They are not school stories qua school stories, nor were they intended as such. How could they be, dealing as they did with a boy who necessarily spent much less than a quarter of his time at school, even during term-time? Nevertheless, I soon discovered that school was entering into these tales with much more of a significance than if it had seeped in as a mere background. Drawing on my own experiences as a teacher in such a school, I found that the local-colour material was beginning to act on other ingredients of the plot in a very encouraging way.

In the first book, for example, I found more than once that there was no need to resort to any mechanical tricks, coincidences or *deus ex machina* devices to get my characters out of a classroom during lesson time so that they could pursue certain lines of private inquiry. In one case an art teacher of the modern go-see-for-yourself persuasion is provoked by their work into ordering them into the school yard to see just what colours turf and a nearby river are. In another, they absent themselves from a mathematics lesson on the pretext of measuring the school hall in connection with an arithmetical problem. Neither of these incidents would have seemed very plausible in 1938.

But these are only minor examples. Earlier in the writing of the same book I introduced a reference to the collection of trip-money – a fairly typical, often wildly irritating detail of modern school life. This was to burgeon into a major plot element. 'What trip?' I asked myself, aiming simply at being concrete. The form-master happened to teach history and social studies, so I made it an afternoon visit to a local museum, a Corporation-owned stately home. Thus, almost by accident, a place called Godwell Hall came into being, providing the heroes with a perfectly natural means of tempting and trapping some lead-thieves and the book with a useful setting for its climax. Again – remembering only *two* such organized outings in the whole of my own pre-1941 schooldays – I can't help thinking that the use of such a trip would have seemed somewhat implausible, too contrived, in 1938.

In *Jim Starling and the Colonel* I found the same school asserting itself not only as a major plot element but also in the very theme. The Colonel of the title is one of the modern day school's most vociferous critics. He believes that too much time is spent on what he thinks of as frills: on trips, activity methods, local historical fieldwork and so on. It is also his conviction that 'modern youth' is pampered, lacking in resourcefulness, soft from constant spoon-feeding. In a speech he tells of a schoolboy of the town back in 1893 who performed a number of athletic and endurance feats. He enumerates them and asks where is the boy who could emulate those feats today. Jim Starling takes up the challenge.

It was a promising plot to work on. The change of conditions in the intervening 70 years gave rise to a number of highly plausible complications. There was, for example, a run between two public houses in a time which had been made to seem impossible by the initially unknown fact that one of them had been demolished in an early urban renewal programme and rebuilt further away. But I must confess that it gave me a certain social as well as artistic pleasure when I found that I could have my hero and his friends unravel this and some of the other complications because of their knowledge of local history – a knowledge gained as a result of the very methods the Colonel was condemning.

So far as I know, fiction writers have only drawn on this catalytic vitality of the modern day-school background as casually as I have done.[1] But one wonders how long it will be before some new Frank Richards comes along and begins to exploit it methodically. School meals; PTA groups; educational visits; expensive and stunt-prolific visual aids; the financing and construction of home-made swimming pools; required uniform and banned hair-styles; journalists on safari into pre-conceived blackboard jungles; critical businessmen – there will certainly be no lack of ingredients for him to work upon, or let work upon himself. Indeed, it may be that soon we shall see the school story as a truly international genre, for many of the methods and situations are as valid in the U.S. and other countries as they are in Britain.

As I mentioned, the school story is just one of the subjects that have received very different treatment in children's fiction at different periods, and it has done so in an organic response to the different social climates of those periods and not, as Miss Gillian Avery seems to think in an attempt to cater to fashionable whims, merely because:

> Writers of the domestic tale have grasped that the 'holiday adventure' story is old-fashioned. With an anxious eye on the needs of the school teacher and librarian and a depressing lack of spontaneity, they write of housing estates and secondary modern school children and a television-minded society; of an ethos they would not dream of practising themselves, and, what is far more important, that they do not enjoy describing.[2]

Another significant change of content with the times is, in British stories for children, far less of the poking of fun at foreigners, or the over-use of foreigners as villains, that Orwell condemned in pre-war fiction. Yet another is the growing admittance into children's stories – as normal protagonists and not as figures of fun or villainy – of certain classes: notably the working classes in Britain and the black races in the U.S. It must be said, however, that some changes are not always for the good or even in line with current attitudes in other branches of fiction. Too often the sort of democratization we have been examining takes place in a spirit of social engineering rather than in the searching light of art. Maybe that is the sort of writing Miss Avery had in mind when making the too-sweeping statement quoted above. It is certainly more difficult to argue against the burthen of her following comments:

> Whereas the nineteenth-century juvenile writers kept pace to a certain extent with the prevalent tastes in adult literature, it is remarkable

---

1. I have also found it useful in a number of other books, particularly *Jim Starling Takes Over*, *Meet Lemon Kelly* and *Lemon Kelly Digs Deep*.
2. *Nineteenth Century Children*.

how this is no longer the case. For years now realism has been the fashion on the stage and in fiction, but those who write specifically for children write with a set of tabus that held good in the days of L. T. Meade and Evelyn Everett Green. They omit (instinctively, not consciously, one feels) all unpleasant traits in a child's personality; all crudity and coarseness. Their children hardly seem to have a physical nature, beyond a good appetite. Family relationships are smooth, mother is always right, father never irks his sons. [That statement we *can* dispute, with overwhelming evidence to the contrary. W.H.] And they add to these tabus which did not exist sixty years ago. It is impossible to talk without embarrassment of religion or to allude to class differences. Truly we are a mealy-mouthed lot.

But that takes us right to the heart of the next topic: the question of the children's author's responsibility to his readers.

Chapter six

Adult responsibility: Authors' and critics'

'After that,' said Gargantua, 'I wiped myself with a kerchief, with a pillow, with a slipper, with a game-bag, with a basket – but what an unpleasant arse-wiper that was! – then with a hat. And note that some hats are smooth, some shaggy, some velvety, some of taffeta, and some of satin. The best of all are the shaggy ones, for they make a very good abstersion of the faecal matter. Then I wiped myself with a hen, a cock, and a chicken, with a calf's skin, a hare, a pigeon, and a cormorant, with a lawyer's bag, with a penitent's hood, with a coif, with an otter. But to conclude, I say and maintain that there is no arse-wiper like a well-downed goose, if you hold her neck between your legs.[1]

In most respects we have there the perfect text for an award-winning picture book. The style is good, the rhythm attractive, the source classical. From the artist's point of view there is everything he could wish for: colour, variety, texture. And from the young child's it is equally perfect, with its giant, its wealth of detail, its occasional jaw-breaking word – and its rudeness.

For most children love rude humour of this kind, especially when it is based on the bodily functions they have had such a tough time – and so recently – learning to control. The Opies rediscovered this when they came to collect verses for *The Lore and Language of Schoolchildren*. 'Genuinely erotic verse,' they noted, 'is unusual. . . . The usual group of youngsters whispering together, passing some verse to each other and giggling, though they refuse to tell what it is, are probably interested in

---

1. *Gargantua and Pantagruel* by Francois Rabelais. Tr. by J. M. Cohen.

nothing more sordid than the deeds of nature, an intimate garment, or a crude word.' And they go on to quote, amongst other things, the old counting-out verse:

Eeny, meeny, miney, mo,
Put the baby on the po,
When he's done
Wipe his bum
Shove the paper up the lum.

It is a strange comment of human fashions and values that when I was a child the 'clean' version, approved by teachers and parents who would have chastised us for using the one above, began:

Eeny, meeny, miney, mo,
Catch a nigger by his toe . . .

But to return to Gargantua. In spite of all its advantages and attractions, no publisher nowadays – not even Penguin Books who published the Rabelais translation from which I have quoted, nor the Oxford University Press who presented the Opie findings – would dream of offering that passage as the basis for a picture book for children. And few editors would press the matter.

Now Rabelais has been a long time dead and probably wouldn't have cared a toss, one way or the other, had the question arisen during his lifetime. After all, he was writing for adults, not children. But what of the children's authors who are alive? How does the problem of what is suitable and what is not affect them? Where, in fact, should they draw limits, assuming they have an active sense of responsibility towards their readers?

In this matter one can really speak only for onself, using one's opinions as a focus for the general argument. First, however, let me describe a plot for a children's story which an American author put to me not long ago. A tough, sincere, fearlessly honest writer, whose account of his own childhood in Harlem has not only reached best-seller status in the U.S. but has also won him a great deal of well-deserved critical acclaim, he was telling me of a collection of children's stories he had in mind. They too, he explained, would be about Harlem. They too would be about the sort of kid he was. But this time they would be *for* children, O.K.? Then he went on to outline one of the tales – about a boy of 6 or 7, playing in Central Park and, suddenly taken short, going into some bushes. 'He's in a hurry, see, he's eager to get back into the game, and as soon as he's through he reaches out, grabbing around, for a handful of leaves. And he grabs a handful, but they're too crispy, this being the fall, so he looks at them to see if there's any softer ones.

And – hey, baby! – what's this? There *is* a softer one, just right, perfect. But it ain't no leaf. It's a five-dollar bill. . . .'

It is in fact a fortune for the boy. He looks around, still in a hurry, only this time not to rejoin the game but to run all the way home and bear this treasure to his mother. But there's nothing suitable, only the bill – 'and he ain't for using *that*.' So he doesn't bother, and runs home anyway, and is scolded for the state he arrives in, until he shows what he has found.

The story, as my friend is capable of writing it, would have great charm, expressing without the rancour of some of his adult work the exact truth about what it is like to be a child in such a place. It is the sort of truth that other children would respond to at once and the force of the momentary dilemma would soon dispel any tendency to snigger. It would of course make an excellent subject for an adult story about childhood, but – since there would be nothing in it that a child couldn't clearly understand and sympathize with – it would still make an excellent subject for a children's story about a child. Yet I had to tell him that it would stand very little chance of being published as one.

It could be argued that to publish in a children's book either the Rabelais passage or my friend's tale would be a gratuitous act, that there are plenty of other, less contentious themes to present, that deliberately to go out of one's way to be 'broad-minded' or 'outspoken' can be as intellectually offensive as to be militantly censorious. One is reminded of the progressive kindergarten in Mr Mordecai Richler's *Cocksure*, where the swinging Miss Tanner, during a lesson on the Marquis de Sade, asks her small charges to give other words for 'member', solemnly listing them in all their increasing coarseness on the blackboard until someone ('now that her back was turned') suggests 'Tea-kettle'.

Miss Tanner whirled around, outraged. '*Who said that?*' she demanded.

Silence.

'Well, I never. I want to know who said that. *Immediately*.'

Eventually a boy confesses.

'It was me, Miss Tanner,' he said in a small voice. 'I said tea-kettle.'

'Would you be good enough to tell us why, Reggie?'

'. . . when my nanny . . . I mean my little brother's nanny, um, takes us, ah, out. . . '

'Speak up, please.'

'When my nanny takes me, um, us . . . to Fortnum's for tea, well before I sit down she always asks us do we, do . . .' Reggie's head hung low; he paused, swallowing his tears, '. . . do I have to water my tea-kettle.'

'Well. Well, well. I see,' Miss Tanner said severely. 'Class, can anyone tell me what Reggie's nanny is?'

The class offer their epithets, including 'prude', 'repressed' and 'Victorian'. Miss Tanner presses on.

'She is against . . . Class?'
'Life-force.'
'And?'
'Pleasure!'
'RIGHT. *And truth-sayers.* Remember that. Because it's sexually repressed bitches like Reggie's nanny who put truth-sayers like the marquis in prison.'
The class was enormously impressed.
'May I sit down now?' Reggie asked.
'Sit down, what?'
'Sit down, please, Miss Tanner?'
'Yes, Reggie. You may sit down.'

But there are occasions in children's stories where reference to bodily functions or even to coarseness in behaviour or language is necessary – where to evade the issue and ignore the existence of such things is to be as dishonest as it is inartistic. For example, a tale of young campers that goes into immense detail about how they make fires, catch and cook fish, take precautions against storms or gales or insects, apply first-aid, wash clothes and crockery, rig up showers, forecast weather, tell the time by the sun, say their prayers, make plans for expeditions, draw maps, cut their toenails and split hairs, and yet leaves out that cardinal concern of all campers, suitable toilet arrangements – such a tale is as aesthetically incomplete as a rug with a big blank space in the middle of its elaborately detailed pattern. Or, in a more melodramatic type of story, to have the hero or heroine gagged and bound for anything over twelve hours without serious bladder discomfort is to create in the normally intelligent young reader a sneaking doubt about the reality of the whole thing – a dangerous lapse, even prolapse, in his willing suspension of disbelief, or, as Henry James might have said, 'a leak of interest'.

Speaking as a children's author, I should, in cases of that sort, insist on alluding to the facts no matter what the publisher might have to say in deference to some notion of 'taste' or scale of taboos. Such matters needn't be dwelt on, described in graphic or dramatic detail. But they must be mentioned when the context demands it.

Notions of taste, scales of taboos: these are, after all, so very arbitrary. They vary from period to period, country to country, locality to locality, class to class, person to person, and even within the same person – even, that is, within the same person at given times. Stephen Leacock quotes a good example of variation in the first case, from Fenimore Cooper, pointing out that:

> the public of his day was too strict in its ideas to allow a sailor even to shiver his timbers in print. A glance at any of Cooper's famous sea-stories will reveal such terrible profanity as d——l apparently hinting at *devil* and d——e, which may be interpreted with a thrill as 'damme'. Oddly enough in Cooper's day the word 'bloody' had not yet taken on in America its later offensive connotation, so that Cooper was at liberty to write: 'D——e', said the bos'n, 'what the d——l does the bloody fellow mean?'[1]

Variations in behaviour taboos from country to country – often based on religious attitudes – are so numerous as to be hardly worth listing, as are the variations from class to class and person to person. But the schizophrenic aspect is worth dwelling on for a while because in some respects it comes close to the question of the author's responsibility. For example, a man I once worked with was a stickler for the proprieties as far as his teenage daughter was concerned to the extent that he confiscated any make-up he found in her room and flushed it down the lavatory. On the other hand he had quite a salty line in reminiscences about his World War One soldiering days, with which he used to regale the young apprentices working with him. (Indeed, he actually used these tales to increase output, refusing to tell us 'what happened in the ex-Cadi's mother's palace' until we'd checked another transmitter.) Now I don't think he could have been called a hypocrite. In fact his position could be regarded as the completely logical attitude of the ultra-cautious personality. Far less logical – yet still not hypocritical – is the dual standard maintained by a man I know: a man who prides himself on his earthy Chaucerian sense of humour, who pursues his colleagues and friends of both sexes with jokes to match, in absolutely uninhibited language, who is not above relating some of these within earshot of his children, but who would be liable to be very angry if either of *them* so much as uttered a single medium-range obscenity. Obviously, somewhere at the back of his mind there is an uncertainty lurking and a taboo at work. It may be that he has a lingering suspicion that his jokes are immoral, that while he is a lost soul for repeating them his children must be saved. Or it may be that he has one of those common but completely irrational notions that there is an age, a birthday, a definite dividing-line after which obscenity becomes permissible, suddenly harmless, even healthy. Or the phantom taboo may be basically a social rather than an ethical one, founded on a determination that his children will not

---

1. Quoted in *How to Write*.

become, as far as he is able to help it, the crashing bore that his addiction has made him.

With examples such as these teeming all around us, the author whose aim is to present a picture of life as it is has a doubly difficult problem if he happens to write for children. Part of his responsibility, after all, is not to mislead, but to present the truest possible picture, and this simply cannot be done if he is to respect everyone's every susceptibility. People do copulate. Many of them enjoy copulating. They do urinate and defecate. They do talk about such functions – clinically or coarsely. People do swear. People do use colloquialisms. People are often ungrammatical in their utterances. Yet there are taboos to cover the whole gamut, from sex to minor lapses of behaviour and speech. Even elisions are taboo with some people – as if the sliding of one word into another were somehow too vividly reminiscent of the sexual act – and I've heard of teachers criticizing the Leila Berg primers referred to on page 78 because (may God have mercy on the author's soul!) one of the books began with the word 'Who's' instead of the two words 'Who is'.

Crackpots and fusspots apart, an author who bows indiscriminately and completely to all the more serious taboos is bound to falsify his picture of life and even trivialize it. P. G. Wodehouse, himself a great but completely honest and highly intelligent trivializer, knows this well and has freely confessed as much in one of his letters to William Townsend.

> I believe there are two ways of writing novels. One is mine, making the thing a sort of musical comedy without music, and ignoring real life altogether; the other is going right deep down into life and not caring a damn. The ones that fail are the ones where the writer loses his nerve and says: 'My God! I can't write this, I must tone it down.'[1]

Sex itself doesn't present the genuine children's author (as distinct from the hybrid who thinks of himself as a 'young adults'' author, and who deserves all the trouble he gets) with too much difficulty. Up to the age of 12 or 13 it doesn't represent a large part of a child's conscious life, and the author needn't go very far out of his way to avoid it. Coarseness, including the mention of bodily functions, itself often regarded as coarse, is a tougher problem, but can be satisfactorily handled, as I have already suggested, if the writer faces each instance, as it would normally crop up in life, coolly and honestly and deals with it on merit. After all, everything that happens in a story needn't – indeed shouldn't – be presented dramatically, directly, in every detail. Many things can be referred to obliquely – not euphemistically, *obliquely* – either by suggestion or summary. And even swearing can be handled

---

1. *Performing Flea.*

satisfactorily by this last method, by simply saying 'he swore', for example, or, where the swearing was more important than the actual statement made, giving it more prolonged treatment, perhaps of a comic nature, as I did myself in *Louie's Lot*, when a couple of crates of milk fall off the hero's van.

> Over the river of milk, Louie cursed. He cursed the milk itself. He cursed the bottles it had been in. He cursed the crates the bottles had been in. He cursed the floating tops. He cursed the bottles that hadn't been broken. He cursed the road. He cursed the gutter. He cursed the grate. He cursed the van. He cursed his job. He cursed his luck. He cursed the day he was born.

Minor lapses of behaviour – 'rough' behaviour – should not present much of a problem. Many children do behave roughly or rudely and if one is writing about children one simply has to come to terms with this. Certainly if an author disapproves of such behaviour – say a belching contest on top of a bus – he is at liberty to show this disapproval in his text. Some of our supposedly prissy forebears who reacted like that were far more honest and far better writers than the modern milk sops who shy from mentioning this sort of thing at all, and thereby seek to buy with dud cheques a reputation for child-tolerance. Granted, even here a publisher will probably draw a line in certain circumstances, even if the author doesn't. For example, I have written a number of realistic stories about boys of between 9 and 13, and it is a not uncommon pastime among boys at the younger end of that scale in the environment I write about to have 'peeing contests' – to see who can make his mark highest on a wall. Now in one episode I required my bunch of heroes to be engaged in some activity that was innocent in their eyes but objection-able to a passing adult, and I'd dearly have loved to use such an instance. It would, however, have been an indulgence in that for one thing my boys were just a bit too near the top end of the age-group and for another that there was available the even commoner, still objectionable but less spectacular practice of seeing who could spit farthest – so I used that. Even then the publisher – a dear, gentle, middle-class soul who knew much more about international company law than child behaviour – was sufficiently horrified to ask for its removal, to which I flatly refused to agree. I think it was my description of the first possibility even more than a threat to take the book elsewhere that caused him to capitulate in the end. But the point is that the spitting was just sufficient for the pur-poses of the plot and as an indication of the quality of life portrayed, and therefore *had* to remain, while the urinating would have been – shall we say? – a leaning-over backwards.

As for roughness of speech, this is no problem where I am concerned. I can see how objections to its use in dialogue in children's books arise.

I know about the old pedagogical maxim that a teacher should never write examples of bad usage on the blackboard because of the danger of such examples making too strong an impression and being accidentally assimilated. I can fully appreciate that some teachers will feel a similar or even greater concern over the presentation of bad examples in print.

Further, I will grant that it would be impossible anyway to reproduce speech exactly as it is spoken, with all the mistakes, false quantities, hesitations. Personally, I even shy from dropping aspirates in print, or final g's, partly because of the distracting nature of all those pockmark apostrophes and partly because it reminds me too painfully of the sickeningly condescending would-be-humorous use of the dropped *h* in all those ghastly pre-war *Punch* captions. But as a writer I must try to *suggest* that which is there, even if I can't reproduce it. Therefore I must try to suggest rough speech when dealing with characters who use nothing else and to those who would object I must declare that my obligation to do this outweighs my sympathy for their arguments. When all is said and done, which is the more important: to avoid the risk of having a child encouraged in his use of such statements as 'Me and Charlie went with him', or to avoid the bewilderment or suspicion or disappointment that would arise if an obviously rough working-class character were to talk like a bishop? So a stand has to be made on one side or the other, for in this case there is no possibility of a compromise. One can't put all the dialogue of a rough- or colloquially-speaking character into *oratio obliqua*, pointing out that this is how that character would have expressed himself directly had he been brought up in a vicarage instead of a one-up-one-down at the back of a greyhound track in Bradford. Swearing, yes – as I have pointed out. If one writes about the sort of character who, on cutting his thumb, is likely to say, 'Shit! I've cut me thumb!' – one can without much distortion or danger of distraction write: 'He swore. "I've cut me thumb!" he said.' But one simply cannot write: 'He swore and, eliding the first two words and mispronouncing the fourth, said, "I have cut my thumb!" '

The problems of the children's author's responsibility so far described have been comparatively minor ones, even if they do tend to get most attention in any general discussion of the subject. Infinitely more important are those concerning the presentation of (*a*) non-violent, attractive, but physically dangerous behaviour, (*b*) violence itself, and (*c*) deep-seated, often quite natural, but essentially anti-social behaviour, such as that portrayed by Miss Enid Blyton in *Five Run Away Together*, discussed on pages 85–89.

For my first example of a story presenting in a most attractive light a course of action that could result in grave danger for any young imitator, I would cite a book already mentioned in another context:

Walter Macken's *The Flight of the Doves*. This is a fast picaresque tale of an anxious 12-year-old boy who flees with his young sister from their stepfather in England – probably Liverpool – to their grandmother on the west coast of Ireland. This involves sneaking on to a passenger boat in the middle of the night, sneaking off the connecting train in Dublin, getting a lift with a shifty scrap dealer, joining up with a gang of tinkers, and generally roughing it for several days. The children have tremendous luck, especially in the nature of the individuals they encounter, with the bonus of a most sympathetic detective, who – unknown to them at first – keeps an avuncular eye on them for much of the way. To offset these contrivances, however, Macken takes us very close to Finn, the boy, allowing us to share his concern for his seven-year-old sister's health and safety in a number of scenes of sharply observed yet very tender realism. Like this, for instance:

The other part was worrying. Their description.

He opened the bag and got out the food. There wasn't a lot of food left. He wondered how two people could eat so much food in such a short time. He buttered the bread. They had to drink water from the milk bottle. He looked at Derval. She was a bit grubby. He would have to wash her face and hands at least. Then he thought, with a sigh, he would have to do something else as well.

They ate the bread and butter and the few bits of meat they had left, and the fruit. They were now left with the heel of the loaf and some butter. He thought that Derval should be getting hot food, that all this cold stuff couldn't be good for her. But she looked fairly well.

'I'll have to wash you, Derval,' he said.

'Oh, Finn,' she said.

'It'll have to be done,' he said. 'We are both dirty.'

'Oh, all right,' she said reluctantly.

He took off some of her upper clothes and they went to the river and he washed her hands and her face with a handkerchief. She made faces and kept her eyes shut while he did so. Derval was glad he had no soap.

'Derval,' he said then, 'I will have to do something else with you.'

She looked at him anxiously.

'Something nasty?' she asked.

'I'll have to cut your hair,' he said.

'Why, Finn?' she asked.

He explains that the 'Missing' notices about them refer to a boy and girl. But if he cuts her hair short she'll look like a boy, because she's wearing her long pants.

She thought over it.

'I'd like to be a boy, so,' she said. 'It will be fun being a boy, Finn, won't it?'

'I hope so,' said Finn. 'All right. Kneel down there in front of me and I'll start cutting it.'

He got Joss's knife. He cleaned it first of the butter and the crumbs. He saw he would have to use the big blade, and on the other side of it when you pulled something a small scissors came out. He was sure it was blunt but he hoped it would do.

'All right now,' he said.

The knife-blade was sharp. He cut at her hair over her ear. It was long silky hair. It wasn't hard to cut, but he didn't like doing it. It was nearly a foot long. He cut it all around her head. Her head looked very odd. Her head looked as if her hair had been hacked off with a knife. It was very ragged. She didn't look like Derval at all. Then he used the scissors to try and make it look respectable. He didn't have a comb so he had to hold the bits with his fingers and cut them with the scissors. It wasn't too blunt. He tried to shape it like a boy's hair, long on top and close cut at the back of the head. He shook his head over it. There were a lot of ridges, but after all it would grow in a few days.

'Now,' he said.

She shook her head.

'It's funny,' she said, 'not to feel my hair.'

This is a superb bit of writing at any level, but particularly for children. Note the piling up of simple details, drawing the reader into the situation, making us weigh it up to the nearest crust and curl with Finn, making us temporarily Finn himself – as preoccupied as he when answering the girl's question about the fun of being a boy ('I hope so') and as immediately practical – as determined yet anxious – with the next words: 'All right. Kneel down there. . . .' Note too the very marshalling of the details as he cuts the hair, the rhythms and repetitions that match the slow speculative circuit, with its pauses for standing back: 'He cut it all around her head. Her head looked very odd. Her head looked as if her hair had been hacked off with a knife.' Note too the effect of that single word of Finn's – 'Now' – at the end, the mixture of relief, regret and satisfaction that seems so perfectly to sum up the reader's feelings at this point, as well as the character's. Then note the extra brilliant touch, the quick dip into the *little girl's* feelings as she shakes her head. Such warmth, such sympathy, allied to the pace of the narrative and Macken's excellent timing, already mentioned (note here how he makes us wait after alerting us to this 'something else' Finn felt he would have to do), add up to an irresistibly attractive adventure, with *a sense of responsibility* (the boy's) itself forming a major active ingredient and throwing up scores of Crusoelike problems of improvisation.

Thus the very quality of the writing creates the enthusiasms and challenges that could well result in imitation – for this is not any old runaway tale but a story about running away that is told in depth, with drama being dug out of the most prosaic situations. The more is the pity, therefore – in my view – that the author didn't go just that little bit deeper and issue at least one vivid warning, perhaps by way of an episode underlying the very real dangers that children would be more than likely to encounter these days in similar circumstances. Such an episode would not have spoiled the story; rather would it have enhanced it by increasing the tension. But as it is, the sole threatening stranger is thrown up by the plot itself, while the casual encounters – the true danger area – produce only golden hearts and helping hands.

My other examples of portrayals of potentially dangerous but very attractive behaviour concern that notoriously dangerous and attractive element: water. Here are a few sample figures for deaths by drowning in England, Scotland and Wales alone during 1966.

Total number: 1,128.

Total number of children under 15: 329 (i.e., over 25 per cent).

Number of children in the 5–14 group (i.e., the group we are most closely concerned with in this study): 192.

Of these 192 cases, 2 occurred in the home, 4 on farms, 10 in mines or quarries, 7 on industrial sites, 156 in 'other places', 12 after 'submersion with a small boat', and 1 unspecified.

The 'other places' figures for this group break down thus: inland waters, coastal waters, street and highway, public buildings. They are available in the breakdown for England and Wales only, where during 1966, a total of 119 children in the 5–14 group were accidentally drowned in these 'other places' – 87 in inland waters, 31 in coastal waters and 1 in a public building.[1]

Books or no books, children do of course love to play with, in or on water, and anyone writing about children can hardly fail to reflect this interest that so often amounts to a passion. Nor indeed does it behove authors to avoid the subject, or even to avoid getting their characters into dangerous situations connected with water. What they should avoid, however, is attractively presenting such situations without sufficiently underlying the danger. In *Pirate's Island*, Mr John Rowe Townsend offers a somewhat alarming example of inadequacy in this respect.

Here again we have a twelve-year-old hero with a younger girl companion, and the first thing to notice is that unlike Finn and Derval, Gordon and Sheila are not absolutely compelled to embark on dangerous behaviour in order to escape from an even more dangerous situation. The constructing of a home-made raft to float on a city canal is simply a rather interesting, rather jolly thing to do, and even though it does have

---

1. Figures supplied by the Royal Society for the Prevention of Accidents.

a purpose – to get them to a tiny man-made island in the middle of the waterway – this purpose is in the same low key as far as the boy is concerned, for he doesn't really believe the little girl's wild imaginings about buried treasure. It is then essentially a typical, everyday, loose-endish venture, of the sort that a child reader in a similar state of semi-boredom might undertake or might be inspired to copy.

The raft is basically a large upturned table – not, one would think, the most stable of bases for such a purpose. Yet Mr Townsend fails to make anything of this fact, his mind apparently running too swiftly on isn't-it-great-to-make-things-with-your-hands lines. As the job nears completion, Gordon voices this. 'I know it isn't quite like the pictures. . . . You don't see them hammering away for hours in the pictures and pulling nails out that have gone in wrong.' Well, it's a good cultural point to make, but just here, one feels, the reader's nerves should be made to tingle at the prospect of pulling more important things than nails out of a more dangerous element than wood. True, Gordon himself has certain reservations, but Gordon has been built up as a fat softie, and rather cowardly. So when he reflects thus:

> Although the idea of sailing the raft was exciting, whenever he thought of actually taking it out on the black waters of the North-west Junction Canal he didn't feel too keen. His sense of caution was more strongly developed than his sense of adventure.

– any thoughts the reader has of finding an old table for himself are given an impetus rather than a damping down – the impetus of a challenge. Similarly, when a note of warning is sounded by an elderly man – 'Well, have a good trip. And be careful. You only live once. You've a long way to go till you reach my age, eh? Don't take any risks' – it is the stereotyped, conventional, low-powered one that children are so often tired of hearing, not the sort that appeals to their good sense through their imagination. And the fact that the man in question is presented as something of a pig-headed old fool for keeping his life's savings at home doesn't add to his appeal as an adviser.

Mercifully, in one way, Mr Townsend is not at his best in this book, and his account of the delights of first sailing on the raft is not likely to stir young imaginations through the power of the prose.

> The raft was heavy, and hard to steer. But they were elated – Gordon at the success of his carpentry, Sheila at the romance of being on the water. The next half-hour was sheer enjoyment. They managed to propel themselves a hundred yards or so along the canal, passing under the viaduct.

This is not the recreating of a highly adventurous situation. This is adult conceptualizing on such a scene. We are *told* 'they were elated' but we are not *shown* their elation. We are *told* that it was 'sheer enjoyment' but we are not shown why. We don't get the feel of the raft, the motion of the water, any sudden tendencies to tilt or spin. We are not given any of the actual thoughts of the children – their fears, their fantasies. And with this lack of realization of the enjoyment there is also a lack of realization of the danger.

That is why I say it is only *in a way* merciful that Mr Townsend was not on top form. For, unhappily, the floating of rafts on deep waters is tempting enough in itself, as an ungarnished prospect – and could still stimulate emulation. And the great pity is this: that had the author thought himself more deeply into his subject he would probably have given a far more vivid account of the venture and one that would have been as satisfactory artistically as socially.

Here is another makeshift craft on its maiden voyage – this time an old abandoned rowing boat that a group of small boys rehabilitate. Potentially almost as dangerous, and equally fascinating to children, it is a situation that Mr Roger Collinson deals with in perhaps a clumsier fashion than Mr Townsend dealt with his (this is from his first book, *A Boat and Bax*), but with a lot more imaginative force.

> They pushed the *Albatross* out into the river again, boarded her, and paddled downstream for a hundred yards or so. The fun and excitement of being afloat again dispelled the cloud of bad temper that had hovered over them on shore. The swaying of the boat beneath them, the plashing of the paddles, the lines of little whirlpools the blades left behind, transported them to a world of pure delight. Even Worm, mechanically baling in the stern, sloughed his sardonic mood, and entered with abandon into the joy of make-believe.
>
> By the time they had fought off a pirate galleon, sunk an enemy submarine, escaped from the gaping jaws of a dozen crocodiles, rounded the Cape in the teeth of a hurricane, and narrowly avoided being smashed to match-wood by an iceberg, they felt in need of a rest. They looked for a suitable shallow landing, jumped out of the *Albatross* and drew her nose up out of the water. They sprawled on the grass and examined the blisters they had worked up on the palms of their hands.

At this stage no note of danger has been sounded, but the author soon makes it quite plain, through the plot, without preachiness, that such pastimes are for reasonably good swimmers only. Already, in fact, he has had the three boys deciding to bring their swimming trunks when messing about with the boat – ostensibly to free themselves from worrying about getting their clothes wet – but the trunks are faded, well-used, and it is taken for granted (*a*) that the boys can swim, and (*b*) that they're engaged on an undertaking in which swimming is a vitally necessary skill. Now, after the launching, the point is elaborated. Bobby Bax's younger sister, the ten-year-old bespectacled and bookish Maggie, has come along for the ceremony, and has indeed named the 'ship' with a bottle of lemonade. (A squirt only – for the kids have other uses for the stuff and, as one of them drily observes, breaking the whole bottle over the bows might 'smash the sides in'.) But they are reluctant to let Maggie sail on her – mainly and simply, one suspects, because she is a girl and inclined to fuss, but also partly because, as the same dry observer points out, 'It's unlucky to have women on a ship'. The clincher, however, comes from Bobby – who very shrewdly throws back at her a recent boast that when it comes to looking after their young brother, she is the more 'responsible'. 'Besides,' he tells her, 'you know you can't swim yet. It wouldn't be *responsible* to sail with us until you can.' Thus the author, very skilfully, issues his warning, his reminder, openly – yet at the same time obliquely – through the mouth of a respected character, one of the children concerned in the adventure. The fact that it comes in the guise of a purely diplomatic move, a neat bit of juvenile one-upman-ship, does take some of the immediate force off the warning note, certainly, but by planting it in this way he ensures that it will stick in the reader's mind and quietly take root there. It is a technique known to most teachers. However, Mr Collinson is not content with this alone, and he follows it up most amusingly and convincingly by having Maggie a few chapters later, engineering that Bobby be detailed to teach her to swim, and this in turn is followed by a scene in the public swimming baths, during which the bravely trying girl is pulled under by a young lout. Again the incident is handled lightly, but with just enough detail to underline the seriousness of the matter. Margaret, for example, goes down with a 'gurgling scream' and there is a black side to the following satirical passage:

Jugears and Worm were already pulling Margaret to the side, while all the girls screamed with terror. One or two were already composing speeches in their minds suitable for the occasion: 'When they pulled her out, I thought I would have fainted. She was all blue and her arms were stiff. I shall never get over it . . . never, never, not as long as I live.' The same heart-broken friends were secretly quite vexed when Margaret began coughing and spitting out mouthfuls of water, and generally making it quite clear that she was not drowned yet by a long way.

Nevertheless, ensuring that the real point is not undervalued or over-looked, the warning direct is put into the mouth of an adult who has already been presented sympathetically, as something of a hero-figure: the swimming instructor. 'I saw everything. You might have drowned that girl – as it is, it'll be a miracle if we ever get her near water again. Get out, and don't show your face in here again.'

Mr Collinson, it should be added, is himself a teacher – a member of a profession only too well aware of the unavoidable difficulties and anxieties and responsibilities involved in being *in loco parentis*. Children's authors are in a very special and intimate way similarly placed – though without the threat of possible legal repercussions continually hanging over them – and it would be as well if they were to remind themselves of this more often than many of them seem to do. Far from being incompatible with their work, a lively awareness of this situation could positively enhance it, for, as we have seen, a fulfilled responsibility to one's art practically ensures fulfilled responsibility to the reader. And morally the position seems to me to be abundantly clear: *if a children's writer accepts the benefits of a subject's fatal attractiveness to children, then he must handle that subject with the very greatest care.*

It wasn't until I was sixteen that I first had my jaw broken in a fight, by a kind of improvised karate chop – and I shall never forget the experience. Nothing I had read in comic-books, magazines, children's novels or adult thrillers, and nothing I had seen on the stage or on the screen, had prepared me for it.

First there was the shock – a stinging sensation as of a simultaneous pricking of a score or so of needles, lasting for no more than a second and followed immediately by a numbness. Then came the pain, very severe and lasting for hours. Then came the discomfort, which went on for days, and a recurrence of the really excruciating pain whenever I tried to eat. Finally there was the inconvenience of going for X-rays and treatment, which went on for weeks.

Since then I have watched enactments of similar blows, and read about them, with a certain cynicism – for in almost every case in which they occur in popular fiction, in prose, strip cartoon or on the screen, the result is so clean, so uncluttered with consequences, so lacking in truth as to be positively indecent. One cowboy bashes another around a saloon – giving and receiving blows any one of which would be at least twice as damaging as the one I received – yet what happens? Hero or villain, the victim gets up after being stunned for a few seconds, rubs his jaw, works it from side to side, and goes off threatening vengeance but otherwise quite healthy.

Now just as I was completely unprepared for the actual consequences of such a blow, so was my assailant – who'd had the extra benefit of some 25 to 30 years' seniority and therefore a greater opportunity of finding out the truth of the matter in his reading and filmgoing. In fact I'm not sure which of us was the more upset and horrified, and it has always since then seemed to me quite reprehensible for a writer to portray in great detail such acts of violence without showing in equally great detail their likely effects.

Again the question of art enters into the matter. The greater the artistry the greater the essential truth, and the greater the essential truth the greater the good. Not writing about violence descriptively will never cause it to diminish. Nor *will* writing about it descriptively cause it to diminish unless its often disgusting, always painful consequences are shown in some detail. Then, indeed, there is likely to be a diminution – if, that is, there is such a thing as human sympathy at all. Yet this consequential aspect is precisely the one that our self-styled cleaners-up of the popular arts would seek to suppress. The sight of blood, they argue, or of a messy exit wound in a shooting scene, or the puckered bloody criss-cross of flesh in a knifing incident, is harmful because it is likely to stir up the urge to do violent acts. In this, it seems to me, they are assuming an ubiquitous, almost universal barely latent sadism – that realistic details will be responded to by a pathological gloating if not actual emulation. So they will, no doubt, in a small number of clinical cases, but the more general reaction is likely to be one of repugnance – the same sort of healthy repugnance felt by the 'cleaners-up' themselves – for while there is perhaps some latent sadistic streak in most of us there is also an equally strong, if not stronger streak of compassion. It often strikes me as being ironic that these people should be so ready to deny the likelihood of healthy reactions in others – as if they themselves formed some kind of superior minority in this respect.

In adult fiction there is a great deal of physical violence, just as there is – and because there is – in life. Some of it is honestly treated, with equal weight being given to the act and the consequences; some of it is grossly distorted, with undue attention being given to the act alone; and much of it is rendered completely innocuous-seeming, in the Western-saloon ruckus manner I have already described. But let us see what happens when a very great novelist handles the subject of a beating.

D. H. Lawrence, in *Sons and Lovers*, doesn't attempt to disguise the sheer animality that the situation calls up in the victim as well as the aggressor.

. . . before the younger man knew where he was he was staggering backwards from a blow across the face.

The whole night went black. He tore off his overcoat and coat, dodging a blow, and flung the garments over Dawes. The latter swore savagely. Morel, in his shirt-sleeves, was now alert and furious. He felt his whole body unsheath itself like a claw. He could not fight, so he would use his wits. The other man became more distinct to him; he could see particularly the shirt-breast. Dawes stumbled over Paul's coats, then came rushing forward. The young man's mouth was bleeding. It was the other man's mouth he was dying to get at, and the desire was anguish in its strength. He stepped quickly through the stile, and as Dawes was coming through after him, like a flash he got a blow in over the other's mouth. He shivered with pleasure. Dawes advanced slowly, spitting. Paul was afraid; he moved round to get to the stile again. Suddenly, from out of nowhere, came a great blow against his ear, that sent him falling helpless backwards. He heard Dawes' heavy panting, like a wild beast's; then came a kick on the knee, giving him such agony that he got up and, quite blind, leapt clean under his enemy's guard. He felt blows and kicks, but they did not hurt. He hung on to the bigger man like a wild cat, till at last Dawes fell with a crash, losing his presence of mind. Paul went down with him. Pure instinct brought his hands to the man's neck, and before Dawes, in frenzy and agony, could wrench him free, he had got his fists twisted in the scarf and his knuckles dug in the throat of the other man. He was a pure instinct, without reason or feeling. His body, hard and wonderful in itself, cleaved against the struggling body of the other man; not a muscle in him relaxed. He was quite unconscious, only his body had taken upon itself to kill this other man. For himself, he had neither feeling nor reason. He lay pressed hard against his adversary, his body adjusting itself to its one pure purpose of choking the other man, resisting at exactly the right moment, with exactly the right amount of strength, the struggles of the other, silent, intent, unchanging, gradually pressing its knuckles deeper, feeling the struggles of the other body become wilder and more frenzied. Tighter and tighter grew his body, like a screw that is gradually increasing in pressure, till something breaks.

Then suddenly he relaxed, full of wonder and misgiving. Dawes had been yielding. Morel felt his body flame with pain, as he realized what he was doing; he was all bewildered. Dawes' struggles suddenly renewed themselves in a furious spasm. Paul's hands were wrenched, torn out of the scarf in which they were knotted, and he was flung away, helpless. He heard the horrid sound of the other's gasping, but he lay stunned; then, still dazed, he felt the blows of the other's feet, and lost consciousness.

Dawes, grunting with pain like a beast, was kicking the prostrate body of his rival.

So Lawrence applies the whole of his imagination to the act and spares us none of the details. As a fight it is superficially exciting, of course, but at every stage the author is reminding us – without stopping to preach – of the *possible* consequences of each blow, each kick, each tightening of the grip. To an adult reader there is the added horror of the spiritual consequences – of Paul's possession – of what happens to him as a man under such pressure. But it is the attention Lawrence gives to the actual physical consequences to Paul that concerns us most here, and we should note that it is equally close.

Dawes has left the young man lying in the field – 'and dimly in his consciousness as he went, he felt on his foot the place where his boot had knocked against one of the lad's bones. The knock seemed to re-echo inside him; he hurried to get away from it.' (Note, incidentally, the effect of that plain matter-of-fact description of a boot knocking against a living bone – so much more accurate and vivid and sobering than any glib euphemistic jargon like 'putting the boot in', used to veil the true nature of the act from the perpetrator's or spectator's conscience.)

Morel gradually came to himself. He knew where he was and what had happened, but he did not want to move. He lay still, with tiny bits of snow tickling his face. It was pleasant to lie quite, quite still. The time passed. It was the bits of snow that kept rousing him when he did not want to be roused. At last his will clicked into action.

'I mustn't lie here,' he said; 'it's silly.'

But still he did not move.

'I said I was going to get up,' he repeated. 'Why don't I?'

And still it was some time before he had sufficiently pulled himself together to stir; then gradually he got up. Pain made him sick and dazed, but his brain was clear. Reeling, he groped for his coats and got them on, buttoning his overcoat up to his ears. It was some time before he found his cap. He did not know whether his face was still bleeding. Walking blindly, every step making him sick with pain, he went back to the pond and washed his face and hands. The icy water hurt, but helped to bring him back to himself. He crawled back up the hill to the tram. He wanted to get to his mother – he must get to his mother – that was his blind intention. He covered his face as much as he could, and struggled sickly along. Continually the ground seemed to fall away from him as he walked, and he felt himself dropping with a sickening feeling into space; so, like a nightmare, he got through with the journey home.

Everybody was in bed. He looked at himself. His face was discoloured and smeared with blood, almost like a dead man's face. He washed it, and went to bed. The night went by in delirium. In the morning he found his mother looking at him. Her blue eyes – they were all he wanted to see. She was there; he was in her hands.

'It's not much, mother,' he said. 'It was Baxter Dawes.'

'Tell me where it hurts you,' she said quietly.

'I don't know – my shoulder. Say it was a bicycle accident, mother.'

He could not move his arm. Presently Minnie, the little servant, came upstairs with some tea.

'Your mother's nearly frightened me out of my wits – fainted away,' she said.

He felt he could not bear it. His mother nursed him; he told her about it.

'And now I should have done with them all,' she said quietly.

'I will, mother.'

She covered him up.

'And don't think about it,' she said – 'only try to go to sleep. The doctor won't be here till eleven.'

He had a dislocated shoulder, and the second day acute bronchitis set in.

I have quoted this at such length because in my view it is a model of how violence should be dealt with, due weight being given to all its aspects: the actual blows, the possible consequences, the actual consequences. In *Saturday Night and Sunday Morning* (the very title of which reflects this roundness), Alan Sillitoe gives us a similarly comprehensive account of a beating, when a couple of soldiers attack Arthur Seaton. John Braine, however, attempting an almost identical scene at the end of *Room at the Top*, is not quite up to it.

He struck out with his fist; I sidestepped, but not quickly enough, and he hit my cheekbone, cutting it with something (a ring, I realized afterwards). But I thought it was a razor, so I hit him in the Adam's apple. He gave a sound half-way between a baby's gurgle and a death-rattle and staggered away from me, his hands to his throat.

'You dirty bastard,' his friend said, and tried to kick me in the groin. More by good luck than good management I turned sideways; but not properly as the PT sergeant had taught me; his foot landed home on my thigh and I lost my balance and went down with him on top of me. We rolled about on the pavement like quarrelling children; I was trying to keep him off and he, I think, had no idea in his head that wasn't based upon making me suffer as much as his friend (whom I could still hear choking with agony) had been made to suffer by me. He got both hands around my throat and began to squeeze; a black and red stream of pain spread like lava behind my eyes. My hands had lost their strength and I couldn't move my legs and I could taste blood from my cut cheek and smell his hair-oil and the laundered stiffness of his shirt and orange and fish and dog from the gutter; the lamp-posts shot up suddenly to a hundred times their height like bean-flowers in educational films, taking the buildings with them in elongated smudges of yellow light; and then I remembered another of the PT Sergeant's maxims, and I spat in his face. He recoiled instinctively, his hold relaxing for a second; then I remembered a lot more things and within thirty seconds he was in an untidy heap on the pavement and I was running as fast as I could down the street.

The details of the actual kicks and scratches and blows are given convincingly enough at first, but they tend to weaken towards the end of the passage and we become aware of a second struggle – the inferior writer's struggle to invent that culminates in the almost ludicrous 'then I remembered a lot more things' and the author's running with his hero as fast as he can from the scene to which he too isn't equal. As for the consequences, Mr Braine doesn't seem to have been able to visualize them beyond a paragraph describing the disorder of the hero's dress, a few bloodstains and the expression of disgust on the face of a woman on the tram *he* catches. Thus it is an outsider's view, a non-participant's in more senses than one.

In children's stories about children, violence of the brutally deadly kind discussed above need never figure at all frequently, simply because it so very rarely occurs in their own experience – the usual playground fights being comparatively innocuous tussling matches. But where it does crop up naturally in a plot – and this will generally be in the type of children's story dealing mainly with adult characters – then an attempt should be made to treat it, if not at the same length, then certainly with the honesty and balance and total engagement displayed by Lawrence above.

Unevenness, lack of balance, the failure of an author to follow through artistically and logically: these are so often at the root of what is potentially harmful in children's (to say nothing of adults') fiction. So far we have been discussing this in relation to physically dangerous activities and violence, but perhaps the most important of the three major problem areas is the one involving the sort of deep-seated anti-social behaviour that manifests itself in indiscriminate contempt for or hatred of whole classes of people – because it is the most insidious in its growth and widespread in its effects. At one end of the scale we have social snobbery and cliquishness, at the other we have nationalist hysteria, class and race hatred, ghettoes and gas chambers.

That is why I have already been moved to criticize so strongly Enid Blyton's *Five Run Away Together*. Children do tend to be cliquish, spiteful, intolerant and, in so far as the author presented them in this light she was doing a good job – a much better job in fact than many a more highly praised children's author. Where she failed was in not making it clear that such behaviour as George's towards Edgar and Julian's towards Mr and Mrs Stick was as irrational at first as it was reprehensible at any time, that spite and contempt may come easily to children but are none the pleasanter for that – and where she aggravated her failure was in giving this behaviour her positive approval, in such passages as the one quoted on page 86, and in the obvious relish with which she has the children bandy about such names as 'Spotty Face' for Edgar and 'Stinker-dog' for the Sticks' dog. Here indeed, in the matter of the dog, Miss Blyton touches the very core of childish malicious irrationality, and it is worth following this thread with some care.

Right at the start, George's dog, Timmy, is presented as a brave, lovable, faithful, clever animal; the Sticks' dog a mangy-looking creature with 'a dirty white coat, out of which patches seemed to have been bitten, and its tail was well between its legs.' Now this in itself is no worse than a rather clumsy piece of scales-tipping on the author's part. A better writer might have seen the advantage of giving the unpleasant characters a nice-looking well-dispositioned animal, not only to throw their unpleasantness into higher relief but also to act as a sympathetic focus – but there is nothing particularly unfair or distorting about the choice of the dog as it stands. When Timmy goes for it, however, and is dragged off, a certain sentimental grossness begins to creep into the narrative:

> Timmy gave a whine, and put his head down on his paws. He licked a few hairs from the corner of his mouth. It was sad to be tied up – but anyhow he had bitten a bit off the tip of one of that dreadful dog's ears!

Even so, a claim can be made that the author is still within her artistic rights if we allow that a dog might just possibly reflect on a recent fight in this somewhat human way.

But from then on the 'dreadful dog' is persecuted unmercifully by Timmy, children and author alike. Timmy woofs, and George explains: 'Timmy says he hates Stinker's miserable tail and silly little ears', in practically the same breath as she has said, of the 'nasty creature' Edgar Stick: 'I hate his pimply nose and screwed-up eyes'. Julian says: 'Hallo, Stinker! . . . Had a bath yet? Alas, no! – as smelly as ever, aren't you?' Timmy has another go: 'Stinker gave a woeful howl' (and note how the author gives her silent blessing to the jeering name the characters have substituted for 'Tinker') 'and tried to escape. But Timothy had him by the neck and was shaking him like a rat.' Later the good Timmy growls and Julian cautions him:

> 'Timmy, keep to heel! Growl all you like, but don't bite anybody – yet!'

Timmy's growls were really frightful. Even Mr. Stick put himself at the other end of the room. As for Stinker, he was nowhere to be seen. He had gone into the scullery at the very first growl, and was now shivering behind the wringer.

And two pages further on, Timmy follows Julian out of the room, 'disappointed that he hadn't been able to get a nibble at Stinker'. There follows a lull in the persecution of the mongrel when the Five run away and hide on a nearby island, but he's never far from their thoughts. They muse on what's happening back at the cottage.

'I guess the old Sticks are glad we've gone,' said Dick. 'Spotty Face will be able to loll in the sitting-room and read all our books, if he wants to.'

'And Stinker-dog will be able to wander all over the house and lie on anybody's bed without being afraid that Timothy will eat him whole,' said George.

Then, as the lull is about to be broken by the intrusion of the Sticks, Timmy notices it first. He 'had smelt something exciting – he had smelt a smell he knew – a dog-smell – and he meant to find the owner of it and bite off his ears and tail!' There is an immediate set-to between the dogs, the inevitable result of which is a victory for Timmy over the 'bleeding, whining mongrel'. But the children call him off (their concern having been over the danger of being discovered, of course, and not out of any sympathy for the vanquished) and in their hiding-place 'Timmy growled softly, wishing that he could go and find that Stinker-dog again! It had been lovely to bite his ears hard.'

Timmy invariably growls on sensing danger as well as at the prospect of sport; Tinker invariably whines. At his next appearance – when the children are making use of the echoes in a cave to frighten the Sticks – 'poor Stinker began to whine pitifully. He was frightened almost out of his life. He pressed himself against the floor as if he would like to disappear into it.' The children find this very gratifying. ' "We heard old Stick yelling to us to clear out," said George, "and he sounded scared stiff. As for Stinker, we never heard even the smallest growl from him." '

The enemy-dog's next appearance is in daylight, when he explores the courtyard of the island's inevitable ruined castle with his owners, 'his tail well down'. His persecution continues when Mr and Mrs Stick leave him for a while with Edgar – 'Spotty Face' to the children – and George, hiding on the cliff above, picks up a clod of earth 'and flung it high into the air. It fell all over Stinker, and the dog gave a yelp, and scuttled down the hole that led into the dungeons.' There he stays until the Stick parents return, when:

A dismal howl came echoing up from below the ground. It was Stinker, terrified at being alone below, and not daring to come up.

'Poor lamb!' said Mrs. Stick, who seemed much fonder of Stinker than anyone else.

'What's up with him?'

Stinker let out an even more doleful howl, and Mrs. Stick hurried down the steps to go to him.

Poor lamb? Talk of fondness? Is the author faltering here? Shall common human sympathy be allowed to break in, even at the cost of spoiling the fun, the sneaking pleasures of the pack? For the next chapter or so these questions are left unanswered, as the author concentrates on the two major developments in the plot – the discovery by the children that the Sticks haven't come to search for them but to hide away a little girl kidnapped by a gang, and the Five's own kidnapping of Edgar Stick. But when the dog is next mentioned a curious thing happens. The Sticks are about to row back to the mainland to see if they can find out something about their son's disappearance:

'What about Tinker?' said Mr. Stick, in a sulky tone. 'Better leave him here, hadn't we, to guard the entrance to the dungeons? Not that there will be anyone here, if what you say is right.'
'Oh, we'll leave Tinker,' said Mrs. Stick, setting off to the boat. Julian saw them embark, leaving the dog behind. Tinker watched them rowing away, his tail well down between his legs. Then he turned and ran back to the courtyard, and lay down dolefully in the sun. He was very uneasy. His ears were cocked and he kept looking this way and that. He didn't like this queer island and its unexpected noises.

For once, Miss Blyton treats him objectively – apart from the slight sneer implied in the tail's being *well* down – even to the point of giving him his real name. Is this a further softening of attitude, a continuation of the faltering noted earlier? Significantly, two paragraphs earlier, we had witnessed, with Julian, Mrs Stick's concern for the missing Edgar: ' "Goodness knows what he's going through – feeling frightened and lonely without me" ' – and here at last it seems that humanity will indeed be allowed to break in, to the great advantage of the narrative and the benefit of the young readers. After all, it is a quite natural reaction on the woman's part, and could lead to an equally natural secondary reaction of remorse and fellow feeling for the kidnapped girl's parents. But it is through Julian's eyes we are seeing this at the moment and:

Julian felt disgusted. Here was Mrs. Stick talking like that about old Spotty-Face – and yet she had a little girl down in the dungeons – a child much younger than Edgar! What a beast she was.

Quite a natural boyish view, of course. But the point is – and this is the crux of the whole matter – shall the boyish view be allowed to prevail, become the official view, the author's own view, and hence the young reader's, who will naturally incline towards it anyway?

This perhaps accounts for the apparent hesitation, the softening of tone with regard to Tinker, which follows in the next paragraph or two. 'Freudian' as applied to slips of the pen or tongue usually suggests the involuntary release of an unpleasant thought. Here, in the use by the author of Tinker's real name, we might well be witnessing a Freudian slip in reverse: the involuntary release of a pleasant impulse.

But we are soon back to vicious childishness. Two pages later, the imprisoned Edgar spots his dog.

> 'There's Tinker!' suddenly cried Edgar, pointing to a bush some distance away. Tinker was there, hiding, quite terrified at seeing Timothy again.
> 'Fat lot of good Stinker is,' said Julian. 'No, Timmy – you're not to eat him. Stay here! He wouldn't taste nice if you did eat him!'

And with that we know that the broader human aspects will never be allowed to develop, that Mrs Stick will remain the puppet she has been most of the time. So has the Emperor Julian decreed it, and his creator humbly submits to the decree in the very next lines, where it is back to 'Stinker' for her too: 'Timothy was sorry not to be able to chase Stinker round and round the island. If he couldn't chase rabbits, he might at least be allowed to chase Stinker!' and 'Stinker' it continues to be – with everything else this usage implies – to the very last page, where Julian says farewell to the arrested Sticks on behalf of all concerned in the following terms:

> 'Good-bye!' he called, and the other children waved good-bye, too. 'Good-bye, Mr. Stick, don't go kidnapping any more children. Good-bye, Mrs. Stick, look after Edgar better, in case *he* gets kidnapped again! Good-bye, Spotty-face, try and be a better boy! Good-bye, Stinker, do get a bath as soon as possible. Good-bye!'

What sickens one is the *gleefulness* of the persecution of this innocent animal, reflecting as it does the gleeful totality of the children's hatred of the Sticks, and the way the readers are encouraged not only to approve of this but to participate in it through the author. And what surprises and disappoints one is the fact that this author could, as has been suggested several times, have made a much better job of the narrative had she followed through more frequently, taking up the human implications of some of the twists in the plot. She had the sharpness of observation, the timing faculty and a sense of responsibility that was sufficiently well developed in other matters. Safety considerations are always very carefully taken into account, and generally raised through the medium of Julian (who lays down the law about how to behave near the edge of cliffs as conscientiously as any Nazi SS officer anxious for the well-being of his men), while in some matters of child psychology the author is as clinically considerate as any other Froebel-trained teacher. Here, for instance, is how Julian salves his little sister's feelings after scolding her (so very properly, of course) for falling asleep on sentry duty:

'Don't make excuses,' said Julian. 'It only makes things worse if you do. All right – we'll give you another chance, Anne, and see if you are really big enough to do the things we do.'

But though they all took their turns, and kept a watch on the sea for any strange vessel, none appeared. . . .

'Better go to bed now,' said Julian, when the sun sank low. 'It's about nine o'clock. Come on! I'm really looking forward to a sleep on those lovely heathery beds that Anne has made so nicely!'

But in the one supremely important area of human relationships – between people of different upbringing, habits and outlook – the author seems to be blind to the consequences of her attitudes, seems in fact to be herself as irrational and as abandoned in her irrationality as a child, and this probably accounts for much of her enormous popularity with children. That is why I have spent so much time on this particular book, for it highlights a type of irresponsibility that by no means died out with the jingoistic anti-foreigner fiction that Orwell wrote about. Reading it, I was put in mind time and again of another children-on-an-island story: a story in which the quality of the writing is much higher but many of the attitudes portrayed are just as primitive. The only difference in this last connection is that William Golding did not present the gleeful witch-hunts and elated self-righteous viciousness of his *Lord of the Flies* children in a favourable light, with his full approval, and for the approval of child readers.

As we have seen, an author's responsibility to his readers is a very important factor in fiction for children, amounting to a social duty to handle certain themes and attitudes with the greatest circumspection. The job of a critic of children's fiction is therefore doubly difficult if he is to do it properly, for it is incumbent upon him to take this responsibility-factor into consideration as well as to evaluate the artistic elements of style, validity, readability, and so on.

Now we have also seen that the artistic elements are very often tightly bound up with the question of responsibility. The fulfilment of a keen sense of responsibility can enhance a work artistically, just as artistic integrity – the writer's urge to follow through honestly and comprehensively, often in spite of personal prejudice – will usually result in his discharging a social responsibility without his being aware of it.

But there will be times when a children's author's keen sense of responsibility will lead to certain detours or retreats. These may not necessarily be inartistic in themselves, but they will always be liable to misinterpretation by critics who are not aware of their significance or importance, or of the extra burden placed on the shoulders of a conscientious children's writer. Where this burden leads to clumsiness, of course, the critic's duty is to say so – but he should always be aware of the reason for such clumsiness and be all the readier with his praises when the extra weight is handled gracefully or even – as will sometimes happen – is turned to artistic advantage.

Furthermore, because a critic's recommendations may be expected to carry some weight with parents, teachers, librarians and others concerned with choosing books for children, he shares the children's author's responsibility in a very real way. The praising of a seemingly artistically well-done book (or of a seemingly highly readable one) that might lead to the jeopardizing of a reader's life or a poisoning of his personality, without mentioning such hazards, is as serious a failure on the critic's part as on the author's. So is the ignoring of an immensely popular work merely because it is deemed to be inartistic or downright trashy and therefore unworthy of the critic's attention. It may be trashy, inartistic, insipid or generally mediocre – but it may also be dangerous, physically or morally, with its very popularity multiplying and heightening the hazards.

All this suggests that the criticism of children's fiction requires more space than the criticism of adult fiction if justice is to be done to it and an essential service to the public performed. But what happens in reality? Because of slow-dying attitudes to children's fiction as 'kid's stuff', it is shoved very much into the background. As mentioned in an earlier section (pages 31–32) editors of newspapers and magazines tend to dismiss it entirely or, even where they are more enlightened and sympathetic, to get it over with in two or three quick rushes per year. (Though the U.S. has a much better record than the U.K. here, with regular and much more frequent review space being given to children's books in periodicals like the *New York Times Book Review Supplement* and the *Saturday Review*.) The result is that many snippetlike 'reviews' in the popular daily press are the work of junior members of the staff, hard-pressed for time, who are only too prone to make a quick précis of a book's blurb. Granted, from an author's point of view, this blurb regurgitation is commercially not a bad thing, since blurbs (which authors often write themselves anyway) are always extremely favourable, but to the public such reviews can obviously be of little value. Hardly any more useful are the gimmicks that some editors indulge in – presumably in an effort to brighten up what seems to them to be a drag. At one end of the scale, for instance, books might be given to children to review, and especially to the children of celebrities – a procedure that has the added advantage of seeming to be completely logical. So it is of course, up to a point – that point being where a skilled adult reviewer finishes canvassing his own children's or his friends' children's opinions and begins to take them into account when making his *own* assessment, which will naturally envisage other children, with other tastes or reading abilities. As they stand, however, the fifty or so solemn words by Adrian (aged 11) or Sara (who is $8\frac{1}{4}$) are about as likely to be useful as a review of *Lord Jim* by a deckhand, or *Lady Chatterley's Lover* by a gamekeeper.[1] Then at the other end of the scale we have the well-known critic of adult books charged with the task of being mistily reminiscent or waspishly sociological or brilliantly facetious according to his usual persona.

Where more sympathetic and knowledgeable skilled critics are used, they are still rarely given the space for lengthy quotation and analysis – and it should be especially noted here that the duality of concern in children's fiction, the intertwined questions of social and artistic responsibility, often require the lengthy disentangling of the various threads, through extensive quotation, in order that a work be properly appraised. Granted, even adult-fiction reviewers are seldom given the space in which to delve deeply, through analysis, but there is a whole field of criticism in volume form in which they may extend themselves and their inquiries, to say nothing of the literary quarterlies and similar journals. By comparison, the books on children's fiction and the journals willing to find room for the subject form a tiny, almost negligible patch. And even here, the habits formed in the workhouse of the more popular sections of the press seem to cling, so that comparatively little advantage is taken of their opportunities by critics who are given their head. Broad surveys are undertaken rather than studies in depth, with the result that each book discussed is so often given little more space than it would have had in a friendly newspaper or weekly review. The squaring of children's preferences and needs with artistic accomplishment in relation to single books or authors – a subject requiring whole chapters or volumes – tends to be ignored or skated over. And where lengthy quotations are given they are too often presented only in the course of paraphrasing a plot or as the subjects of eulogy. Again and again one comes across quotations heralded or followed by such thin unsubstantiated comments as: 'What child could resist the following pen-picture?' or 'This is a masterly piece of writing' or 'Here is a characteristic example' or 'The social milieu is indicated in the second paragraph' or 'Just how far from real children they were will be seen from the following extract' or 'Here is how the author describes the scene' or 'A fine piece of realistic observation'. What we wish to know is *why* the critic thinks a

---

1. Which reminds me of the time – though on a ·different level – when a weekly newspaper gave a children's book of mine with an archaeological theme – *Lemon Kelly Digs Deep* – to their agricultural correspondent.

piece of writing is 'masterly' or 'fine' or 'characteristic' or 'irresistible to a child'. We need closely pursued investigations and closely argued conclusions. We need, in fact, studies of children's fiction of the same calibre as such classics in the adult field as *Seven Types of Ambiguity, Enemies of Promise, The Liberal Imagination, The Craft of Fiction, The Great Tradition, Theory of Literature* and *The Wound and the Bow*.

The same eulogistic surface-skimming habits are also carried over, one suspects, into the field of awards. (And perhaps I had better add that I write this as an award-winner myself.) Much is made in citations of qualities like wisdom and tenderness, of styles that are 'at once flexible, colloquial and evocative', of atmospheres that are 'uncanny', themes that are 'rare', craft that is 'refined', conceptions that are 'imaginative', writing that is 'inimitable', developments that are 'inevitable', art that has 'matured', power of imagination that is 'concentrated', instruments of craft that are 'subtle and delicate' – yet very little attempt is made to qualify let alone justify such terms, even when the opportunity is presented in compilations such as the British Library Association's *Chosen for Children*, from which most of the phrases quoted above were drawn. It is little wonder really that Mr Brian Alderson was moved to complain about the same association's Carnegie Award procedure that 'it would add greatly to our confidence in the association if the announcement of the awards could be coupled with an intelligent critical account of the chief books considered, together with an elucidation of the reasons for selecting the winners.'[1] And, apropos the need for critics of children's fiction to take into account the total situation – involving questions of social responsibility as well as artistic merit – it is significant that the Lambeth Borough Children's Librarian, joining in the same correspondence, could point out (*a*) that while serving on the awards sub-committee she had not had a reasonable opportunity to read even once three of the titles put forward before the meeting at which the short list was drawn up, ('There had been one week beforehand in which to consider a total of 45 titles'); (*b*) that because the children's librarians serving on the sub-committee were all in supervisory posts, none could honestly claim 'day-to-day contact with children or knowledge of their reactions to the books'; and (*c*) that many of the books selected in the past were 'hardly read at all by children'.[2]

Perhaps some day we shall have a body of children's fiction critics whose skill and authority can be relied upon in cases such as this, and whose sense of responsibility will, collectively, match that of the children's authors. Indeed, the signs are (and the Carnegie Award

---

1. In a letter published in the *Times Literary Supplement* and quoted in *The Bookseller*, 6 July 1968.
2. Quoted in *The Bookseller*, 20 July 1968.

controversy is only one of them) that we shall. But these things take time, and meanwhile we should remember that the critical function can also be performed by the concerned individual: the person sufficiently aware of the subject's importance to make his own investigations and comparisons and draw his own conclusions, preferably after discussion with others equally concerned. In the present circumstances, teachers and librarians in particular have a considerable critical responsibility to discharge.

Chapter seven   Fiction in education

As we have seen, fiction plays a very large and important part, or complex of parts, in the life of a growing child. Apart from its more narrowly educational uses and applications in the classroom – sometimes as an instrument in the acquisition of a skill, sometimes as a sugar-coating, sometimes merely as a subject for examinations – it is constantly offering a child models on which to base speculations of his own, as well as a means of further exploration of his total environment. To establish and maintain successful communication with children on *any* subject, therefore, it is essential to have a thorough acquaintance with what is available in the field of children's fiction.

Some colleges concerned with the training of teachers are aware of this and make efforts to refresh students' minds with supplementary courses on the subject, of varying degrees of comprehensiveness. Others seem to trust to luck, perhaps rashly assuming that the students are near enough to their own childhood reading. What is really required, in my view, is a thorough systematic study that is not an off-shoot of the work in either the regular English course or the education course, but is the product of a combined operation: a joint effort on the part of the English, education and library staffs, with supplementary lectures by specialists in other subjects. An art lecturer, for example, might deal with illustrations in children's books, and aspects of the comic strip; a social historian with changing fashions in subject-matter; a mass communications specialist with fiction presented on television, film and radio, perhaps with a side-glance at fiction in advertising and popular magazines.

At the basis of such a course would be a critical examination of fiction for children not only from a literary point of view, but also a social one (which would be given equal weight) taking in the aspects of responsibility discussed in the last chapter. The course would not therefore confine itself to 'good' fiction for children, or what is generally accepted as 'good'. Popular series and popular authors, comics, television and radio series and serials, would all come under scrutiny. And at all stages and in all branches, the accent would be on the contemporary. It is all too easy, but of far less value, to become entangled in a dilettantish or even scholarly way with the *history* of children's fiction – though this could of course be briefly touched on, with particular reference to broad and possibly recurring trends.

Even when examining works in this field from the literary critical point of view, attention should not be confined to stylistic points any more than it would nowadays in the adult sphere. Instead, it should be directed in a more comprehensive way to deal with characters, settings, motives, psychological patterns, philosophical considerations etc., and thus the examination will naturally have to cover part of the adult fictional field – as it did at the beginning of this study – to consider also the presentation of children there. Indeed, the two threads that have run through this book – the 'about' and 'for' in connection with children and fiction – would be close to the heart of such a course, and student teachers might pursue a number of related lines of psychological inquiry that could be of great immediate practical value in the acquisition of professional skills.

Child characters, vividly drawn and documented and imaginatively developed, are after all logical subjects for child study, particularly where general discussion by large groups is a feature of the method of study. Naturally, there is no satisfactory substitute for an actual, living, readily and more or less constantly available child for individual study, but when opinions are likely to diverge and even conflict and must therefore be compared and discussed, certain difficulties arise. The student may have made a thorough study of young John X, a member of a class at the teaching practice school – in so far as any such study can be thorough when confined to a few waking hours of the subject's life, possibly quite outside the home environment and certainly outside the more secret or even simply private recesses of that environment. The tutor may also have made a fairly thorough study of the same child. But the only fruitful discussion of the child is likely to be between these two, because as far as a third party is concerned, a student who has not himself made a study of that child, they will be talking about not one hypothetical subject but two: the boy as the first student presents him and the boy as the tutor presents him. Furthermore, there will be the question of reaction to contend with: the problem of how far the studied child's behaviour has been influenced by the personality of the observer-reporter in each case. Far better, for general discussion purposes, would be the study of a child character in fiction – the more fully and skilfully portrayed the better, of course. Then Maggie Tulliver or the Young Marcel in *Remembrance of Things Past* or David Copperfield would be available to all – the same Maggie or Marcel or David in the same environments and situations – and conflicting opinions about the behaviour and personality and potentialities of such a child could be more instructively argued, with fallacies or misunderstandings more readily traced and tracked down. It is true that even with the creations of the best artists certain inherent fallacies or misunderstandings might exist, but these themselves could form an equally fruitful basis for discussion.

One way of conducting such an examination of fictional children in a more compact and precise manner than by straight discussion would be to use the various methods of recording personality at the disposal of teachers and other educationalists. This would have the additional advantage of offering a test of the tests, as it were, and of underlining for the students the importance of taking subjectivity into account when making such assessments. One of the most valuable short investigations I ever undertook as a teacher started as a matter of idle curiosity more than anything else, when my own annual attempt at rating the personalities of a class of twelve-year-olds happened to coincide with a rereading of *David Copperfield*. What – I found myself wondering – would Mr and Mrs Murdstone's assessments of David have been had they been required to fill out a similar record card prior to the boy's transference to Mr Creakle's school?

Thus, under *Self-confidence*, I decided that Mr Murdstone would have bestowed an E – 'diffident, nervous, lacks self-confidence' – bearing in mind his own attempts at tutoring the boy. His wife, on the other hand, might well have written C – 'normally confident in familiar circumstances' – no doubt with more than a twinge of bitterness as she weighed the qualifying phrase.

Similar conflicts of opinion were deducible under *Prevailing Attitude*, *Sociability* and *Conscientiousness*, but of all the hypothetical assessments, I found those concerned with *Co-operation* the most illuminating. 'Churlish, sullen, not co-operative' – E, E, E! Mr Murdstone could hardly have been expected to restrain himself here, as he wrote with the hand that David had first refused then finally bitten. Mrs Murdstone, however, would have had greater difficulty in making up her mind. An A – 'invariably co-operative and helpful' – might well have suggested itself at first, but then, remembering David's attitude to her second marriage, she would probably have been forced to award a candid D – 'reluctant to co-operate, needs stimulus'. Certainly not E in her case, though, if the following exchange is to be taken into account – an exchange that Dickens might have written expressly to illustrate the teacher-assessor's problem:

'Now, David,' said Mr. Murdstone, 'a sullen obdurate disposition is, of all tempers, the worst.'

'And the boy's is, of all such dispositions that ever I have seen,' remarked his sister, 'the most confirmed and stubborn. I think, my dear Clara, even you must observe it?'

'I beg your pardon, my dear Jane,' said my mother, 'but are you quite sure – I'm certain you'll excuse me, my dear Jane – that you understand Davy?'

A few exercises of this kind would soon drive home the point – not always appreciated by many an experienced educationist – that in making such 'objective' 5-point assessments, one must first be sure that one understands the particular Davy in question and can assess his behaviour in the light of changing circumstances and relationships. In the Murdstone case it is true, of course, that we are dealing with extremes – with a couple of 'teachers' having large personal axes to grind – yet it is equally true that both would be making sincere estimates according to their own experiences of the boy. This leads naturally to the question: Is it possible to make an objective estimate at all, using such cut-and-dried methods? – the answer to which might well appear to be No. After all, the person most qualified to make such an assessment of Davy was Dickens himself – standing in for God and having the benefit of omniscience as far as the boy was concerned – and it took *him* three large volumes to present his assessment. Then again, was not Dickens in some measure writing about himself? How objectively in fact can one assess one's own personality? So questions of educational psychology succeed questions of methodical recording, and questions of literary processes succeed those of psychology, which in turn succeed those of the others again, taking the inquiry as deeply into the heart of the teaching situation as may be desired. Or the emphasis could be shifted more to the literary side – with such tests being applied to the quality of the writing, to the author's ability to recreate convincingly something of the complexity of human relationships, with characters sincerely holding conflicting opinions about certain other characters. Negatively, few things could be more revealing of the inferiority of a writer than a set of identical ratings resulting from an application of what might be called the 'Murdstone Test' (a test that applied to Jesus Christ Himself produces some spectacularly contradictory results, incidentally) – just as few things could be more intriguing than the conflict between an author's obvious rating of one of his characters and the rating that might equally obviously be made by readers and other characters alike. (Not necessarily a sign of inferiority, if we take into account some of the characters Dickens himself seemed to approve of; and sometimes an indication of great art, if we remember Henry James's *The Turn of the Screw* and the strange case of the governess.)

The examination by teaching students of children in fiction is something that has been going on for years, but usually in only a somewhat sporadic way, with Tom Sawyer, as we have seen, whitewashing an occasional fence, or Maggie Tulliver bashing a nail into an occasional doll in various education lectures, without any systematic follow-through being undertaken. Apparently even less appreciated is the value to teaching students of any systematic inquiry into the other aspect of child psychology as applied by successful fiction writers: their understanding of children as *readers*, of their needs and their preferences and of how these often vary at different stages. Perhaps this is because as a rule the traffic between teaching and fiction-authorship is in practical professional terms one-way: with many teachers benefiting from their knowledge of children, becoming increasingly successful as children's authors because of this, and then leaving the classroom to concentrate on writing, either privately or in one of those distraction-proof eyries the education system itself sometimes provides. On the other hand, very few professional fiction-writers, ex-teachers or not, go into teaching. This is understandable – because if they are good they are doing an extremely valuable job educationally anyway, on a much wider scale – yet it is also a great pity, for the basic perceptions of such people, more or less adequate to begin with, become very much sharper, more sophisticated, more flexible, more powerful, in the practice of authorship; and were these to be applied directly in the classroom they could be of immense value. What is needed therefore is a method of ploughing back some of this enriched and fortified talent and realizing its potential benefits in the classroom. It could be done of course by persuading authors – and especially the ex-teachers among them – to return to colleges of education as part-time lecturers, ideally to conduct short courses rather than give occasional lectures. The difficulty there, however, lies largely in the matter of persuasion. Even part-time teaching or lecturing can be terribly demanding on one's time and nervous energy, and the most desirable candidates will largely be those who have already left the profession for that very reason. Consequently, neither wild horses nor substantial fees are likely to bring many of them back in this way. But there is a course that is at once more practicable and cheaper: a study of their works along the lines suggested.

Thus the methods used by children's authors to seize the readers' attention on the very first pages of their books might be adapted by teachers and applied to the first minutes of lessons introducing new topics. From the smoothly, soothingly familiar through the odd or puzzling to the startling and sensational: the elements of such fictional openings would be assessed for their possible value as baits and traps in relation to subject-matter and the age or sex or intellectual capacities of the class. Here, for example, are a few opening passages from stories suitable to be read to quite young schoolchildren:

(a) One day Tim Rabbit found a pair of scissors lying on the common. They had been dropped by somebody's mother, when she sat darning somebody's socks.

Alison Uttley. Ten Tales of Tim Rabbit

(b) Tim Rabbit crept out one night and went exploring. He didn't take a lantern because there were lights everywhere in that countryside for little rabbits to see their way.

Ibid.

(c) Little Maria that morning – and this is a good many years ago now – was dressed in a black and white frock with a flounce to it.

Walter de la Mare. Collected Stories for Children

(d) A man had three sons and he was fond of them all. He had no money, but the house in which he lived was a good one.
'To which of my three boys shall I leave my house?' thought the old man.

Wanda Gag (ed.). Tales from Grimm

(e) The green front door of number thirty-two Windsor Gardens slowly opened and some whiskers and two black ears poked out through the gap. They turned first to the right, then to the left, and then suddenly disappeared from view again.

Michael Bond. Paddington Helps Out

(f) Paddington sat up in bed with a puzzled expression on his face. Happenings at number thirty-two Windsor Gardens, particularly breakfast, always followed a strict time-table and it was most unusual for anything to waken him quite so early.

Ibid.

(g) 'I'll do it all,' said Rodney, holding out his hand for some money. Mother felt in the silky inside of her handbag and brought out a scented ten shilling note.

William Mayne. The Yellow Aeroplane

(h) There was a golden apple-tree and it grew in the king's garden. Every night the apple-tree blossomed and bore golden fruit. But every morning the fruit was gone.
The king said, 'Who will keep watch and catch the thief who steals my golden apples?'

Ruth Manning-Sanders. The Glass Man and the Golden Bird
collection, based on Hungarian folk tales

All of these openings present certain familiar objects and concepts – mothers, scissors, sock-darning, lights in the dark, little girls' frocks, fathers, sons, houses, apples, and so on – and in this respect they are fully in line with the old and perfectly sound pedagogical precept of proceeding from the known, the familiar, the everyday, to the unknown. It is a precept drilled into every student-teacher, and most of them apply it conscientiously throughout their careers, often to lesson material for older children. But although the precept is perfectly sound it can also be damnably dull in its results – as witness those dreary geography topics openings that begin with 'The Food on Your Breakfast Table', embellished but scarcely brightened by pictures of bacon and cereals and sugar and coffee with strings attached to them and inset pictures of pigs or wheatfields or coolies at the other end.

Now in exactly the same way, the openings of stories can be damnably dull when use is made of the same precept, and what is required of course is a touch of imagination, a twist of the familiar, a new cast of light on it, a care to introduce *at once*, if only in a word, a touch of that unknown which is after all the whole purpose of the journey – teacher's or story-teller's – into the unknown. Thus in the first example quoted above the scissors take on a lively significance from the very fact that Tim Rabbit has found them outdoors, and is therefore away from parental super-vision, and could therefore do harm with them if he isn't careful. In the second example he is again alone, this time deliberately escaping parental supervision by *creeping* out. And it is night. In the third example the tone is very low-pitched indeed, but de la Mare saves it from being dull by that one small word 'that' – *that* morning – a morning therefore in which something of moment is going to happen. The dramatic use of the question-raising pronoun in opening sentences is very widespread in all forms of fiction. In (g) we see another example, where the reader is prompted to wonder what the 'it' is that the speaker is going to do on his own. It is a device untranslatable into terms of teaching technique, but the theory behind it – the immediate arousing of curiosity coupled with the promise of something unusual – can be so transferred. So too can the introductory problem – another favourite with authors and a technique widely used by teachers because of its obvious direct peda-gogic applications. Thus the house-money problem in (d) and the tricky double problem of who-done-it and who's-gonna-catch-him in (h). Mystery of a more immediate kind is another common bait – the directly presented mystery of the slowly opening door in (e), or the unusual awakening in (f) for example. Here, however, in the former, we can have another category still, depending on the quickness of the reader or hearer: the pseudo-mystery, or perhaps *mini*-mystery, which will puzzle but intrigue the duller child and delight the quicker, who will be able to anticipate its early solution. This in fact is one of the most useful devices, with its two-way swings-or-roundabouts effect, that any teacher or author can employ.

As children get older, the element of familiarity can with greater safety be played down or dropped altogether, and the puzzle, the oddity, the highly dramatic or astounding be presented nakedly. Most authors are aware of this, and the following examples are typical of thousands of openings in stories for children of 8 and upwards.

(a) The First Lord of the Admiralty was unpopular at Pin Mill.
(*With a bunch of children? Why? Here, in* Secret Water, *Arthur Ransome introduces the unfamiliar without any preamble whatsoever, though the readers would have to be intelligent enough and sufficiently informed to know of the exalted nature of the post.*)

(b) Pushing his belongings in a squealing wheelbarrow Chancy set out for the Ohio River fifty miles away.
(*Sid Fleischman.* Chancy and the Grand Rascal. *The odd use of the vehicle is arresting in itself; the stating of the actual distance snaps on the handcuffs.*)

(c) It was a lovely afternoon during the first week of the summer holidays. Birds warbled, a little breeze bent the heads of the dandelions, and on the window sill of Mrs. Dunn's kitchen a sweet-smelling blackberry and apple pie lay peacefully cooling on a tin plate. Then slowly and silently, from an upper window, a strange contraption began to descend upon the unsuspecting pie.
(*A peach – or should we say a blackberry and apple? – of an opening from Jay Williams and Raymond Abrashkin in their* Danny Dunn on a Desert Island. *How many teachers have harnessed this perfect blend of gleeful anticipation and mystery by opening a topic with a similar silent unannounced demonstration of a similar contraption? Ideal for most scientific topics, obviously, but readily applicable to many others.*)

(d) 'I don't mind it at all! My name is Leonard Dacre Allen, and Leonard means lion-heart; and I am named after Major Dacre, and he is out at Sebastopol, firing cannon-balls every day, and I am never afraid.'
(*The stirring up of gleeful anticipation again, this time indirectly, by the skilful ensuring that the reader shall be aware at once that not only is this a braggart talking, but a very shaky one. Note the question-raising 'it', too. From 'Leonard, the Lion-Heart' by Charlotte M. Yonge, reprinted in* Village Children.)

(e) He woke up suddenly, as if from a deep sleep full of unrecoverable dreams. He was very uncomfortable. The light was too bright, even through closed eyes, and there was something sharp and hard jutting into one of his shoulder blades. His head hurt too.

He moved his right arm in search of something familiar, a sheet or a wall, and found a quite different feeling – hundreds of rough, scratchy lumps on a warm but slimy surface, like iron pimples. Familiar, though – barnacles on a sea rock. He was lying on a rock. He opened his eyes and sat up.

(*The familiar in a most unfamiliar and disturbing light, again with the use of a pronoun to present a minor mystery – in this case the identity of the 'he'. Actually he is a boy who has been accused of witchcraft and sentenced to death by drowning. Many a history lesson could be enlivened by this old fictional device of plunging into the middle of an action at one of its most dramatic points. From* The Weathermonger *by Peter Dickinson.*)

(f) I did not know where I was.

I had awakened, it seemed, to a bright afternoon. No matter in what direction I looked I could see rolling hill country neatly divided up by grey stone walls. Here at my feet – for I was standing at a point where the lane was crossing a ridge so that I was raised above the surrounding country – was a field quite white with daisies. Purple clouds were going along the horizon. Where was I? Never in my life before had I seen this lane nor this field of daisies; yet even as I looked at them they nagged at my memory as though I had previously seen them in a dream.

(*A double mystery – for not only is the narrator puzzled about* where *he is, he soon finds out he is equally perplexed about* who *he is, in this story of pursuit and lost memory,* The Spirit of Jem *by P. H. Newby. And mystery succeeds mystery sentence by sentence in the first pages, as the narrator realizes he has been running hard and wonders why.*)

(g) It was morning, and James Douglas awoke frightened. Perhaps it was because the light had not been turned on, and the morning city light itself was gray and cold, hardly different from early evening. Maybe it was because of the three old women, one bending over the sink, one standing against the wall opposite his bed, one sitting at the table, her head bent over an empty dish. Maybe it was because he had been thinking about how to run away from school when he went to bed the night before. Maybe it was because it was a cold November Monday in Brooklyn. He closed his eyes and pretended to sleep.

(*Yet another awakening scene to open a story with. It is surprising how frequently they occur – as if the author's purpose, to arouse the reader's attention, tended to crystallize itself symbolically in the described situation. But here, in* How Many Miles to Babylon? *Paula Fox handles her mystery rather badly as far as child readers are concerned, for to them it will have no clear-cut solution – as each of Mr Newby's has in the preceding example. It is true that James's frightened feeling, inexplicable though it is, can be psychologically valid, and adult readers would appreciate this. But not children, who are likely to feel let down by such apparent mystification for mystification's sake. Nevertheless, the curiosity aroused by the three old women and the promise of a spell of truancy will probably carry them over their disappointment on the mystery score.)*

Care to make openings arresting is not confined to younger children's fiction, nor should it be confined to younger children's lessons. As aesthetically delicate a writer as Virginia Woolf was by no means above employing a very flamboyantly startling bit of business in the first sentence of *Orlando*. ('He – for there could be no doubt about his sex, though the fashion of the time did something to disguise it – was in the act of slicing at the head of a Moor which swung from the rafters' – which has its educational parallel for me in the occasion when the physical education teacher petrified us seniors one day by unfastening his pants and slipping them down with the words: 'Are you familiar with the use of these?' – to introduce the topic of suspensory bandages as it turned out.) An even more aesthetically abstruse writer, Nathalie Sarraute, regularly opens on a note of subtle multiple mystery (e.g., 'Once again I was not able to restrain myself, I couldn't help it; and although I knew that it was rash of me and that I risked a snubbing, tempted, I went a little too far' – from *Portrait of a Man Unknown*). The seemingly prosaic Trollope was a master of the enticing opening ('In the latter days of July in the year 185–, a most important question was for ten days hourly asked in the cathedral city of Barchester, and answered every hour in various ways – Who was to be the new Bishop?'), while Emily Brontë did much to lighten the reader's burden, or help him to shoulder it willingly, in the extraordinarily but necessarily complex early chapters of *Wuthering Heights*, with this first sentence: 'I have just returned from a visit to my landlord – the solitary neighbour that I shall be troubled with'. But perhaps the opening that sums up the whole question most adequately – with its own enticements built into its cynical dissertation on the subject – is J. D. Salinger's in *The Catcher in the Rye*:

If you really want to hear about it, the first thing you'll probably want to know is where I was born, and what my lousy childhood was like, and how my parents were occupied and all before they had me, and all that David Copperfield kind of crap, but I don't feel like going into it. In the first place, that stuff bores me, and in the second place, my parents would have about two haemorrhages apiece if I told anything pretty personal about them. They're quite touchy about anything like that, especially my father. They're *nice* and all – I'm not saying that – but they're also touchy as hell. Besides, I'm not going to tell you my whole goddam autobiography or anything. I'll just tell you about this madman stuff that happened to me around last Christmas before I got pretty run-down and had to come out here and take it easy.

Many teachers who are faced with the task of presenting material to the Holden Caulfields, the students who *don't* 'really want to hear about it', will have recognized the need to get straight to 'this madman stuff'. Salinger – and other authors of his calibre – will show them how, even where there are no actual madmen.

Capturing the attention of children is one thing; retaining it for comparatively long periods and sometimes over considerable stretches of time, is another. Again it is something a children's author must learn to do in short stories, full-length books and perhaps in serials as well, if he is not to starve or be driven into changing his job. And again teachers – for whom failure in this respect results in suffering rather than starvation or resignation – could learn much from the way authors set about this problem. (Though it should be understood that this comparison in no way disparages teachers, for while the author is under greater compulsion to acquire this expertise he has also the enormous advantage of being able to do it away from the distracting demands on his time and attention that the actual physical presence of his readers, in groups and classes, would create.) Student teachers then might with considerable advantage be invited to study the ways in which successful children's authors *unfold* their narratives and the tricks they use to maintain suspense and, at a gentler level, constantly keep alive the reader's curiosity to know what happens next. As I have suggested more than once already, not all of such devices will be immediately transferable to the teaching situation, in the sense that they can be lifted directly from their context and applied to the form of words a teacher might use to introduce a subject or continue with its discussion. At those stages where direct verbal exposition is used, of course, then such a transfer will be possible. But the main result of a study of this kind will be to alert the student teacher to the constant necessity to arrange and reveal in the most enticing manner possible the facts and ideas he wishes to get across to his class – whether they're to be presented in words or pictures or by demonstration or through activities. The order, the grouping, the holding back here and the darting forward there: these are everything. If they're absent the most potentially exciting historical episode will fall flat; if they're present the description of bottling gooseberries will hold an audience entranced. Careful scrutiny, sentence by sentence and paragraph by paragraph, will reveal how an author achieves this in his own potentially dull patches (usually the 'summary' linking passages between dramatically presented incidents), as we have seen many times earlier in this study, and particularly in Chapter Two. But perhaps the most fruitful areas to scrutinize at first would be the chapter endings, to examine the grip with which an author steers or draws his reader into further instalments of his narrative. An intelligent application of the various devices used here could do much to strengthen links between lessons, especially when a series is required to deal with a single topic.

So far we have been looking at fiction in education in relation to the reader and – in a more specialized way – to the training of student teachers. About the *practice* of fiction in schools and colleges, as it is usually undertaken, I must confess a keen scepticism. As a professional author, with years of experience behind me, I know only too well how difficult it is to work to a schedule, even when the units are days – so much work per day. With authors, this reluctance to sit down to write is often not so much a matter of laziness as of a fear that as soon as they pick up their pens or strike the keys of their typewriters they will begin to distort the concepts and images they wish to convey. Thus this starting difficulty exists even when the incentive and inspiration and ideas are there. How unutterably unreasonable it is, therefore, to expect children to sit down and write, or continue to write, stories during firmly fixed half-hour or forty-five minute periods. How unutterably unreasonable it is indeed to expect them to sit down and remain sitting down at all during such an activity, when grown men and women whose very business it is to write fiction need so often to do other things as part of the process: to pace about, for example; or stand up at a high desk; or play records; or stare out of the window; or lie flat on their backs; or drink three stiff very dry martinis in quick succession; or shout at the cat; or make love to their secretaries; or pick their noses. . . . Especially unutterably unreasonable is this when the children in question haven't the vocabularies, the simple prose technique or sometimes even the basic physical handwriting skills to keep pace with their imaginations, which are so inclined to run away with them when they *are* inspired and ready to go.

And yet countless text books and courses require children to write stories. Even in examinations young candidates are still often required to do this – and on such asinine subjects. As recently as the nineteen-fifties, for example, the determinedly go-ahead British county education authority of Leicestershire was year after year setting 'stories' as subjects in its 11-plus examinations. In some cases beginnings were given, the children being required to hack out suitable middles and ends and tack them on. In others, only slightly less unintelligently, news reports or advertisements were given, and the children asked to build stories from the bare details. As for the nature of the details and situations posited, here is a selection: (*a*) a boy and girl see a man hide something in the chimney of a ruined cottage and then drive away; (*b*) a couple of children are stranded by the tide and forced to spend a night in a cave;

(c) two children come home from a ramble, tired and dirty, their clothing torn, carrying a dead rabbit; (d) a prize rabbit is advertised in Wednesday's paper as having been lost on Monday, and on Monday afternoon Harry Brown finds it. Clearly (a) and (b) are likely to conjure up, and seem to be calculated to conjure up, swag and smugglers and all the paraphernalia of the cheapest kind of professional fiction. The other two are at least more promising in that respect but – without the essential *personal* touch – destined to be pedestrian at their best. How much more interesting and stimulating they would have been had the setters had the imagination themselves to put the subjects squarely in the arena of each child's own personal experience by stipulating in the first case, say, that the two children be 'you and your best friend', and in the second, instead of this Harry Brown nonentity, 'the naughtiest (or laziest, or stupidest) boy in your class.'

It is hardly surprising therefore that the British 'Plowden Report' on Children and their Primary Schools (1966) should have this to say on the subject:

> It is becoming less usual for personal writing to take the form of an invented 'story'. Save for exceptional children who have a story telling gift, and should be given the opportunity to use it, this type of writing tends to be second rate and derivative from poorish material. The great story can change children's ways of looking at the world and at themselves; but poorer story writers often have more influence, in the short run, on children's style because their conventions are mechanical and easily borrowed. In the long term, the quality of children's reading will certainly influence their writing.

> The best writing of young children springs from the most deeply felt experience. They will write most easily and imaginatively about their homes, their hobbies and interests, about things seen and done in science, mathematics, geography and on school visits. When relationships are good, the slower children often achieve most when they have talked over with their teacher the day to day experiences of school and family life. In a few sentences, a child from a fourth stream can portray her mother: 'she is not tall or short and quite ordinary looking. She is patient and good natured and helps us in all we do. She always gives in to my sisters and to me. She says sometimes, she wishes she was dead.'

This is all very well, but unfortunately it misses a far more important point about the educational value of good fiction, which is essentially therapeutic rather than aesthetic. No course involving children in making up stories should aim at turning out polished little story-tellers or impressive material for school magazines or education authorities' shop-window compilations or even for that matter such home-truths as the one quoted, for educationists to get dewy-eyed about and mistake for good writing. Instead the aim should be to derive from such a course that greatest educational value of all, which is – as I have stressed again and again – the stimulating and strengthening of the speculative imagination and therefore of the individual's capacity for human sympathy.

The act of writing imaginatively about people, of seeking to represent truly their probable behaviour in the light of their personalities and environment can radically affect the views of a writer of integrity. Many an author must have been pulled up by the realization that a given character, with a given background, upbringing and set of habits, would not after all really behave in a way that would illustrate so perfectly the author's political or religious ideas. Art has little truck with prejudice, as propagandist authors and their readers have always discovered, and when Arnold Bennett described the really great novelist's essential characteristic as being 'a Christ-like, all-embracing compassion'[1] he was speaking of a professional, technical prerequisite as much as a moral one. Stevenson was rather more explicit:

In all works of art, widely speaking, it is first of all the author's attitude that is narrated, though in the attitude there be implied a whole experience and a theory of life. An author who has begged the question and reposes in some narrow faith cannot, if he would, express the whole or even many of the sides of this various existence; for, his own life being maim, some of them are not admitted in his theory, and were only dimly and unwillingly recognized in his experience. Hence the smallness, the triteness, and the inhumanity in works of merely sectarian religion; and hence we find equal although unsimilar limitation in works inspired by the spirit of the flesh or the despicable taste for high society. So that the first duty of any man who is to write is intellectual. Designedly or not, he has so far set himself up for a leader of the minds of men; and he must see that his own mind is kept supple, charitable and bright. Everything but prejudice should find a voice through him; he should see the good in all things; where he has even a fear that he does not wholly understand, there he should be wholly silent; and he should recognize from the first that he has only one tool in his workshop, and that tool is sympathy.[2]

To help to make and keep minds 'supple, charitable and bright'; to forge the tool of sympathy not simply to equip a few for writing but to equip everybody for living, in all its aspects: this, surely, is what education itself should be about. Fictional projects in schools therefore should

---

1. *The Journals of Arnold Bennett*, quoted by Miriam Allott in *Novelists on the Novel*.
2. *The Art of Writing*, quoted by Miriam Allott in *Novelists on the Novel*.

aim at stimulating the kind of *involvement* that makes a good writer and be relatively unconcerned about the actual finished products. The very acts of production, and of speculation prior to production, are what matter here, and the questions of limited technical ability and talent needn't arise. Indeed, there is hardly any need for the written word at all. Thousands of teachers have for years been helping their students to create fiction of a kind in spontaneous dramatization sessions. Nevertheless, to be really valuable, certain limitations or requirements must be made and certain positive directions be given, even in this form, otherwise the childish running away of the imagination will only take place at a faster gabbled pace.

To illustrate the sort of limitations and requirements that should be made in situations of this kind, and the response they might have, let me describe a project that I developed with a class of about 20 backward boys, whose ages ranged from 12 to 14 (average reading age 8.8, reading age range from 5.8 to 14.0).

As so often happens in teaching, the immediate objectives were comparatively limited and framed without reference to the larger strategic gains that actually resulted. Disturbed by the possibility of certain harmful effects of the boys' private comic-reading, I wished to awaken in them a more critical attitude – indeed, in many cases, *any* critical attitude – towards the subject-matter of the strips. In particular, I wished to expose to them (*a*) the deficiencies of the Cult of the Short-Cut – endemic in the sort of comic books they read – whereby all problems are solved by characters endowed with superhuman powers, usually at the pressing of a button or the donning of a special garment or the utterance of a certain phrase; and (*b*) the lack of individual character in the protagonists, and especially in the heroes and heroines, who, when stripped of their gimmicky trappings and crude distinguishing marks, were pretty well interchangeable from story to story.

Now the type of criticism I wished to foster was of the blunt destructive type, the sort that boys like these could be expected to take to most readily, and even in those days I knew that the best exponents of that form of criticism tended to be those who were themselves practitioners of the criticized art. For it isn't so much a question of professional jealousy as of professional insight, of being able to detect more easily than the non-practitioner the shirked problem, the off-day or the urge to finish a job quickly. Especially the shirked problem, which is of course at the very heart of the Cult of the Short-Cut.

Obviously, I couldn't make practitioners of these boys in the sense that they should draw and script their own comic-strips, any more than I could reasonably expect even the best of them to write their own stories. What they could all do, however, was make up and tell a tale – and consequently it was on oral lines that I conducted the project.

We began with a class tale – a story made up from individual suggestions guided where necessary by me, in much the same way as the more
orthodox 'oral composition' – after I had pointed out that all that was to
happen in the story had to be 'possible', with no ray-guns or magic
cloaks or Bond-type gadgetry. What was more, I insisted that the
protagonists should have distinct personalities of their own, and to ensure
this (to say nothing of adding spice to the venture) I stipulated that the
three principal characters be three of the boys in the class, who were to
behave (or misbehave) throughout the narrative in a manner we should
expect of the three originals. Then I asked for a basic situation (I called
it a 'title') and – since it was early October – someone suggested 'Potato
Picking', which was adopted.

The three boys – whom I shall call A, B and C – I had chosen carefully for their strong characteristics. A was a tall scruffy delightfully
amiable lad with a passion for collecting odd items of junk and the linked
reputation of being an amateur detective. (His most glorious achievement
had been to discover a dismantled Sten gun hidden in a dry-stone wall,
and this had led directly to the arrest of a couple of extremely dangerous
post-office hold-up men.) B on the other hand was the smallest, neatest
and most nervous boy in the class and C was renowned for his sly mischief. So there at once they were in the eyes of the class: B scared of
getting dirty, C throwing potatoes at the other two, and A – what else? –
stumbling over a trail of old coins. This was the first of many storybook
clichés to be dug up with the potatoes – but since we got plenty of argument about what each character was likely to do next, I let them stand:
including the inevitable gang of thieves, the hide-out in the deserted
cottage, the tyings-up, the escapings, and the happy ending in the
police station with its suitable reward. But everything that happened
was possible. Every difficulty was tackled with hands or feet or teeth or
even the bit of broken glass in the corner of the cellar, and not by
the introduction of midget wireless transmitters built into signet rings.
Granted, I had to nudge the narrative in that direction at first, but it
wasn't long before the brighter ones latched on to the idea, shouting
down any stupid short-cut suggestions from the Superman-fixated.

Some of the ideas were excellent, by any standards. In the tale, one
of the boys secretly escaped. (B, because he was the smallest and able to
squeeze through the coal hole – which provoked much laughter because
B was also the fussiest about his appearance.) He set out to fetch help.
At this point I tossed in a bit of atmosphere, suggesting that it was getting
dark and misty. Later, after B had successfully and *plausibly* surmounted
several difficulties, he saw a police car. Here I cut in again to suggest that
a switch of scene back to the cellar would be interesting and could be
made exciting by the robbers' discovery that B had escaped. 'But what,'
I asked, anxious to avoid coincidence almost as much as I wished to

eschew the superhuman, 'would cause one of the robbers to go down into the cellar at this point?' 'Sir,' came the answer, 'you said it was misty, didn't you . . . Well it must be getting a bit cold then, and one of the robbers thinks he'll go down and pinch A's coat.'

The boys, every one of whom had contributed to the tale, were enthusiastic about the project and eager for more. So I obliged by giving them each a simple basic situation (e.g., At the Baths, In the Churchyard, Blackberrying) and a couple of classmates as characters. I allowed them a week in which to make up their tales, after which they were asked in turn to tell them to the rest of the class. The results were predictable. One or two were surprisingly good, others were lame, and some were hopelessly dull. And of course nearly all were about robbers: robbers surprised, robbers triumphant, robbers foiled. There was also quite a lavish use of short-cut devices and flat undistinguished characters. I'd expected that, too, but since each tale was followed by a bout of candid criticism from the class, all was grist to that particular mill.

'They could of been *any* boys, sir!'
'Yergh! He can't even ride a bike, never mind a Nellycopter!'
'Where'd this helicopter come from, anyroad?'

By the time the last boy had gone back to his place, nursing his wounded artistic susceptibilities and muttering protests at his critics, I felt they were ready for the real thing. So I produced a comic-book, described a certain episode (admittedly a juicy chunk of Supermania) and flung it to the critics, who pounced on it just as hungrily as they'd pounced on the tales of their wretched comrades and proceeded to tear it – Superman's cloak and all – to tiny shreds. Then, still pressing on to the critical objective I'd had in mind from the beginning, I got them to look through their own comic-books at home, find particularly stupid passages, bring them to school and explain *why* they thought them stupid.

Looking back, I can't help levelling at myself the same charge for not seeing the very great creative possibilities of the project: the positive benefits that it could bestow by inculcating the habit of sympathetic speculation – of trying to imagine how others, with their limitations, qualities and idiosyncracies, might react in certain situations. Had I done so I might have developed the idea further, making it a regular feature throughout the whole of the two years each group of the boys was with me. As it was, I was content to have achieved the limited objective and to congratulate myself on discovering, as I wrote at the time, that 'a healthy critical attitude' towards what I regarded as the comic's worst elements lay 'not very far beneath the surface of even the dullest schoolboy's consciousness'. What I failed to see – or rather failed to pay due attention to, for it is of course the reverse side of the critical coin – was the healthy potentiality for human sympathy that also lay there, a potentiality that needed only careful regular guided stimulation through the creation of a form of fiction to be fulfilled.

Personally, if I were to be put in charge of similar classes again, I should be prepared to give up large portions of my 'general subjects' timetable to this kind of oral activity – whether in the periods designated for English or those allotted to 'Social Studies' or 'Civics' or even 'Religious Knowledge'. (Isn't the activity described infinitely more valuable spiritually, then, than making clay models of shadoofs, or studying the story of David and Goliath, or tracing geographically the wanderings of the tribes of Israel?) Fortunately, with backward children one's timetables are sufficiently flexible to accommodate such extended projects. With abler children, however, the pressure to pack more academic substance into a timetable is, rightly or wrongly, much heavier. Nevertheless, work along the same lines can be conducted here without poaching any time at all from the more orthodox, often sacrosanct areas of the schedule, and in this the very ability of the children concerned – to write and read with some fluency – could help considerably. Thus, with average-to-bright children of 9 to 11, preliminary oral work in creating fiction in the way described above could be followed by writing, reading and reckoning activities that would continue to stimulate the speculative faculties and create sympathetic habits of mind.

Yet again I must stress that by this I do not mean by the writing of complete stories – an activity unsuitable even for much older children unless they should personally and enthusiastically opt for it. Instead I am thinking of the logistics involved in the creation of fiction: the preparation of the elements, the components, the details of character and background and situation that most professionals have to deal with, consciously or unconsciously, whether in elaborate notes or in jottings on the backs of old envelopes, before they embark on the actual writing of the story. In Chapter Four we saw how seriously and carefully writers like Stevenson and Conrad made such preparations, using maps, charts, tables, lists and so on, and it is work of just this sort – with its involvement in concrete detail – that children find most fascinating. Furthermore, it is the sort of creative work that they will be likely to find most satisfying too, because it can be done in small manageable units of *work that creates its own inspirations* and therefore needn't wait upon a favourable mood.

During the oral story-making sessions preliminary to this, emphasis will naturally have been placed on the familiar: the environment familiar to the children; the characters drawn from what they know of their own friends and acquaintances. On turning to the more advanced written logistical activities, these links with the familiar should still be retained, but with the gradual and balanced introduction of certain unfamiliar elements. Thus a class might be asked to construct new personalities to be introduced into their own environment: a new boy or girl, or a new teacher. This could be done through guided discussion, compositely, by the class as a whole, or by small groups, or by individuals – probably by each method in turn. But the emphasis should in all cases be firmly placed on facts. What are the newcomer's physical statistics and features? How old? How big? How handsome? How healthy? What are his mental characteristics? How clever? How good-tempered? His tastes? His phobias? What is his background? Other members of his family? Where from? What sort of living conditions? And so on and so on. As the basic facts are determined, certain others will begin to suggest themselves, and so the true creative process will have begun – through figures, bare notes, pictures, photographs, maybe graphs and tables and extracts from reference books (in relation to backgrounds and origins, which should always be as geographically valid as possible). And then, when a sufficiently detailed picture of the newcomer has emerged, the final breath of life can be administered by placing him in the known context. How will the young Jasvinder Singh from Karachi – with the qualities and attributes and shortcomings we have given him – react to life in our own town or village, and to being a member of our school and class? How – just as important – will the townsfolk and classmates and teachers we know react to him?

Later, the reverse process can be applied. Villages or parts of towns might be invented, with street-plans, shops, services, local industries all particularized. Danger areas can be added: the treacherous reaches of a river, the road accident black-spot, the condemned buildings. Then into this charted, timetabled territory, known characters – the children themselves and their acquaintances – can be introduced.

The largest fictional units will probably be incidents, and these needn't be spectacular where so much of the fascination lies in the creation of plausible detail and the speculations involved. Many will suggest themselves as the details begin to emerge. How, for instance, will an invented new teacher, endowed with a fiery temper and a phobia about children who talk out of turn, get on with the real young X, who is notoriously unable to hold his tongue when his enthusiasms are aroused. Naturally, the teacher in charge of such a project will be alert for such possible catalysts and inject them, preferably by suggestion, in the early stages wherever possible. And when detailed preparations have been built up and the various natural possibilities explored, there can occasionally be introduced certain given situations: a period of heavy rain followed by flooding, say. How will this affect a certain actual or invented area, or a certain actual or invented person? Or the given catalyst could take the form of an advertisement (and here the 'Lost' notice really will creatively come into its own); or a news report; or even a school report. At first such bolts from the blue, or loudly knocking opportunities, will best emanate from the teacher, but later the children themselves might be asked to provide them – particularly in relation to the characters and environments built up by others.

As I have stressed all along, nothing elaborate need be produced by way of a complete story, fixed and polished for presentation in booklets or the school magazine. In effect, however, something much more elaborate and infinitely more interesting and rewarding will have been built up: a whole complex of potential stories based on a network of sympathetically observed and speculated facts involving such disciplines as mathematics, geography, history and science, as well as English. For – as I have pointed out many times earlier – fiction in its speculative aspect runs through everything in the whole educative and civilizing process, from the simplest arithmetical problem to and beyond the Quantum Theory, just as influentially as it does from the merest pre-pre-pre-primer to and beyond the most abstruse 'Exagmination round His Factification for Incamination' of a literary work in progress.

That is why one of the most important recommendations of the British 'Plowden' committee was for fiction 'to form part of the permanent collection of books in every school' and why every teacher, librarian and parent would do well to bear constantly in mind Paragraph 595 of that committee's report:

> We are convinced of the value of stories for children, stories told to them, stories read to them and the stories they read for themselves. It is through story as well as through drama and other forms of creative work that children grope for the meaning of the experiences that have already overtaken them, savour again their pleasures and reconcile themselves to their own inconsistencies and those of others. As they 'try on' first one story book character, then another, imagination and sympathy, the power to enter into another personality and situation, which is a characteristic of childhood and a fundamental condition for good social relationships, is preserved and nurtured. It is also through literature that children feel forward to the experiences, the hopes and fears that await them in adult life.

There was really no need for the committee to continue into the tautology and banality of the next sentence: 'It is almost certainly in childhood that children are most susceptible, both to living example and to the examples they find in books.' The question of example is a relatively minor one and its citation a hangover from the days when education was regarded as a largely passively receptive process and not the dynamic creative giving and taking process it must be. As I hope this study has helped to prove, the committee had already accurately assessed the immense potential value of fiction in education when they spoke of the preservation and nurturing of 'the power to enter into another personality and situation'.

Appendices

Appendix A

Some notes on the editing of British and American English in children's stories

The need for good Anglo-U.S. relations has probably never been greater than it is today. In this connection few people to whom the matter occurs at all will deny the importance of a regular interchange of children's books between the two countries. Good relations are based on understanding, and true understanding – deep and instinctive – is best developed at an early age: fostered unconsciously as a by-product of continuing sympathetic interest. And since, in books, sympathetic interest is aroused most naturally and strongly by well-presented fictions, the work of authors, editors and publishers in this field deserves the greatest consideration in two of the main senses of the word: careful thought by the technicians involved and a measure of respect and encouragement from the various official representatives of the two nations. My immediate concern here is with the former.

The problem facing the technicians (authors, editors, publishers) revolves around changes in texts: whether to make them or not, and, if so, to what extent. The arguments for and against – often quite forcefully put and staunchly maintained – vary in quality. On the anti-change side the most cogent is the one that insists on retaining the national flavour, the individuality, the quiddity of a British or American story. After all – the upholders of this line generally continue – that is where the great value of such a book lies in the field of international relationships: in its ability to present and hopefully to teach something of the country of origin's way of life. A less positive argument on the anti-change side, but one that still deserves respect, is that put forward by some Britishers: 'We had to adapt as children to the idioms of American films – why shouldn't they go to the same trouble over our books?' Another British anti-change argument – far less worthy of serious attention but one that is put forward with great emotive force and must therefore be taken into account – is the snobbish one that equates anything American with cheapness, shoddiness, meretriciousness. This most often arises in the neighbouring field of historical film drama, with some such outraged or derisive cry as: 'They even had Christ (or Genghis Kahn) speaking with a Texan (or Brooklyn) accent!' – as if the originals themselves had in fact spoken pure Oxford (or Cockney).

On the pro-change side the arguments are usually less emotional and the range is narrower. There are, at one end of the scale, the authors, publishers and editors who are anxious to remove *all* the possible causes of difficulty in *any* work. These are the players-for-safety who pursue what might be called the line of least sales resistance – usually relying on slick packaging and promotion to ensure a steady turnover – and whose accountancy systems leave little scope for either careful and prolonged authorial-editorial deliberation or the taking of calculated risks. For all the lasting international-cultural impact their products make they might just as well stick to native work (which they usually do, unless some particularly profitable deal can be swung by using foreign plates or texts or printing arrangements). At the other end of the pro-change spectrum, however, there is the argument that is as much artistic as commercial or educational: that difficulties great enough to disrupt the reader's willing suspension of disbelief too severely (i.e., severely enough to make him lose interest in the story) are to be avoided at all costs.

Authors are as a rule anti-change on principle. They know, either instinctively or through experience, that quite often even a single word cannot be changed without causing a displacement in the context – a displacement that is more or less undesirable but which must at any rate be taken care of. Now many editors are unaware of this. They may feel, with justification, the need for a change to be made, but unless they also make whatever delicate but *telling* readjustment may be necessary in the context, something of value will be lost. All the author sees at first, when such an uncompensated-for change has been made without his consent, is the loss. So, the United States being some 3,500 miles away from Britain, frustration, exasperation and anger often result, with tedious consequences, and an over-jealous artistic author's behaviour will tend to mirror that of the cooler over-commercial publisher. While the latter says, 'Change everything that is unfamiliar to the readers and so be on the safe side', – he will, for a similar safeguarding reason, say 'Change nothing'. But in my view the more important artistic consideration remains: in transferring a children's book from one country to another some changes really are necessary and the fact that they can be troublesome to deal with (though they *needn't* be, as I hope to show) is irrelevant.

But what sort of special factors make for the irksomeness mentioned above?

Broadly speaking, there are three:

1. The very distance involved. To be completely satisfactory to both sides, proposed editorial changes should be discussed between the two parties, with reasons and/or objections carefully explained. Ideally this should be done face to face or at least over the telephone. To deal with such matters by correspondence, going into all the relevant details with the delicacy and tact often required in such a situation, can be prohibitively time-consuming.

2. Individual limitations. This is where the delicacy and tact mentioned in *1* above come in. Editors (and authors) are rarely fully conversant with *all* the differences in language, customs, flora, fauna, etc. within their own country. In the U.S. this is particularly exacerbated by the very size of the country. Thus a British friend of mine could complain that a relative's book was turned down by one American editor because much of the interest was centred on owls – and 'American children were not familiar with that bird'. Now possibly owls are rare in those parts of the country that editor lived in and came from – but America is, after all, the land of Owl Creek, with some thirty species listed in most of its bird books. Had the issue been concerned with change rather than rejection, it is easy to see how tempting it would have been for the indignant author to write quoting such an authority as Roger Tory Peterson and giving a list beginning with the Acadian Owl, the American Hawk Owl, the Arctic Horned Owl, and on through the Barred, the Boreal, the Burrowing, the three Floridas, the Montana and the Nebraska, to the two Texans and the Western Burrowing. With or without a stiffening of invective (e.g., 'And anyway, dummy, there are thousands of British kids who never see or hear owls from one year's end to the next – and that didn't invalidate the book over here, did it?'), such a counter-correction would be hard to take in a letter (especially in a firm where correspondence passes through other hands and a simulation of editorial omniscience is obligatory) – whereas over the telephone or, better still, a quiet drink, the matter could be speedily, satisfactorily and even good-humouredly settled.

The owl instance is an extreme one, granted, but within my own experience similar types of difficulties have arisen, though these were generally settled happily, on the spot. Once it was the introduction of a ferret that was in dispute, with one editor (a Chicago man) saying there was no such animal in the States and that American children would therefore be perplexed by its appearance even in a British setting, and another editor (from rural upstate New York) scornfully asking him where the hell he'd been brought up, never to have seen a ferret. Similarly, I have known conflicts of opinion between Americans over the native use of 'shop' and 'store', 'clerk' and 'assistant', 'toward' and 'towards', and many other pairs involving apparently hard-and-fast Americanisms.

3. Manufacturing processes. When a British book is taken by an American publisher, or vice versa, one of two processes is usually followed: either (a) it is reset and reprinted entirely; or (b) the original type is used. In the case of (a) no special technical difficulties are involved when making necessary alterations. The original copy is used as a manuscript on which the amendments may be marked in the usual way, and the new edition is set up from that. But with (b) – which is cheaper and therefore quite frequently adopted by smaller publishers – the process becomes more complicated. Making changes to the existing type is rather like making changes to page proofs: within certain narrow limits whatever is substituted must take up a similar amount of space to that taken up by the original word or phrase or passage. So while 'toward' for 'towards', or 'honor' for 'honour' presents no real problem to the editor, it requires great verbal dexterity to provide substitutes for idiomatic expressions, or the explanatory amplifications or contextual reshufflings required to make certain native customs or usages comprehensible to the non-native reader. Sometimes in these cases recourse is had to a prefatory chapter, sometimes to a glossary, sometimes to footnotes – but when the material is part of a story, a delicately balanced fiction, a fragile other-world, whatever method is chosen and whatever the ingenuity of the editor, the author's close collaboration is essential if too many disjunctive bumps are to be avoided. (And one such bump, if big enough, is one too many, it must be remembered.)

But what of the changes themselves?

Processes, distances and individual personal susceptibilities apart, what special difficulties of judgement are likely to be met with here?

On the face of it, spelling and punctuation should present none. The substitution of 'traveling' for 'travelling' or the use of double quotation marks instead of singles is hardly likely to make any calculable difference to the flow or feel of a story. Personally, wherever American or British usage permits two forms of spelling the same word, I prefer the one that is common to both languages (for instance, 'theatre' rather than 'theater'), but I should never waste time disputing such a point if an editor should hanker after the exclusively American spelling. After all, most professional authors frequently make such stylistic concessions inside their own country whenever similar but indigenous alternatives are decided according to the 'house style' of the publisher concerned. But although an author may regard such matters as trivialities, he will, if he is artistically conscientious, become far more cautious in his judgements the moment they have to be applied *between* quotation marks, single or double. In works of non-fiction, for instance, it should be regarded as more than a quirk of academic punctiliousness to insist on printing a quoted passage exactly as originally written, whether according to

British or American usage. Most American editors would, I think, see the sense of this and be prepared to respect it. (Up to a point, anyway – that point being the punctuation mark that would normally occur just after a quotation in a sentence containing that quotation, where, according to strict American usage, it would be brought within the inverted commas, as if the original writer had used it.) In works of fiction this respect for what was originally said or written (or supposed to have been said or written) is even more important. Thus, in a story set in Britain, it would be completely illogical to Americanize the spelling of a quoted letter, supposedly written by an Englishman, or of a quoted extract from a British newspaper or public notice. And, similarly, even though there is every justification for Americanizing the spelling of something a British character *says* (since spelling is directly relevant only to written language and not to speech), it would be quite wrong to Americanize the idiom or the usage of certain words, for then the author and/or editor would be perpetrating one of the basic errors in fiction-writing, by having someone speak 'out of character'. Granted, a child-reader may be puzzled by certain idiomatic expressions or forms of words presented in this way, but in this case he will be *prepared to be puzzled* – he will not be surprised to find a foreigner using strange terms, he will indeed rather expect it. Consequently there will not occur the disruption that would have attended the same perplexity had it cropped up in a narrative passage, where it would have reminded him forcibly of the actual *writer* rather than the supposed *speaker*.

Sometimes, of course, a character's speech may be so shot through with strange idiom that it slows down a reader's progress to a mechanically dangerous pace – to the pace at which the thread of a narrative is lost. Indeed, this can happen with British readers confronted with too much of some British dialect they are unfamiliar with. In such cases then, the sensible thing would seem to be to replace some of the idiom with plain speech – but plain speech that is universal English, not American. Again the same problem may be magnified to the point where a publisher has to decide to change nothing or not publish a work at all. I am thinking here of the sort of story that is supposedly a written account made by one or more of the characters – a narrative in letter- or diary-form, or an autobiographical chronicle of some other kind. When a good fiction-writer chooses such a form, he does so because it is important that the reader believes, if only for the duration of the reading, that this really is a diary, or series of letters, etc. But if the supposed writer is an Englishman and, for no specified reason, he is presented as writing American English, the precious illusion is soon destroyed.

Another aspect of Anglo-American editing of children's books requiring very careful handling arises in relation to differences of a social or political kind. Shall the words 'City Hall' be substituted for 'Town

Hall', for instance, or 'Police Chief' for 'Chief Constable'? What does one substitute for the British 'grammar school' or 'public school'? How does one deal with GCEs, O-levels and A-levels? Once again I would insist that no American-for-British exchange take place within the supposed utterances of a British character. Outside the quotation-marks, however, such changes could be made, I think, provided that the Town/ City Hall or police officer is merely mentioned in passing and the actual designation doesn't have a special bearing on the course of the story. With school systems, admittedly, the borderline between background and significant detail is straddled. For example, when one points out, even in passing, that a British child character goes to a grammar or public school, one is making a certain statement about that child's level of intelligence or social background. One may consider it very much to the credit of the Americans that there is no equivalent ready indicator in their society, but it makes it terribly hard for a British author and his American publisher when it is necessary for them to make the same point without long, complicated explanations to the reader – even supposing that the book is to be completely reset and there is the necessary space at their disposal.

But at this point it would perhaps be more instructive if I were to give a summary of all the alterations that were felt to be necessary in preparing a book of my own for the U.S. public, with an account of some of the factors that were taken into consideration in a few of the more difficult cases, and – most important of all – a description of our methods of working.

The book in question was *Louie's Lot*, published in Britain in 1965. It was my thirteenth children's novel and none of its predecessors had at that time been published in the U.S. According to the various agents and British publishers handling American rights, this had not been for want of their trying – but in every case their attempts had been met with a reiterated 'too British for the American market'. For a time it looked as if *Louie's Lot* would meet with the same response, in spite of my personal hope that this would be the book to make the breakthrough. My reasons for this hope were fundamental: the leading character being a milkman whose enterprise and initiative had in them something typically American. When, however, I expressed this hope to my British publisher, one of the people handling American rights there wrote back as follows: '. . . although I enjoyed it enormously, I don't really feel that it is something we will be able to sell in America. This is simply because the younger generation in America have never heard of milk bottles as all their milk arrives in paper cartons!'

This was, in fact, incorrect. There are still many places in America where milk comes in bottles. And even if it had been true, it was hardly a valid point: lack of direct experience of a thing cannot be equated with not having *heard* of it; while lack of experience, direct or indirect, is no barrier to one's becoming interested in a story. But authors tend to be hypersensitive in matters of this sort, and, not realizing then that the basic premise was factually incorrect, I allowed my hopes to be damped.

In the following year, however, I accepted an invitation to work in the U.S. for a spell and, after living and working there for some time, I managed to get various publishers interested in some of my British books. The result was that early in 1967 *Louie's Lot* was accepted by an American firm – the first of my children's books to make the journey. Needless to say, it was a source of great satisfaction to me, particularly in the light of the British publisher's remarks, and at the time I was inclined to put the success down entirely to personal initiative on my part and the previous lack of success down to shortcomings in those making earlier attempts to sell my work over there. I now feel that in this I was a good bit off the mark. My presence in America helped, certainly, but not so much on account of any winning quality of personality or skill in promoting my work as *because I was there on the spot to deal with all the editorial queries likely to arise.*

These were numerous. In all there were over 250 small but necessary changes to be made and, since this was a case in which the American publisher was to print from the British plates, each substitution had to fill approximately the same amount of space. By letter this would have gone on for months, consuming many working hours on both sides of the Atlantic. By telephone it would have cost a fortune. And, because of the aforementioned element of tact that is invariably called for in such matters, there would have been a constant danger of misunderstandings.

As it was, the task couldn't have been accomplished more speedily, economically or pleasantly. The American editor went through his copy at leisure, marking all suggested alterations and queries, and then – when he was ready to discuss them – I spent a couple of hours with him one Sunday morning at his home, going through them one by one – agreeing to some, rejecting others, and in each case reaching a mutually satisfactory solution. He respected my knowledge of the British setting and, above all, of the characters I had created; I respected his knowledge of the American language and the child readers there. And – in the light of what I have written both in this appendix and elsewhere in the book about too-facile judgements – I think it not irrelevant to add that as we sat there working on the book that Sunday morning, not forty miles from New York City, we were interrupted by the rattling of bottles as the milk deliveryman came up the drive!

The alterations fell roughly into six main categories, some of them overlapping: *Spelling, Money, Geographical, Social, Usage,* and *Idiom.* They may be broken down as follows:

Spelling
Surprisingly few words were involved. To be precise, there were two: *honour* and *centre* – though there were several instances of each. This is somewhat unusual in a story of this length (about 30,000 words) and may perhaps be explained statistically by the fact that I had deliberately restricted the vocabulary in the first place. Thus there were fewer chances of divergence in spelling.

Money
Since the book concerned a milk round all the activities involved in such a business, money – and particularly the collecting of money – played rather a large part. So again, although there were few actual words or phrases in need of changing, there were recurring instances of each. Colloquialisms such as *bob* and *quid* were translated into *shillings* and *pounds* in most cases, and allowed to stand only in the few places where their meaning was apparent from the context. (And even here it was necessary to explain to my American friend that these particular colloquialisms always take the singular case.) With *pounds* itself it was also deemed necessary to slip in the words *in cash* whenever there was the possibility of a confusion with pounds in weight. All mention of *half-crowns* or *half-a-crown* had to go, lest any remaining confusion be worse confounded, thus anticipating the country of origin's switch to decimal currency.

Geographical
Very little explanatory change was necessary here – the action taking place wholly in a single close urban setting. Since it was obviously a *British* town, we decided that most of the main points of difference would be taken for granted by an American child anyway. There was one instance, however, in which an ingrained habit of thought might have proved confusing. I had written at one point: *You could never tell with the weather*. But in most parts of the American land-mass meteorological conditions are in fact pretty stable and predictable, so the potential mystery was cleared up by the insertion of the word *English* in front of *weather*.

Social
As already hinted, references to the English school system caused some difficulty here. Most of the boys seeking jobs with Louie on the milk round go to the local secondary modern school. But to make the comically expressed but nevertheless serious point that a job with Louie made certain intellectual demands and was much valued by the boys, their parents and local employers as an excellent character-training ground, I had included a number of grammar-school boys, as former helpers and

as candidates for a vacancy. In the educationally much more democratic context of the United States, these differences would have been meaningless, unless carefully explained. Fortunately, the story didn't once have to take the reader into any of the actual school premises, so references to modern and grammar schools were silently obliterated. Some of the original point was lost, but where the essential official difference between a grammar-school boy and a secondary-modern-school boy did have to be stressed we reverted to the basics. Thus, when Louie starts upbraiding a grammar-school boy for making a mistake in a calculation (albeit a deliberate one), and the following exchange takes place in the British version:

'You go to the Grammar, don't you?'
'Yes.'
'You taken your G.C.E. yet?'
– we decided to change it to:
"You think you're a brainy kid, don't you?"
"Yes."
"You taken your exams yet?"

Time and again, when considering changes in this category, I have come across a similar kind of democratic bringing-down, often from a pompous or portentous level – a sort of gentle musket-echo from the War of Independence. Personally, I found it rather pleasant in this case to join in when demoting a *Lord Mayor* to a more readily identifiable *Mayor*, lower-casing the *Law Courts*, and transforming a *master* into a *teacher*. As an ex-National Serviceman I was delighted though astonished to find that a *charge* – in the sense of *putting someone on a charge* – would be incomprehensible to American children, even if as an author I was hard put to it to find a substitute. On the other hand, it gave a much less favourable glimpse of the American social and political background when the words *niggled* and *niggly* had to be changed to *needled* and *jumpy*, because of their quite fortuitous and etymologically completely unconnected reminiscence of the word *nigger*. British purists might scoff at such a change's being requested, let alone acceded to. Admittedly, it is fundamentally illogical – if the foundation referred to is a strictly verbal one. But there is such a thing as the logic of situation, which in this instance I read thus: the word *is* reminiscent of *nigger*, *nigger* is a most violently explosive word in the U.S., its use can cause great physical suffering, many children are not capable of reasoning in this way before using it, this is a children's book, therefore let's by all means use a less potentially harmful substitute. Had this been a novel for intelligent adults, British or American, I should probably have insisted on retaining the words in exactly that form on the grounds that it is more harmful to make such concessions to ignorance at that level than it is to risk even violent misunderstanding. In short it is yet another instance of

what I consider to be a case of a children's writer's *special* responsibility
to his readers.

Usage and Idiom

By far the largest number of alterations came into these two categories,
which, because of their close relationship, I have combined here. Some
of the commonest will be familiar to most people who read fairly widely
and keep their ears open when listening to American dialogue on the
screen, whether or not they have any direct experience of the U.S. Thus
round became *around; towards,* toward (though I understand the former
is still often preferred in some Southern states); *had got to, had to; lorry*
or *van, truck* (though *van* is retained for furniture removal vehicles);
chemist, druggist (in the sense of a shop-keeper who sells drugs etc.);
ladder (in a stocking), *run; biscuits, crackers* (though *dog biscuits* would
have been all right); *zip, zipper; pumps, sneakers; braces, suspenders;*
jersey, sweater; banger, firecracker; and the old perennial, *two weeks* for
fortnight. And of course, the subject being what it was, the substantive
round (as in *milk* or *paper round*) cropped up on nearly every page, to be
changed to *route.* Rather less common than any of the foregoing, but
still occurring quite frequently, were such words as *verge* (of road),
which became *edge; rise* (in wages) becoming *raise;* cigarette *ends, butts;*
bottom (of lane), *end;* and such constructions as *got to know,* which was
changed to *heard; doing sums, figuring* (with attendants like *tot up* changed
to *add up,* and *get it to* becoming *figure it at*); *call round, stop in; go on*
(as in 'How did you go on?'), *make out; going on* (as in 'How are you
going on?'), *doing.* Where colloquialism crystallized into slang the
changes that had to be made were often drastic. For *blower* we had to
revert to *phone,* there being no commonly-known equally-colourful
equivalent; *fly customer* was tamed into *wise guy; mix things* became *make*
trouble; telly, TV; packed in, finished; a bother on, trouble; mucking
about, fooling about; he's not half mad, he's mad; get set on, get the job;
smarmy, fancy; shower, rabble; dafter, crazier; chip in, interrupt. Indeed,
as the work proceeded, it became quite interesting to me to note how
very conservative the Americans often are in this respect compared to
the British – contrary to the common pre-war schoolteachers' com-
plaint about an almost total American slanginess.

Regarding logic or taste, sometimes the American expression seems
to have the edge, sometimes the British. For example, to speak of a
cigarette *butt* where we should say cigarette *end* is an improvement in
that it makes for greater precision. (The *end* could mean the lighted
end.) But while the adherence to a universal *around* helps a writer to
avoid such semi-comic ambiguities as *the fat man looked round,* it does
strike me as giving a pedantically blurred edge to such statements as
he went the long way around. Similarly, just as I was glad to be rid of the,

to me, faintly irritating British use of *that* in such expressions as *just that bit tighter* (irritating when used to excess by presumptuous salesmen, from the door-to-door drummer to the glossary magazine ad-writer, in such exhortations as 'Save now for that holiday abroad!'), which became *just a bit tighter*, I regretted the loss involved in having to delete in such statements as (of a tall man) *and he was broad with it*, the last two words, which seem to me to add another dimension to the description (with an oblique reference to tall men in general).

It will probably not have gone unnoticed that a certain element of bowdlerization crept into one or two of the changes already mentioned – or, to be more precise, a form of back-dated or archeological bowdlerization. For instance, many British people who normally wouldn't dream of swearing will blithely call some group of whom they don't approve *a shower*, without realizing that this originated as one of the drill-sergeant's favourite descriptions for a bunch of new recruits (a *shower of shit*); while *mucking about* has similar vulgar origins. Perhaps it is some national trait – call it a faculty for compromise, or hypocrisy, or a readiness to turn a blind eye – that allows such expressions to be adopted so unquestioningly over here, but with the Americans the tendency is, as in other areas of life, all or nothing. As if to illustrate this, as well as compensate me for the suppressed *shower* etc., the editor offered me a round 'Oh damn!' where I had originally written a mild 'Oh heck!'

Such corporate unintended obscenities and profanities are one thing – they might well have slipped past young American readers as they often get by mature English non-swearers. But the unilateral unintended obscenity is another matter. By this I mean the word or phrase that is perfectly innocent in one language or society but is palpably obscene in another. Quite apart from any moral attitude he may have on the question, a fiction-writer, like a schoolteacher, simply cannot allow such slips to occur. They are too disruptive. The mood, the suspension of disbelief, the whole atmosphere can be shattered beyond repair by them. So I was doubly grateful to my editor for saving my milkman's moral character by having him, in the course of his duties, *wake* people up in the morning rather than *knock* them up (which, to U.S. ears, would mean having sexual intercourse with these customers). Not actually obscene, rather less open to misconstruction, but nonetheless potentially distracting in a surrealist way, were the numerous references to Louie's *fags* (U.S. slang – with *faggots* – for homosexuals) – which became, with alacrity, *cigarettes* again (there being no common colloquial equivalent). And amusing though these instances may seem (and indeed *were*, as far as we were concerned) it is not difficult to imagine the embarrassment they might have caused if they'd had to be dealt with by correspondence, at a distance of 3500 miles, between total strangers.

Of the remaining changes, two or three are of special interest in other ways. The alteration of *pin tables* to *pinball machines*, for instance, reminded me again that it is we supposedly more leisurely British who tend more to abbreviate (c.f. our deplorable *fridge* for refrigerator, or *zip* for *zipper*). I was also intrigued, from a socio-cultural point of view, to find that a reference to *comics* as a place where one usually finds jokes would not do. Nor would *comic strips*. Apparently in the U.S. these have lost so much of their original exclusive affinity to humour that the link had to be more precisely determined. Hence – since the word occurred in dialogue – an example of a humorous strip well-known in both countries had to be found, with Louie eventually upbraiding his giggling assistants with: 'If you want jokes there's the TV. . . . Or the Andy Capp strips. In your own time. Not the Dairy's time. . . .' Another interesting social comment is, I'm sure, bound up in the change we had to make from *slimming* to *dieting*. Judging from this, the American woman is more pragmatic and far less optimistic about the outcome of whatever weight-reducing programme she embarks on. At all events it seems to me to be preferable on grounds of verbal accuracy, as indeed do so many American alternatives.

The reason for the rather unusually high incidence of idiomatic changes in this particular book was that it was written in a colloquial, easy, story*telling* style – with a narrator other than the author himself lurking just below the surface. This meant that idiomatic expressions appeared frequently in the narrative passages, where, for the reasons discussed above, they had to be dealt with far more drastically than those appearing in the dialogue. On the other hand, it did mean that I could introduce, quite naturally, a new short opening chapter, in the same chatty tone, preparing the reader for some of the more intractable peculiarities of the English scene – and fortunately room could be found for the extra couple of pages even though, as I mentioned earlier, this was a case where the American publisher was using the British plates.

Since then I have approached the problem from several different directions. Some of my British books have been completely reset and reprinted, giving me wider scope in the actual physical process of making alterations – enabling me to rewrite whole passages where necessary, in order to preserve the original British flavour and yet make my meaning clear to young Americans without breaking the illusion or altering the storyline. Often this can be done quite simply and economically by rearranging the context slightly to make the meaning self-evident, or by offering – where stylistically possible (as in the colloquial *Louie* narrative) – short bursts of synonyms. Here is an example from *Louie's S.O.S.*, where the sentence:

And you can't make enemies without one of them, one day, trying to nobble you

became:

. . . trying to fix you, frame you, nobble you

– thus enabling me to retain throughout the book that pleasant, colourful and very versatile British colloquialism. Similarly the money question in *Louie's S.O.S.* could be very neatly settled through dialogue, with:

'You promised me another quid when the job was finished'
becoming:

"You promised me another quid when the job was finished. Another pound, Winks. Another twenty shillings"

– which is perfectly in keeping with the speaker's impatient finger-flicking tone. A far less satisfactory method was applied to some of my *Birdy Jones* books, however. This was another deal involving the use of British publisher's plates, but instead of making individual alterations to fit the spaces, it was decided to leave the British text as it was and have footnotes do the work of interpreting. At the time, the idea appealed to me as a literary experiment – an attempt to use footnotes in a humorous way – but it failed because to do each of these books the same justice as was done to *Louie's Lot* would have required far too many footnotes for comfort – artistic or physical. (Many of the bottom margins would have had to be two or three inches wide to accommodate the extra material!) In the event, too many words and phrases had to be left unexplained.

My conclusions, then, are as follows. The best way of preparing a British children's story for the American public is for the author to make the changes himself, preferably after some direct experience of living in the U.S., in close collaboration with a native editor with whom it is possible to have on-the-spot consultation. (Naturally, it also helps immensely to enlist the aid of an American child, of the appropriate age, to read the British version and make notes of all perplexities – though care should be taken to allow for any *individual* limitations or blind-spots the child may have.) Ideally, the book should be completely reprinted (i.e., the type itself reset) and, wherever possible, the use of footnotes or glossaries avoided. A similar process holds good, of course, when preparing an American children's book for the British public.

Finally, two corollaries.

(1) Reverting to my original observation concerning the valuable contribution an interchange of children's fiction can make in the field of Anglo-American relations, perhaps the best course of all would be for children's authors to write at least some of their stories directly for the transatlantic market – presenting British characters in an American setting, or vice versa – and so avoiding any necessity for the kind of surgery, elegant or otherwise, discussed above.

(2) Bearing in mind the considerable amount of delicate and concerted work required on the part of author and editor in *satisfactorily* preparing a book for a foreign *English*-speaking public (i.e., preserving

its general interest without sacrificing its specifically national qualities) one can only wonder at the destructive possibilities likely to be involved when a work is translated into a language the author doesn't understand. Alerted by my researches into the Anglo-American question while preparing this Appendix, I was moved to puzzle out a few pages of one of my translated books in a language I am – to put it at its best – least unfamiliar with. I was horrified at the amount of crude compression that had obviously been perpetrated – at the reduction of the original to a bare almost synoptic storyline. Most contracts giving a licence for translations carry a clause insisting on their being 'faithful to the original', with no unauthorized cuts etc., and it seems to me that the time has come for the people handling an author's subsidiary rights – whether literary agents or the original publishers themselves – to pay much closer attention to the quality of work appearing under that author's name in other languages. After all, quite apart from the moral issues involved in such matters of stewardship, it is in the long run the regard in which that name is held by the reading public in any country that determines the size of the financial returns from which an author's representatives take their cut.

Appendix B

A further note on illustrators and the 'kids' stuff' complex

Although the following extract concerns a sub-editor's work on a women's magazine, it underlines horribly amusingly a tendency that may sometimes be detected in the work of those who illustrate children's books. Happily, book editors tend on the whole to have a less cavalier attitude towards their basic material. Note, incidentally, the feeling underlying the final paragraph quoted, illustrative of another point made in Chapter Two.

Subs had to wait for illustrations to come in before cutting stories or serials because the passages that had inspired the drawings were lifted out for captions. Sometimes an artist, clearly unmoved by the narrative, slapped down whatever came into his head. Since artists never ever redraw, many a baffled sub has stared down at some lavish piece of art work, striving to find a connexion. If we couldn't, what we had to do was insert a telling bit of prose which linked drawing to tale. The story couldn't be changed so it wasn't always easy. Someone once, faced with a mysterious picture of a girl distractedly pushing her hand into her hair and glaring across the dinner table at a man swigging his wine, wrote, ' "Stop," cried Julie. "That's my ear you're drinking!" ' But it never got in. . . .

Then they put me in charge of the kiddies' corner and I sat there being auntie something-or-other, cursing and judging finger-paintings from the under-eights until I got quite fond of them.

(From an article by Harriet Chare about her experiences on the staff of *Modern Woman. The Times*, 9 March 1970.)

181

And for a similar striking of the 'kids' stuff' note, consider the following, which came at the end of an account of the work of the novelist and critic Janice Elliott:

> All her books now take around nine months, no matter how long they happen to be.
> She sits at her big upright typewriter overlooking the pond and the quince tree every weekday morning from 10 till two. Sometimes she works weekends as well.
> The only book that did not take around nine months was *The Birthday Unicorn*. Maybe being a children's book had something to do with it, but it took only three weeks.

So the old fallacy is trotted out once more – in *The Times* again, too – this time by Malcolm Winton. Why, one wonders, didn't it occur to him that since the book was considerably shorter than Miss Elliott's adult novels it naturally took less time to write – just as an adult short story would take less time to write?

Appendix C

Some further examples of good narrative technique employed outside prose fiction

1. The unfolding of a process exploited in a stage play
The following is an extract from a newspaper article discussing a new play:

One of the most absorbing experiences in theatre-going which has recently come my way was to sit in at David Storey's 'The Contractor' at the Royal Court, watching that now famous marquee being put together and subsequently dismantled. Every criticism of the piece that I have read has borne witness to the compulsive interest of its action. . . .

It is a plotless play. Yes, but is it? The building of that marquee in the first two acts, and its dismantling in the third, constitutes a plot in itself. It holds your attention enchained while a complicated action is carried through, and it's only with an effort – I'm speaking here only for myself – that you can pay attention to the chatter of the human beings involved. It is a plain, absorbing documentary. Yes, but is it? If your taste is for symbolism, you can read into it as much as you please, and make it an allegory of human life.

Alternatively, it is an example of Mr Storey's sense of character. Well, perhaps. It's true that the chattering humans who cause the rise and subsequent fall of the big tent ring true when you have time to think of them. But it was their characteristics rather than their characters that the author showed us.

No, none of the labels will stick. All one can say is that while this piece certainly hasn't a plot in the ordinary sense of the term, Mr Storey has found for it as perfect a plot-substitute as can ever be devised. It has enough simplicity to commend it to the general public, enough complexity to please more demanding tastes.

W. A. Darlington. *Daily Telegraph*, 3 November 1969.

For an equally good example of a modern British process-tracing play, the writer could have mentioned Arnold Wesker's *The Kitchen*, with its enthralling study of a morning's work in the kitchen of a large London restaurant, where the action – or the plethora of concerted actions – rises to a crescendo as the porters, the butchers, the vegetable cleaners, the various chefs and waitresses cope with the lunchtime rush. In Wesker's later – and to my mind much weaker – play, *Chips with Everything*, the highlight for many critics and playgoers was a scene in which the intricate process of stealing coke from an RAF camp's fuel dump is traced through.

2. Expertise as entertainment

Although marquee builders *per se* haven't yet taken to the stage as entertainers in their own right, certain other types of experts have. Perhaps the best-known are those who appear regularly on television with cookery or gardening or do-it-yourself hints. Naturally, a basic interest in the skills involved will account for a certain amount of the following – but it is the experts who attract large general audiences, including hundreds of thousands of people not particularly interested in preparing food or potting plants or fixing pelmets, who will offer the most pertinent examples of the skilful use of narrative technique. 'Personality' does enter into it of course, and so does a flair for showmanship. Mrs Fanny Cradock's evening dresses (in the kitchen!) form a case in point. But even more important as far as her performances are concerned is the care she takes to highlight special difficulties before they occur in the demonstration – to present the awful possibility in good time, to cross the tightrope bridges before she gets to them. 'And now we come to the *really* tricky bit. . . .' 'This *should* rise into a light crisp batter. . . .' 'And that's the reason . . . (*pause while she performs some short but impressive feat of manual dexterity*) . . . why this so often ends in *complete* disaster.' The comments I have quoted from memory, and the subject – whether tart or flan, fish or fowl, cocktail snack or main dish at a dinner party – has gone. But the recollection of their utterance, with Mrs Cradock's tense and slightly breathless delivery, and the riveting chair-edge reaction they produced, is still sharp and enjoyable. (And when one comes to consider it, doesn't the wearing of such gorgeous *and vulnerable* dresses for such often messy tasks itself heighten the awful-possibility element, especially in female eyes?)

In a less histrionic manner Mr Clement Freud often captures the non-enthusiast's attention in his magazine articles on similar topics. Here he is discussing the preparation of asparagus:

In certain respects asparagus is like turkey; there are two parts to it and both need different cooking times and methods. In the case of turkey you can get string and truss the whole bird so tightly that cookery aimed midway between the white and the brown meat is reasonably successful.

When it comes to asparagus, you have a very much better solution. The stalks require cleansing and scraping and comprehensive boiling. The tips need to be treated with great care and should be steamed.

You can cook asparagus as do the Transylvanians: cut off the tips and steam them; take the stalks and boil them. This is satisfactory but unsubtle (as, indeed, are the Transylvanians).

What you should do is to stand the asparagus upright and find a saucepan that is taller than the tallest spear (if necessary use a knife to cut down the asparagus from the stalk). Get some wire and bend it into a loop a little bigger than the bunch of asparagus and use the rest of the wire to ensure that the loop remains more or less in one place, halfway up the pan.

Perspicacious readers will already have guessed the end of this ploy. Stand the asparagus in the loop in the pan, add salted boiling water up to one inch from the tips and put on a lid. Par for the course is about 15–20 minutes, depending on the circumference of the asparagus.

Daily Telegraph Magazine, 12 June 1970.

The magnetic element there does most assuredly not derive from the witticisms or the travel-chat, which at first sight might appear to be the clue to Mr Freud's popularity in this field. In fact in the present case neither the wisecrack nor the National Geographic bit could be said to be sparkling. What does attract and hold the attention is first the posing of the problem in a clear, graphic and challenging manner and then the gradual revealing of the solution in such a way that the 'perspicacious reader' is drawn on step by step: curious at first, then in anticipation, then in a desire for confirmation of his own perspicacity. (And note especially the timing here: the wait he imposes after the sentence '. . . you have a very much better solution' – when what he presents at first is rather the antithesis of any solution, is in fact the detailed challenge, as if he had actually written '. . . you have a very much *trickier problem*'.)

In a very similar way did Mr Freud's illustrious grandfather take *his* readers along infinitely more difficult paths: careful to give the clearest possible view of each step and casting just enough light on the next or next-but-one to stimulate the reader's enthusiasm as well as preserve his interest. In the following passage the problem – or the complex of problems – is the immemorial one of dreams: where they come from, how they are formed, what they mean. That is sufficiently fascinating to hook the attention of any reader, one might imagine – but how to keep that attention along the intricate paths that this expert had himself been led along is quite another matter.

> The dream-work is the name for the whole sum of transforming processes which have converted the dream-thoughts into the manifest dream. The surprise with which we formerly regarded the dream now attaches to the dream-work.
>
> The achievements of the dream-work can, however, be described as follows. A tissue of thoughts, usually a very complicated one, which has been built up during the day and has not been completely dealt with – 'a day's residue' – continues during the night to retain the quota of energy – the 'interest' – claimed by it, and threatens to disturb sleep. This 'day's residue' is transformed by the dream-work into a dream and made innocuous to sleep. In order to provide a fulcrum for the dream-work, the 'day's residue' must be capable of constructing a wish – which is not a very hard condition to fulfil. The wish arising from the dream-thoughts forms the preliminary stage and later the core of the dream. Experience derived from analyses – and not the theory of dreams – informs us that in children any wish left over from waking life is sufficient to call up a dream, which emerges as connected and ingenious but usually short, and which is easily recognized as a 'wish-fulfilment'. In the case of adults it seems to be a generally binding condition that the wish which creates the dream shall be one that is alien to conscious thinking – a repressed wish – or will possibly at least have reinforcements that are unknown to consciousness. Without assuming the existence of the unconscious . . . I should not be able to develop the theory of dreams further or to interpret the material met with in dream analyses. The action of this unconscious wish upon the consciously rational material of the dream-thoughts produces the dream. While this happens, the dream is, as it were, dragged down into the unconscious, or, more precisely, is submitted to a treatment such as is met with at the level of unconscious thought-processes and is characteristic of that level.

At this point, Freud digresses for a paragraph to give his critics a lambasting. He then proceeds:

> The dream-work, then . . . submits the thought-material, which is brought forward in the optative mood, to a most strange revision. First, it takes the step from the optative to the present indicative; it

replaces 'Oh! if only . . .' by 'It is'. The 'It is' is then given a hallu-
cinatory representation; and this I have called the 'regression' in the
dream-work – the path that leads from thoughts to perceptual images,
or, to use the terminology of the still unknown topography of the
mental apparatus (which is not to be taken anatomically), from the
region of thought-structures to that of sensory perceptions. On this
path, which is in the reverse direction to that taken by the course of
development of mental complications, the dream-thoughts are given
a pictorial character; and eventually a plastic situation is arrived at
which is the core of the manifest 'dream-picture'. In order for it to be
possible for the dream-thoughts to be represented in sensory form,
their expression has to undergo far-reaching modifications. But while
the thoughts are being changed back into sensory images still further
alterations occur in them, some of which can be seen to be necessary
while others are surprising.

I have chosen to break off the quotation at that point to underline the
'come on', almost cliff-hanging technique employed by the great
psychologist, with its talk of surprises and promise of strange reports.
To follow him farther along this fascinating path, one should consult
his *Jokes and their Relation to the Unconscious* (translated by James
Strachey), Chapter VI, from which the passage has been taken, or,
better still, his equally brilliantly *narrated* study, *The Interpretation of
Dreams*. (In which, incidentally – as well as the prolific use of analogy
and anecdote – he employs for the very basis of the book the fictional-
type model of an imaginary walk. 'First comes the dark wood of the
authorities (who cannot see the trees), where there is no clear view and
it is easy to go astray. Then there is a cavernous defile through which
I lead my readers – my specimen dream with its peculiarities, its details,
its indiscretions and its bad jokes – and then, all at once, the high ground
and the open prospect and the question: 'Which way do you want to
go?" ' From a letter to his friend, Fliess, quoted in *The Interpretation of
Dreams*, translated by James Strachey.)

3. Timing – related to expert analysis of games skills
In recent years, along with the instant-replay technique used in television
to show key passages of play moments after they have occurred, there
has been developed a refinement which allows the instant-replay passage
to be shown also in slow-motion. Thus in a game of soccer, we see:
1. a goal being scored 'live' – as it happens;
2. the same, repeated at normal speed;
3. the same, repeated in slow-motion.

For the viewers, the interest in (1) is obvious: they are watching the
awful/delightful possibility (according to which team has scored) being

realized. Their interest in (2) is often of the same intensity, but – since the awful/delightful possibility has in fact been realized – the interest cannot wholly be derived from the same source. Here, then, emerges a more conscious interest in *process*, though largely in the historical sense – 'How on earth did *that* happen?' or 'Who's to be given the credit (or blame)?' being the chief questions here.

One can understand these reactions. But to account for the undoubted popularity of the slow-motion replay (of an incident, it should be remembered, that has probably been re-shown at normal speed several times before reaching this stage) one must remember the basic attraction of a process when carefully and clearly presented. Given a good expert commentator, like Mr Jimmy Hill, the slow-motion replay is looked on with all the pristine curiosity about 'what happens next' with which the live incident was initially regarded – except that this time it is the next movement, the next swerve or check or spurt, the next change of position of a body, a limb, a muscle that intrigues one. And, of course, the words 'given a good expert commentator' are of key importance here.

(A similar chain could be traced in a recent highly successful television series, *The Golden Silents*, presenting and analysing comedy in early silent films. First the audience laughed with a normally-run example; then part of the same sequence would be run through again, often in slow motion, as the expert described how some especially spectacular sequence of slapstick acrobatics had been achieved by the actors and technicians.)

4. Wealth of detail plus . . .?

There is something about the order, as well as the nature, of the detail in the following small-ad – taken verbatim from a weekly local newspaper – that has more to teach about narrative technique than many a textbook on the subject. Note how the 'plums' (in terms of narrative-appeal, of course, not of bargain-hunting) seem to break into the humdrum catalogue at precisely the right points to awaken, or reawaken, interest.

Goblin Sweeper, £3 10s.; Grundig Tape Recorder, £10; Washing Machine, converts to Washing-up Machine, suitable for school or hotel, £8; old-fashioned, portable Gramophone with Records, £5; several spare Motors for old Gramophones, £1 10s.; Electric Toaster, £1 10s.; Cage for dog in back of car, £3; Silver Compact, £3; small occasional Table, in light oak, £4; six pairs of grocery Scales, £1 10s. pair; 4 ft. 6 in. Box spring with interior sprung mattress with button-back headboard, £5; 26 × 1½ Boy's Cycle, Sports Model, £8; small Dumb Waiter, £2; eight Insurance Scholls, £3; two large Mirrors, 5 ft. × 1 ft., £1 each; wrought iron Companion Set with coal scuttle,

£3; Armchair, £4; Burco Boiler, £2 10s.; 4 ft. Wardrobe with Dressing Table, £17 the two; small Round Table, £5; several slabs of black and white marble, £1 each; two-seater Settee with Armchairs, green colour, modern, £11; two single size Beds, £1 10s. each; upright Hoover, convertible, £5; small Cupboard with formica top, £2; small kiddies Wardrobe, £2; two Chest of Drawers, £1 10s. each; Sideboard, £3; small Chest Drawers with Cupboard, £2 10s; one pair Waggon Wheels, £6.

5. Practically everything

The following extract contains practically everything in the way of narrative technique without telling any consecutive story – dealing with not one but a whole series of delightful/awful possibilities (mainly awful), plus, in a large measure, the fascination of watching part of a highly skilled professional process, plus a considerable wealth of detail. It is taken from what might be thought a very unlikely source: Book Two of Carl Flesch's *The Art of Violin Playing: Artistic Realization and Instruction* – a highly technical (and equally highly regarded) treatise. The section is headed 'Hindrances in Public Performance' and the subsection quoted from is headed 'Spacial Hindrances'.

Hereby we understand hindrances outside the radius of the player's person and of his instrument, and which are called forth by certain peculiarities of the space surrounding him, above all, of the *concert platform*. It is hard to imagine the number of circumstances operating unfavorably which originate in this apparently most insignificant component of the concert hall. There is the *"freshly scrubbed"* platform which, especially in little provincial towns, has been thoroughly washed with soap and water before the concert, in honor of the event. In the evening the evaporating moisture, favored by the heated temperature of the concert hall, develops invisible clouds of steam, which envelop the instrument and the strings, make the latter's tone seem veiled, and put both strings and artist out of tune. *Creaking* noises of the platform, usually a result of the use of wood not sufficiently seasoned, belongs in the category of acoustic hindrances. They seem preferably to accompany accented bow-strokes, in which the more strenuous movements of the body weigh more heavily on the platform. Here the danger exists that instinctive fear of these disturbing noises may limit the activity of the right arm, under which again, the power of expression as a whole will suffer. The copious *floral* decorations too, so often arranged on the platform on jubilee celebrations of famous composers or conductors, to enhance the festal spirit, increase the humidity of the air and also exert an unfavorable influence. When the platform *slopes* too much, as is the case with most theatre stages, the player leans too far forward and is in danger of losing his balance.

(*Ole Bull* is said always to have played in heelless shoes for this reason.) The platform may also be too *high*, something which may be fatal to the player inclined to giddiness or agoraphobia, and who feels he is standing on the edge of an abyss.

Lack of space on the platform, especially when the artist is playing with an orchestra, can indispose an artist for the entire evening. He has agoraphobia in every direction. Too close to the concertmaster's desk, he is afraid of knocking against it. Besides, the first violins are playing all too close to him. If he steps back a little too far, he gets in the way of the conductor's baton, while immediately before his feet there yawns an abyss. And woe to him if, in addition to such space-limitations, he has a "long range" conductor as an accompanist, one who thinks no beat gets its full value unless it be more than a yard long. The collisions which unavoidably result under such circumstances have already permanently damaged many instruments and friendships. Here, too, should be mentioned the sight, at bottom a gratifying one, of a platform on which a circle of auditors surrounds the player. In addition to all the drawbacks already mentioned, the artist must also suffer from the reaction of the listeners, who personally radiate a warmth as ardent as their enthusiasm. If he has his performance at all in mind the player will ruthlessly clear the way, and get sufficient room for his movements before beginning.

Now as to the *temperature* of the surrounding space. The thermometer should never exceed 20–24 degrees Celcius (approximately 65–69 degrees Fahrenheit.) In halls that are too *cold*, the instrument will not "speak" well, the fingers do not get warm enough, the fingertips remain hard and inelastic, and the bow-hairs are too tensed. When the temperature is too *high*, we have increased perspiration, the strings get out of tune, the tone sounds veiled, the fingers slip on the fingerboard and the strings as though on a saponaceous substratum, and the sureness of the whole hand is noticeably diminished. Only the experience of years will familiarize the artist with the defensive measures he must apply in such cases. Above all, a few hours before the concert, he should try *personally* to investigate the temperature conditions of the hall. He will then still have time enough to alter them in the one or the other respect. Conformity between the temperature of the artist's room (at the concert hall), and that of the hall itself is also very important. For, of course, the temperature of the hall is relative in so far as it will seem the higher the colder the room which the artist has occupied *before* his appearance, and vice versa. In such cases it will be well, without attracting attention, if he enter the concert hall a few minutes before he begins, in order to accustom his instrument to the temperature.

Appendix D

The Bobbsey Twins books

Formula-books, though usually of low literary merit, can tell us much about the condition of fiction in any given sphere and the assumptions and calculations of its mass marketers. In the U.S., probably the closest parallel to the Blyton 8–11 yrs books in style and popularity are those in the long-running series about the Bobbsey Twins. Originated in the first years of this century by Laura Lee Hope, they have in recent decades been produced by a team of writers working under that name. From time to time the books are subjected to revision, with colloquial usage going through the typewriter as well as the more obvious background details, though it is interesting to note how the slang expressions (never very heavily drawn upon) always seem to be about ten years behind the times even in the latest editions. More interesting from the British point of view, however, is to see in what ways the Bobbsey books conform to the Blyton formula, and where they significantly differ, especially now that they are becoming increasingly available in the U.K.

The first thing one notices is that here again certain basic requirements are strictly, even quite clinically, catered for. The books are usually around 180 pages long. There is a similar tendency for the child heroes to extend their explorations to the periphery of the familiar, as suggested in the titles, *And the Country Fair Mystery* and *On a Bicycle Trip*, though when they go farther afield, as in *The Bobbsey Twins in the Land of Cotton, Visit to the Great West, In Tulip Land*, and *At London Tower*, there are always strong links with their home at Lakeport, sometimes with opening and closing scenes being set there and invariably, wherever they happen to go, with Mr. and Mrs. Bobbsey and the faithful cook, Dinah, being in the offing.

The authors are rarely quite as tight as Enid Blyton in their plotting, but they are obviously equally alert to the need to *unfold* their narratives: to keep constantly in the reader's view some awful or delightful possibility. This they tend to achieve by keeping up a brisk flow of incident – a simple linear flow, with no real complications, no eddying sub-plots or cross-currents, to disturb the reader's easy concentration or tax his memory. Much of this brisk incident is totally irrelevant to the main plot and seems to be inserted on the conjuror's principle of keeping the patter flowing. One frequently used generative source lies in the clumsiness or waywardness of the younger set of twins, Freddie and Flossie. For instance, in *Mystery at School* one of them knocks over a stack of cans in a grocery store, while the older twins are making one of their interminable investigations. No clue is found in the ruins of the stack; its destruction provokes no tell-tale reaction from the assistant or any bystander; it is simply a lively irrelevance that fulfils the eight-to-eleven-year-old readers' demand for constant activity.

But accident-proneness is about the limit the authors will go to in presenting character. Even physical descriptions are sparse, confined to such epithets as 'good-looking', 'pretty', plump', and 'handsome' for the heroes and their friends, and 'thin and swarthy' or 'burly' for villains and others. Indeed, the only really close detail ever supplied in the Bobbsey books seems to be that concerning food, with Dinah ever ready to pop up at the right moment with strawberries and ice cream topped with chocolate syrup, or country ham and candied sweet potatoes, or:

> big platters of crisp fried chicken . . . two blue bowls filled with creamy potato salad, packages of thin bread and butter sandwiches, potato chips, deviled eggs, pickles, olives, and crisp celery stuffed with cheese. There was also a bowl of cole slaw decorated with slices of pimiento

– which is an extract from *The Bobbsey Twins' Adventure in the Country* and not some Gourmet Picnic Cookbook, as might be expected.

The rest – in spite of such dietary excursions – is a total drizzly thinness. While there is a complete absence of the vicious snobbery discussed in the body of this book, there are also no Blytonian shafts of shrewdness in presenting motivation. There are no psychological surprises. Grown-ups and children alike are utterly predictable in everything they do. And this might not matter so much if the anaemia didn't extend to the narrative lines. Tightness of plotting and complete relevance of incident can be safely disregarded in stories for this age-group, as we have seen – especially when a richly inventive and observant mind is at work. But the regular blatant making of melodramatic mountains out of incidental molehills is something that cannot readily be condoned. For instance, the Bobbsey authors have a healthy respect for cliffhangers without a sufficiently robust talent to match it. Thus we get a procession of chapter endings of this sort:

> Just then Flossie cried out, 'Oh, Mommy, the train's wobbling!'
>
> (End of Chapter 10, *Mystery at School*)

followed by:

> The other twins waited breathlessly to see what the train would do.
> 'The wind's blowing it,' said Mrs. Bobbsey. 'But don't worry about our falling into the water. We're already at the trestle.'
>
> (Beginning of Chapter 11)

A better name for such phony emergencies would surely be 'curbhangers' – of which dubious art the Bobbsey authors are undisputed masters.

This constant angling for cheap thrills plays havoc with timing, of course. One cannot devote to such an incident the space a genuine emergency of that kind would demand without making the book far too long, to say nothing of exasperating the reader after the first few incidents; and in the Bobbsey books the resultant weakening of a vitally important narrative element is further exacerbated by frequent use of the giveaway 'somehow', as in 'Somehow I rode out the gale and began rowing' – from *The Bobbseys' Big Adventure at Home*. Naturally, dilutions and evasions of this kind make for a less satisfying reading experience than if the exciting incidents had been properly validated and fully worked out, but it seems that the Bobbsey writers have reconciled themselves to forgoing these opportunities in the interests of facility of production. So the readers are presented with a diet of canapés – visually attractive, light in hand, highly flavoured nothings – or, since these are children we're talking about, a package of salted peanuts which they find it impossible to keep from nibbling. The low nutritional value goes without saying, but that aspect would not matter so much, I feel, if it were not for the fact that too much of this sort of thing can spoil one's appetite and, worse still, one's very taste for equally pleasant but more substantial fare.

Appendix E

Notes on the Blyton/Bobbsey paradox and 'Goodness' in children's fiction

It is often a source of great perplexity to parents, teachers and librarians who make a thoughtful study of children's books that fiction by Enid Blyton in Britain and the team producing the Bobbsey Twins series in the U.S. should be so immensely popular with many children of the highest intelligence – children with a taste for (and frequent opportunities to read) stories of an obviously high literary quality, including certain works of adult fiction. How can they – it is often wondered – turn with such enthusiasm from an enjoyable experience with a Carnegie or Newbery prizewinning book, or even from Dickens or Twain, to immerse themselves with equal enthusiasm in the comparative utter thinness of a tale by Blyton or about the Bobbseys? In their case it isn't, clearly, a seeking of light relief, of an easy passage for a while. Reading nothing at all would be easier, and it is noticeable that with books of apparently similar lightness these children can continue to be very discriminating – picking them up out of bookish habit, perhaps, but soon discarding them with the flagging of interest.

In the body of the present study I have tried to show how well-constructed and neatly-written the Blyton books often are – and how skilfully the situations are contrived from an applied-psychology point of view. But this still does not seem fully to account for the fact that they are so popular with intelligent bookish children in the face of their thinness of detail and characterization, and one is bound to ask oneself if this negates one's conclusions about the *enjoyableness* of work that is rich in these elements. On the other hand, that enjoyment is just as evident and cannot be discounted, and we are left with an apparent paradox.

It can be resolved, I think, if we remember the point made concerning fairy tales and the de la Mare passage on pages 70–71 and the use of certain stories by lively-minded children as *vehicles* for imaginative explorations of their own: vehicles that must be simple in design, relatively free of given detail, and inviting elaboration. A close analogy would be the sort of educational toys – highly regarded by many adults who would be among the first to banish a Blyton book from playroom or library – which can, because of this same simplicity of design and freedom from too closely identifying detail, be made to serve all manner of purposes in the games of an imaginative child. In fact with this analogy and its own attendant paradox, we come close to resolving the original perplexity: by regarding a book of this kind as 'game-material' rather than an intended work of literature. The *universal* popularity of Enid Blyton's books now becomes easier to understand. A child of limited intelligence, who has nevertheless learned to read with reasonable fluency will derive great pleasure from a Blyton book's mechanical easiness alone; while a child of higher intelligence – to whom that form of easiness is irrelevant – will derive great pleasure from using it as an efficient screen on which to project fantasies of his own. (And for the former type of child there is then the psychological bonus of being able to read and enjoy a book which a more gifted schoolfriend also obviously enjoys.)

This brings us back to the very fundamental question of 'goodness' in children's books. To most children – highly intelligent or otherwise – anything is good which gives great pleasure. (Even naughtiness. 'That was *good*!' they will say, after a particularly mischievous but highly enjoyable escapade.) Responsible adults, however, introduce a moral criterion. ('But will it do them good?' or 'Is it good for them?') Such adults will note that (a) with children of average and less than average intelligence the mechanical ease of a Blyton book becomes its *main* source of pleasure, and (b) these children tend to want nothing more than a repetition of this easy diet until (for mechanical ease produces diminishing returns in terms of pleasure) their interests are caught up in more attractive, non-literary pursuits. So these books are condemned – not without some justification – as being 'not good for them'.

Yet there is a sense in which Blyton books are 'good' even for children of this kind – and even in an adult-inspired moral way. For by attracting the young newly-fledged reader so forcefully they are promoting a certain basic reading fluency that will be of value to that individual later in life, even if he or she goes on never to read anything but newspapers, letters, income-tax returns, instruction manuals and advertisements. Then there is the third aspect of this type of 'goodness' in the case of highly intelligent children who have used the books as 'game-material' to develop their own imaginative faculties – even to pour a Dickensian-inspired richness of detail into that convenient Blytonian mould – just as some gifted professional novelist might borrow a vulgar popular form as a vehicle for his personal flights of fiction, or as a musician might base a magnificent opera on a cheap melodrama. In fact, wasn't Dickens himself in the habit of doing something very similar – except that in his case he manufactured his own cheap moulds? Finally, in this Dance of the Good and the Bad, there must be taken into account the contention I made in the text that there is something definitely 'not good' for any type of child in those books in which Enid Blyton mirrors approvingly and thus – consciously or unconsciously – exploits a certain type of childish social viciousness.

We would do well, then, I think, to take these inevitably shifting standards into account when trying to define or assess 'goodness' in children's fiction generally. (Indeed, one of the aims of the present study has been to point up the necessity for this kind of rethinking.) Certainly we cannot go on making do *solely* with the criteria we apply to good adult fiction (even where, as I am continually urging, we take care not to define such goodness by the midbrow standards obtaining at the turn of the century). Adult readers of fiction are comparatively set in their ways. They know – as so many of them never tire of reiterating – what they like. They can – as they are equally fond of pointing out – take care of themselves. A critic of, say, serious adult fiction can therefore address his remarks to a certain fairly clearly defined audience using certain fairly clearly defined terms, whether his personal predilections are for experimental work or the more traditional forms, the French school or the American. What he – or, for that matter, the regular reviewer of detective novels or thrillers – will not have to take constantly into account are the needs and limitations, the stage of mental development and the likely level of experience, of the books' intended readers.

Appendix F

Children's fiction and television

Since the first edition of this book was published, I have had a number of opportunities both in this country and in the U.S. of studying at close range and in some detail various special considerations that have to be taken into account when originating or adapting material for children's television.

Influencing the situation in all its aspects even more significantly than in the book industry is the old facile Kids' Stuff attitude. The most serious result is that budgets for children's productions are nearly always considerably lower than for corresponding adult programmes. Thus, while there are special scales of minimum payments for teleplays and series and serials laid down in the agreements negotiated by the Writers Guild and the ITCA, there is a kind of apartheid section for schools, children's, adult education and religious programmes, in which the quoted minima are less than half those in the adult teleplay category, and barely more than half in the series/serial section. Whether this differential is reflected in the salary scales for the companies' script editors, producers, camera crews and so on I am not in a position to say – perhaps whatever logic is made to sustain the argument vis à vis writers *is* carried right across the board – but it certainly obtains for the total budget allowed for any one project. So even though a lower-paid writer may not necessarily produce work inferior to that of his higher bracket colleagues (a feat that one may feel to be barely possible, after sampling some of the latter's programmes) – and though a lower-paid writer might even benefit from the 'greater creative freedom' that one script editor swore his children's writers enjoyed ('the less money the top brass lays out the less they fuss over the products') – there still remains the restricting effect of this cheese-paring on the very choices involved and the resultant inevitable drop in quality.

We have already touched on two such effects in the body of this book, where it was pointed out that for swift action and the use of child actors filming—with its opportunities for a piecemeal approach, facilitating trial and error and polish and repolish, to say nothing of its flexibility where juvenile employment laws are concerned—is much more suitable than the standard live/video process. But it is also much more costly, so that in order to have any chance of production at all most children's television drama projects should not:

* have child characters under the age of 14 or 15 (themselves to be played preferably by any 16+ actors who can get away with it);
* have widely ranging settings;
* have outdoor scenes unless these can (a) be satisfactorily simulated inside a studio, or (b) be brought within the compass of the ration of 2–3 minutes filming allowed per half-hour episode. ('No, you may *not* hoard up your filming allowance for a final all-film episode!' one producer told me, looking ready to rap my knuckles with a ruler. 'Because – ' There followed a Kafka-like plethora of calculations and qualifications that defy lay repetition yet did seem to make sense at the time – given that tight little budget.)

Nor do the restrictions end with the disposal of the filming opportunities. Since actors have to be paid (and not, one suspects, at cut rates for kiddie shows) it was also made clear to me that:

* no episode should involve more than 10 different speaking roles (including the principal series characters);
* no episode involving the full quota of 10 should call for extras;

but that:

* an episode involving fewer than 10 speakers might involve extras to the tune of 6 for every one speaking-part foregone. (Always bearing in mind that there were categories of extras – like plain walk-ons who say nothing and merely appear in the background; and 'significant' walk-ons who, though not speaking, are allotted actions that have some bearing on the working out of the plot. These latter get paid at a higher rate, and a sufficient number of them might result in cuts in the quota of the former.)

So much for the character restrictions. There next come those concerned with sets. Two overall considerations have to be borne in mind here, where tight budgets and live/video productions are concerned: the building of sets costs money (again, one fancies, the carpenters and others concerned are not on half-rates for children's programmes); and studio space is limited. Very well then. Sets should:

* be as simple as possible;
* be used as many times as possible within a series;
* be restricted to no more than 2 new ones per episode; and
* be so arranged that even those not used in all episodes should be

good for 2 at least, and preferably in consecutive instalments (which facilitates the economic use of studio space and something put to me as 'back-to-back' or 'double' booking of studio space).

Finally, there are certain considerations a writer for commercial television is expected to bear in mind that are not directly connected with the budgeting but have much to do with financial or politico-financial matters. These concern the break in any half-hour programme. Theoretically this may come anywhere, leaving the artist-writer freedom to extract the maximum dramatic effect even from such an unpromising device. But: since most children's programmes in Britain up to now have started at 5.20 and ended at 5.50 – and: since television advertising rates go up at 5.30 – no writer can expect to get away with a first half running for less than ten full minutes. It may be argued that few would ever find it desirable to, of course. But can this sort of argument be applied to the other break restriction – imposed by the ITA on vaguely cultural grounds – that after the break there should either be a complete change of scene or a significant lapse of time within the same scene?

Perhaps it would make the destructive, debilitating, anti-creative effect of all these purely mechanical restrictions more apparent if we were briefly to compare them with the processes of writing for the printed page. Tight budgets are, heaven help us, not unknown in the publishing world. But while a children's book may be done on the cheap – with rough paper, bad binding, poor illustrations, and so on – the fiction itself remains unimpaired. Granted, its chances of a Carnegie Medal may be ruined, so long as the Library Association's irrational and unfair insistence on assessing the quality of these other things along with the prose is maintained, but the integrity of the work itself will be preserved. No one will have told the author to keep his characters down to ten a chapter, or make sure that most of the action takes place in small cheaply furnished rooms, or be sure to make Chapter One go beyond page ten. The list could be expanded point for point, but I think the drift should be now very apparent: that while art does to some extent thrive on restrictions, as I have pointed out elsewhere in this study, there are limits beyond which only damage can be done, especially when such restrictions arise from a logic totally unconnected with the creative process, and one that, being based on the premise that kids' stuff is by definition less important stuff, is even alien to any thoughtful view of what culture, mass or otherwise, is about.

In the U.S. many of the above remarks about restrictions do not apply, but only because there are so very few programmes for children involving non-cartoon fiction. For some years now there has been an increasing pressure of public opinion for more plays, series and serials of the kind under discussion, and with this pressure there has been a corresponding increase of lip-serving promises from the big networks. Small production units have been formed and experiments have been conducted, but while the Americans have the money for more generous budgeting (any producer interested in children's television at all scoffs at the idea of not using film) there still seems to be a tremendous reluctance to go ahead. After all, the cartoons that are put out on Saturday mornings on all channels are very cheap and they do get the results in terms of viewing figures. But still the pressure builds, and still the companies promise, throwing in a few live general interest shows of roughly the Blue Peter or Magpie type (though compered by solemn children instead of hearty or chirpy young men and women) as a token of goodwill. And now that individual producers are beginning to look around in greater earnest, the Kids' Stuff syndrome begins to operate again, though in a curious way. 'The money is there,' a New York producer assured me, 'and it won't be long before we do get the go-ahead. But first we must have the material to work on and believe me we're desperate to get a look at some good children's novels.' When I pointed out that his country had no mean record in that respect, and asked him why he didn't browse around bookshops himself, he confessed he would have no idea where to begin. 'What about agents then?' I asked. He shook his head despairingly. 'The chances of getting a children's novel adapted for television over here have been so slim that most agents have never even considered trying.'

Another attitude that seems to prevail in children's television in all countries is the one described in the body of this book: the too-facile belief that a story *about* a child or children is necessarily a story *for* children. At the 1971 International Television Exhibition of Programmes for Young People, held in New Hampshire as a means of trying to arouse American producers to what can be done in this field, I was somewhat disturbed to see how many world prize-winners seemed to be falling into this category. Mainly they were documentaries dealing with family life or delinquency, sound competent products such as one may see almost any night on adult programmes (which would have little chance of winning prizes in that sphere), but they did not have anything to say particularly *to* children in a way they might find particularly attractive. But the tendency was not confined to documentaries and there is a risk of its gathering momentum over here as it becomes apparent to more producers that the audience for the 5.20 to 5.50 children's shows has a very large proportion of middle-aged adults. One TV programme executive quoted to me as recently as February 1972 the rather startling figure of some 50% of that audience being over 40 – though maybe this is not altogether surprising when one realizes that this slot immediately precedes the first national news programme of the evening and that many adults may become interested in a certain series by switching on early in the course of a particularly gripping episode. When I asked the same person if the proposed extension of daytime TV broadcasting time would mean more children's programmes, he said he wasn't sure and that a more probable result would be the pushing of the slot back as early as 4.0 to 4.30 – with the old one being filled with adult light entertainment. Would this not at least ensure a smaller proportion of adult viewers for the children's programme then? To which he replied with another question; How many kids are back home from school by four? He was glum, understandably. The Kids' Stuff brigade were obviously at work again.

Finally, there are certain special factors at the receiving end of the television process that should be borne in mind. These were most vividly brought to light (if that is the appropriate term) during the power cuts of early 1972, when viewers began to protest about missing episodes of favourite serials (adults' as well as children's) and asking the BBC and ITV companies to put on repeats or at least issue summaries. This was taken very seriously, as well it might have been, with high-level discussions taking place and committees being set up. (Though one had to smile at the furore over the final instalment of *The Moonstone*, a serial put out by the BBC in the children's Sunday slot but obviously commanding a large universal audience. 'What happened?' demanded caller after caller, apparently unaware that the book itself, in many editions, was so readily available, and indeed had been for something like a century.)

Now the point here is that while power cuts may not always be with us, other hazards are. A viewer may be taken ill in the middle of a serial; he may be delayed and arrive home too late for an instalment; the set itself may break down – and so on. Television, in short, is nothing like so conveniently available as a book or magazine, and while a child may soon fall into a mechanical viewing habit per se – one might call it a goggling habit – it will always be more difficult for him to develop and sustain a *discriminatory* habit because of such uncontrollable factors.

But much more important than availability is the basic question of quality. With so many impediments at the creative and consuming ends one can only conclude that TV will never be able to approach the printed page as a satisfactory medium for children's fiction. In fact it could well be that with the development of TV cassettes, on which properly produced children's films may be made readily available, with collections of tapes being built up in public libraries and schools as well as by private individuals, the regular TV companies may be by-passed altogether in this field – virtual non-starters.

Books referred to in the text

1. Children's Books

Aiken, Joan. *The Wolves of Willoughby Chase* (Cape)

Beacon Readers (Ginn)

Berg, Leila. *A Day Out, Finding a Key, Fish and Chips for Supper* (Macmillan)

Blyton, Enid. *Five Run Away Together* (Brockhampton Press)

Bond, Michael. *Paddington Helps Out* (Collins)

Carroll, Lewis. *Alice's Adventures in Wonderland* (various editions)

Collinson, Roger. *A Boat and Bax* (Chatto, Boyd and Oliver)

Crompton, Richmal. *William* books (Newnes)

de la Mare, Walter. *Collected Stories for Children* (Faber)

Dickinson, Peter. *The Weathermonger* (Gollancz)

Fleischman, Sid. *Chancy and the Grand Rascal* (Hamish Hamilton)

Fox, Paula. *How Many Miles to Babylon?* (Macmillan)

Gag, Wanda. *Tales from Grimm* (Faber)

Grahame, Kenneth. *The Wind in the Willows* (Methuen)

Grice, Frederick. *The Oak and the Ash* (Oxford University Press)

Hale, Kathleen. *Orlando* books (John Murray)

Janet and John Readers (Nisbet)

Johns, Capt. W. E. *Biggles* books (Brockhampton Press)

Kastner, Erich. *Emil and the Detectives* (Cape)

Lofting, Hugh. *Doctor Dolittle's Post Office* (Cape)

Mabie, Hamilton Wright. *Myths Every Child Should Know* (Doubleday)

Macken, Walter. *The Flight of the Doves* (Macmillan)

Manning-Sanders, Ruth. *The Glass Man and the Golden Bird* (Oxford University Press)

Martin, J. P. *Uncle* books (Cape)
Mayne, William. *The Yellow Aeroplane* (Hamish Hamilton)
Nesbit, E. *The Story of the Treasure Seekers* (Benn)
Newby, P. H. *The Spirit of Jem* (Longmans Young Books)
Norton, Mary. *The Borrowers* (Dent)
Ransome, Arthur. *Secret Water, Swallows and Amazons* (Cape)
Richards, Frank. *Billy Bunter* books (Cassell)
Stevenson, Robert Louis. *Treasure Island* (various editions)
Thurber, James. *The 13 Clocks* and *the Wonderful O* (Hamish Hamilton)
Tolkien, J. R. R. *The Hobbit* (Allen and Unwin)
Townsend, John Rowe. *Pirate's Island* (Oxford University Press)
Twain, Mark. *Huckleberry Finn, Tom Sawyer* (Collins)
Uttley, Alison. *Sam Pig, Ten Tales of Tim Rabbit* (Faber)
Vipont, Elfrida. *More About Dowbiggins* or *A Win for Henry Conyers*
    (Hamish Hamilton)
Williams, Jay and Abrashkin, Raymond. *Danny Dunn on a Desert Island*
    (Macdonald)
Wyss, J. D. *Swiss Family Robinson* (various editions)
Yonge, Charlotte M. *Village Children* (Gollancz)

2. Adult Fiction

Baldwin, James. *Tell Me How Long the Train's Been Gone* (Michael
    Joseph)
Balzac, Honore de. *Cousin Bette* (Penguin)
Bennett, Arnold. *The Old Wives's Tale* (various editions)
Braine, John. *Room at the Top* (Eyre & Spottiswocde)
Brontë, Charlotte. *Jane Eyre* (various editions)
Brontë, Emily. *Wuthering Heights* (various editions)
Conrad, Joseph. *Lord Jim, Nostromo* (Dent)
Dickens, Charles. *Barnaby Rudge, David Copperfield, Pickwick Papers*
    (various editions)
Durbridge, Francis. *The World of Tim Frazer* (Hodder & Stoughton)
Eliot, George. *The Mill on the Floss* (various editions)
Faulkner, William. *The Sound and the Fury* (Chatto and Windus)
Gaskell, Jane. *Attic Summer* (Sphere)
Gide, André. *The Coiners* (Cassell)
Golding, William. *Lord of the Flies* (Faber)
Hardy, Thomas. *Tess of the D'Urbervilles* (various editions)
Hemingway, Ernest. *First 49 Stories* (Cape)
James, Henry. *The Turn of the Screw* (various editions)
Joyce, James. *A Portrait of the Artist as a Young Man* (Cape), *Ulysses*
    (Bodley Head)
Lawrence, D. H. *Lady Chatterley's Lover, Sons and Lovers* (Heinemann)
Leacock, Stephen. *Literary Lapses* (Penguin)

Liddell, Robert. *The Deep End* (Longmans)
Patchett, Mary. *In a Wilderness* (Hodder & Stoughton)
Peacock, Thomas Love. *Headlong Hall* (Dent)
Pinter, Harold. *The Caretaker* (Methuen)
Proust, Marcel. *Remembrance of Things Past* (Chatto and Windus)
Rabelais, François. *The Histories of Gargantua and Pantagruel* (Penguin)
Richler, Mordecai. *Cocksure* (Weidenfeld and Nicolson)
Robbe-Grillet, Alain. *The Voyeur* (Calder)
Salinger, J. D. *The Catcher in the Rye* (Hamish Hamilton)
Sarraute, Nathalie. *Portrait of a Man Unknown* (Calder)
Sheridan, Richard Brinsley. *The Critic* (Macmillan)
Sillitoe, Alan. *Saturday Night and Sunday Morning* (W. H. Allen)
Sterne, Laurence. *Tristram Shandy* (various editions)
Tchehov, Anton. "The Steppe" from *The Bishop and Other Stories* (Chatto and Windus)
Thomas, Piri. *Down these Mean Streets* (Knopf)
Trollope, Anthony. *Barchester Towers* (various editions)
Woolf, Virginia. *Between the Acts, Orlando, The Years* (Hogarth Press)

3. Non-fiction

Allen, Walter. *The English Novel, Writers on Writing* (Phoenix House)
Allott, Miriam. *Novelists on the Novel* (Routledge)
Attitudes and Adventure compiled by County Libraries Group of Library Association
Avery, Gillian. *Nineteenth Century Children* (Hodder & Stoughton)
Bennett, Arnold. *Journals* (Viking)
Bowen, Elizabeth. "Notes on Writing a Novel" (Orion II)
Butt, John and Tillotson, Kathleen. *Dickens at Work* (Methuen)
Children and their Primary Schools, H.M.S.O. (The "Plowden" Report)
Connolly, Cyril. *Enemies of Promise* (Penguin)
Cowley, Malcolm. *Writers at Work* (Secker and Warburg)
Crouch, Marcus. *Chosen for Children* (Library Association)
Empson, William. *Seven Types of Ambiguity* (Chatto and Windus)
Flesch, Carl. *The Art of Violin Playing: Artistic Realization and Instruction* (Carl Fischer)
Freud, Sigmund. *Jokes and their Relation to the Unconscious* (Routledge), *The Interpretation of Dreams* (Allen & Unwin)
Kermode, Frank. *The Sense of an Ending* (Oxford University Press)
Kramer, Dale. *Ross and the New Yorker* (Gollancz)
Leacock, Stephen. *How to Write* (Bodley Head)
Leavis, F. R. *The Great Tradition* (Chatto and Windus)
Liddell, Robert. *A Treatise on the Novel, Some Principles of Fiction* (Cape)

Lubbock, Percy. *The Craft of Fiction* (Cape)

Opie, Iona and Peter. *The Lore and Language of Schoolchildren* (Oxford University Press)

Orwell, George. *Critical Essays* (Secker and Warburg)

Rose, Jasper. *Lucy Boston* (Bodley Head)

Stevenson, Robert Louis. "My First Book" from *The Art of Writing* (Chatto and Windus)

Timely Reading listed by Margaret Meek and Norman Culpan (Hodder & Stoughton)

Trease, Geoffrey. *Tales out of School* (Heinemann)

Trilling, Lionel. *The Liberal Imagination* (Secker and Warburg)

Wellek, Rene and Warren, Austin. *Theory of Literature* (Cape)

Wilson, Edmund. *The Wound and the Bow* (Methuen)

Wodehouse, P. G. *Performing Flea* (Jenkins)

A Short Selection of Books About Children's Books

Avery, Gillian. *Nineteenth Century Children* (Hodder and Stoughton) Bodley Head Monographs

Crouch, Marcus. *Treasure Seekers and Borrowers*, ed. *Chosen for Children* (Library Association)

Darton, Harvey. *Children's Books in England* (Cambridge University Press)

Doyle, Brian. *The Who's Who of Children's Literature* (Evelyn)

Eyre, Frank. *Twentieth Century Children's Books* (Longmans)

Fisher, Margery. *Intent Upon Reading* (Brockhampton Press)

Green, Roger Lancelyn. *Tellers of Tales* (Ward)

Kamm, Antony and Taylor, Boswell. *Books and the Teacher* (Brockhampton Press)

Lewis, Naomi. *The Best Children's Books of 1963; 1964; 1965; 1966; 1967* etc. (Hamish Hamilton)

Lines, Kathleen. *Four to Fourteen* (Cambridge University Press)

Townsend, John Rowe. *Written for Children* (Garnet Miller)

Trease, Geoffrey. *Tales out of School* (Heinemann)

Turner, E. S. *Boys will be Boys* (Michael Joseph)

White, Dorothy Neal. *About Books for Children* (Oxford University Press), *Books Before Five* (Whitecombe and Tombs)

Index